I0598728

TRUE LOVE
An Erotic Romantic Suspense

by
George A Bernstein
#2 Best Seller at Amazon "Crime Thrillers"
#5 Best Seller at Amazon "Suspense"

GnD Publishing LLC

GnD Publishing LLC
Palm Beach Gardens, Florida 33418
www.GeorgeABernstein.com
info@GeorgeABernstein.com

Publisher's Note: This is a work of fiction. Names, characters, and incidents are a product of the author's imagination. Locales and public names are sometimes used for atmospheric purposes and may have been altered to meet the demands of the story. Any resemblance to actual people, living or dead, or to businesses, companies, events, institutions, or locales is completely coincidental.

Cover Design by Paradox Book Covers

Ordering Information: Quantity sales. Special discounts are available on quantity purchases of print copies by corporations, associations, bookstores, and others. For details, contact the publisher.

True Love?/George A Bernstein

ISBN: 979-8-9871607-2-5

DEDICATION

To my critique team, Sharon and Fred, who insisted I use my talents at writing love scenes to write erotic romantic suspense. I hope you've found it was a worthwhile task.

TRUE LOVE

~ 1 ~

Alex Jordan eased his six-foot frame forward in his ergonomic, black leather executive chair and skimmed his hands across the polished, burl-cherry top of his antique English desk. His ocean-blue eyes had never seen it so uncluttered in the six years he'd owned it.

Last time to sit there, because he didn't own it any more. It was unneeded in the new life he faced, and so he'd included it in the sale of his ten-year-old biotech firm. NeoWorld, the huge tech firm that bought his baby for a mere 1.5 billion, offered him the COO position with a five-year contract, at a half-million a year, but he intended to cut all ties. His half of the five-hundred million in cash, with his other half-billion in stock, was more than he would ever need. NeoWorld's 1.5% annual dividends on their stock, 7.75 million bucks on his shares, was more than he could ever spend.

Justin Blass, his geeky bestie from before pre-K, and the biology whiz and partner who co-developed their unique product line, received the other half of the sale. He wasn't ready to pack it in, so he agreed to stay on as VP of Tech and Development, with a half-million-dollar annual salary. No pikers at NeoWorld when they spotted real talent.

Alex sighed and rose, glanced around, then lifted a small cardboard box littered with his few remaining personal items, and headed for the door. Glancing back, he ran fingers through his shoulder-length, caramel-colored hair, scanned the room, and sought a sense of emotion. The last six years were spent here, often starting each day soon after daybreak and usually extending well after dark, as he and Justin plotted and directed their growth. It was an upscale move that began, like so many tech startups, in his parents' garage, before growth pushed them into a small, strip-mall office. That was outgrown six years ago and brought them to this Olive Street complex in central West Palm Beach.

Surprised at a lack of any feeling of nostalgia, he shrugged and exited the office. This phase of his life was over, and he wasn't going to miss it—he hoped. All their drive for success had blanketed any room for outside pleasures. Fishing, horses, women … especially women. His only carnal experiences in the last ten years had been with professional escorts. An occasional hooker in the early years when funds were limited, and high-end babes the last five or so, dominated lately by the gorgeous, raven-haired, French succubus, Guila. They'd dine, dance, and then retire to a downtown hotel suite for a night of passion. She was the ultimate lover, and had hinted she'd happily retire into his arms. The thought of those delectable, natural C-cups in his face, his dick trapped inside that tight, wet pussy as she surged against him, was intoxicating, but he hoped to find a woman who might love him for who he was, and not mostly for his wealth.

True love.

Alex paused in the office's bullpen to bid adieu to several of his team, most of whom were retained by NeoWorld. He exited the offices and rode the elevator to the parking garage. His Lexus IS 500 gunmetal gray sports sedan, nestled in his reserved parking spot, awaited him. The carton secured in the trunk, Alex pulled out for the final time. The slot would be relabeled tomorrow. Turning south on Olive, he headed for Okeechobee Blvd., en route west to his sprawling ranch house in Wellington. He needed a few days to organize his future. First thing on his list would be starting a social life. A search for romance. Something real.

He was eager to find such a woman, but cautioned himself not to rush it. There had to be a legitimate connection with him and not his money. Was that even possible? He'd soon find out. He was going to be feted at a dinner the next evening at the West Palm

Beach City Club as this year's American Dream "star."
    Probably not the best place to ignore his new-found wealth.

~ 2 ~

Emma Logan stumbled through the doorway of her ocean-front Hallandale Beach apartment, slammed it shut, and threw the deadbolt. She sagged against the raised panel mahogany and mewed softly as tears trickled across her apple cheeks. Teeth gritted and shoulders shoved back, she pushed erect, and on wobbly knees, made her way into her den where she collapsed on her mocha leather loveseat, wincing from her scraped thigh. A groan escaped her at the sight of blooming bruises on both forearms. Face cupped in her hands, she slumped back and let pent-up tears flow.

The bastard. He might have killed me if he got me inside. At five-foot-four and a hundred-twenty pounds, the auburn hair, twenty-five-year-old woman might seem like easy prey to her six-foot stalker, but the past five months spent on TaeKwanDo training had paid off. Brad's iron grip on her forearms hadn't prevented Emma from delivering a hard kick to his knee. Eyes flared, a grunt hissed between his lips, and he released one arm, allowing her the opportunity to deliver a sharp knuckle-punch, aimed at his larynx. Luckily for him, he'd turned and took it on the side of his neck, but it dropped him to his knees, his grasp of her arms gone. Emma tumbled to the curb next to his Audi and scraped her left thigh, but managed to bounce up and race back inside the North Miami Beach Mall and hide in a Macy's dressing room.

Twenty minutes later, after a cautious reconnoiter, she'd slipped out the malls rear entrance, found her silver Rav4 in the lot, and raced home.

Her well of tears finally run dry, she slumped back on the small sofa, her brain finally kicking in. *What the Hell am I gonna do now? I thought that bastard had accepted the fact we're done.* When Emma spied him outside the mall's entrance, she figured he'd come to try to make up. Abusers always say they're sorry, that they love you, and it won't happen again … until it does.

He'd been sweet and loving when he'd first wooed her. A classic romance: bouquets of roses, dinners at fine restaurants, and concerts. No rush into the sack, either. A real gentleman … until two weeks after they'd pledged monogamy and she'd moved in with him.

One evening, after returning from dining out and dancing, they were discussing something—she didn't even remember what—and she'd disagreed with whatever he said. The hard slap stunned her—but before she could react, he gathered her into his arms with a seemingly heart-felt apology. The following sex had been their best ever. Things cooled for three weeks, until the next time—two head-spinning cracks across both cheeks, followed by rough sex, with him choking her as he loomed atop, thrusting with animal ferocity. A third even more scary event soon after was one too many, and she broke it off, escaping back to her own apartment while he was out, prosecuting a court case.

But Brad Barnes wouldn't take no for an answer. The constant phone calls, text messages, and twice almost breaking down her door finally caused her to abandon the North Miami apartment she just redecorated and for which she was about to renew the lease. She'd memory-wiped and donated her pricy I-phone to Goodwill, and bought a serviceable, simple Android. Only her big sis, Charlene, had her new number. The last use of her old phone was to say goodbye to all her friends and explain why they wouldn't hear from her again. She'd rented this smaller condo at the

Hallandale Beach Arms, in south Broward County, and hoped he'd stop looking for her. But to be safe, she began training at a local Korean martial arts dojo in nearby Davie. She never expected to need the skill, but had been wrong. It seemed Brad intended to capture her … maybe even take her prisoner. As a top Miami-Dade Assistant DA's, maybe he felt untouchable, with many friends among the local cops. If she filed a police report of the attack, it would probably trigger those resources to track her down, and the next time he'd be ready for her.

Emma collapsed onto the small couch, arms clasped across her breasts, eyes again welling into teary pools. Was she really safe there? She didn't know what else she could do. Exhausted, she slipped into a restless sleep.

~ 3 ~

Alex brought his Lexus to a stop at the curb in front of the City Club's dual plate-glass doors and stepped from the sports sedan, accepting a chit from the valet. On the walk, he paused, glanced up at the six-story edifice, and chuckled. The stately, brick building, set back a bit from Okeechobee Blvd., somehow smelled of money. He'd only been there once before, eight years ago with Justin, meeting a banker whose name he couldn't even remember. Nothing had come from that. This time would be different.

He pushed through the doors, found the elevator, and selected "4," the ballroom. Tonight was their annual awards gala, and he'd reluctantly accepted their invitation as a candidate for Entrepreneur of the Year. He'd almost refused, as Justin had, but then realized this might be a chance to meet some new people and broaden his scope—maybe even a woman of interest. He was about to begin a new chapter in his life, so why not start it here? At the worst he'd have a fine meal and possibly renew some old connections.

Exiting the elevator, Alex found the registration desk and located his table assignment and stick-on name tag. South Florida was usually casual dress, but the City Club was upscale and old money, so semi-formal was expected. He'd donned lightweight, navy wool slacks, a pale blue silk turtleneck, and a dark blue blazer. Despite his recent wealth, he'd never needed a dressy wardrobe. Glancing around the room, he realized he should work on that.

Moving deeper into the ballroom, he plucked a flute of champagne and two caviar canapés from trays of passing servers

17

as he scanned the room. It was a crowd of mostly fit men, of which he seemed among the youngest, and flashily decked out women, many, even the older ones, replete in tight gowns or flowing cocktail dresses. He spied his assigned table, Two, up front, near the dais, already occupied by six participants. He settled on the one vacant chair, to the left of a tall, ash-blonde woman, clad in a sleek, sequined, white dress that hugged her sensual body. A sidewise glance appreciated its deep cleavage, barely covering an ample bosom.

Alex canted his head left and held out his hand toward a dapper sixtyish man, replete in a black tux.

"Hi. I'm Alex Jordan."

"Ahh." The guy stroked his thin, salt-and-pepper mustache, and accepted the shake. "One of tonight's honorees, aren't you?"

Alex chuckled. "Undeserved, I'm sure. And currently unemployed." He swiveled toward his female companion. "And you are?"

"Thursday D'Angelo, events editor for *Elite* magazine." She proffered a white lace gloved hand. "Friends call me Trudy, and please, no wisecracks. My mom named all of us by the day of the week we were born. Trudy is sort of old-fashioned, but my friends seem to like it." She chuckled. "So, from what I've heard, the sale of your company precludes the need of a job, doesn't it?" Bright ruby lips tilted into a wry smile.

He nodded. "Trudy works for me," and took her fingers in his, paused, and then brushed his lips across them, supposing that's what was expected. A newbie on the social scene, he was unsure of proper protocol. "Yeah. It provides unaccustomed freedom." He studied her hazel eyes and swallowed, suddenly a bit short of breath. "Ten years of nose to the grindstone left little time for recreation." He grinned, back in charge of his heart. "I plan to change that." He nodded toward the dais. "So, you're here on assignment?"

"Yes. And to have a good time. Also hoping for an interview." She patted his hand. "I admit, I finagled this seat so we could meet. The young billionaire is a compelling story." She winked. "I had no idea he'd also be so handsome."

Alex's cheeks bloomed pink. "I'm just an average guy, overworked and a bit out of shape." He appraised her for a moment. "And, I must admit, I expected magazine editors to be a bit dowdy, and not nearly so beautiful." He blushed again at such uncommon—for him—boldness.

"That's so sweet of you," lips tilting into a soft grin, as she turned her attention to the table and the shrimp cocktail just arrived. Dinner service had begun. "I bet now that you have some free time," she bit into a shrimp, finishing it before continuing, "maybe you'll spend time getting fit, if that's what you think you need."

"Well, my community has some pickleball courts in the park, so I'm gonna learn the game, and maybe play my way into shape."

"Pickleball, huh?" pivoting toward him as salads arrived. "I've just picked it up myself. It's all the rage, it seems."

"Yeah, well, easier than tennis, I guess. Anyone can pick it up pretty quickly." He chuckled. "I understand the scoring is the most complicated thing about it."

"Uh huh." Salads finished, they turned their attention to tender filet mignons, bracketed by roasted red potatoes and French beans.

Their meal consumed in silence, Alex kept appraising Trudy with sidelong glances. She was a graceful and sensual woman, and certainly no dummy. Just the kind he hoped to find. Had Lady Luck dumped a prize in his lap so quickly? If she were actually interested. She was there for her magazine, so maybe an interview with one of the awardees would break the ice.

Dinner finished, they were drawn to a triumphant trill from the band as the waiters marched in for the traditional parade of the flaming dessert, baked Alaska. Cakes were deposited on each table, and waiters sliced and served portions to the guests, augmented by hot fudge sauce. The City Club knew how to pull out all the stops.

An hour later, the tables were cleared and four awards had been presented. Alex was feted as the Entrepreneur of the Year and received a lovely Orrefors crystal vase, inscribed with his name and date. Not much of an orator, his comments were brief, with thanks to his partner, Justin Blass, whom he credited with most of the heavy lifting.

Back at his table, Trudy rose to meet him as he set his award on the table, took his hand, and led him to the dance floor. She snuggled close, cheek to cheek, as they swayed to the rhythm. They spoke little, enjoying the contact, her warm breath teasing his ear.

Alex swallowed and tried to control a growing erection. Where was this going? They'd just met, but somehow she felt like an old flame in his arms. After two dances, body-to-body, they left the dance floor, and Trudy drew him to the bar where she ordered a dirty martini, and he a Black Label Scotch on the rocks.

"It's a beautiful, cool evening." She nodded toward the balcony. "I'd love to catch a breath of fresh air."

"Let's go, then." He offered his arm, and she hooked hers through. They strolled across the floor, headed for the dual, sliding-glass doors, leading to a veranda.

~ 4 ~

They leaned against the wrought-iron railing, forearms resting atop as they gazed at the moonless sky, black velvet, strewn with puffs of cotton and thousands of tiny diamonds. A cool, salt-laden breeze wafted across their faces as they sipped their drinks in silence, their shoulders and hips brushing lightly together.

"Beautiful, isn't it?" Trudy tilted her head, pivoted slightly toward him, and laid an arm on his.

"Yes, made more so with you here—the perfect accent to a stary night." *Wow! Where the hell did that come from?* "Sorry." He chuckled. "The drink, the award, you, this," gesturing toward the Intracoastal. "Suddenly I'm waxing poetic."

"Nothing to be sorry about," her face inches from his. "I'm flattered, and frankly, happy you feel that way." Her fingers found his cheek with a caress through his shoulder-length, caramel hair, resting finally on the back of his neck. "I researched you ... *all* of you ... and knew I found the perfect—"

He cut her off, one hand at her back, surprised at his sudden boldness as his lips softly found hers. Her arms flung around his neck as he pressed her to him, their bodies molded into a single fiery unit. Lips no longer tentative, parted as tongues fenced and teased, their pelvises moving in a teasing, erotic dance. Though Alex hadn't had a real girlfriend for over ten years, Gulia, his favorite French-Canadian escort, had been an expert at kindling passion, lessons he'd learned well over the years. No surprise he'd become hard, and Trudy surely noticed that he was unusually well endowed.

After several minutes of heated kisses and roaming hands, they eased apart, panting for breath. She trailed fingers across his crotch, teasing what she found there.

"Ooh-la-la. Look what I've done," giving a wicked smile.

"You're a siren, you witch." He chuckled. "And, I think meeting you tonight was kismet." He stood back, hands on her hips, and sighed. "I've not had a serious relationship with a woman since ... well, ever. I sense a special connection with you, but I don't want to rush things if you're not—"

"Ah, Alex, I *never* rush into a relationship. Too easy to get hurt." She gripped his biceps. "But, somehow, this feels different ... special ... kismet, as you said." She slipped against him, arms crossed behind his neck, and planted a brief, sensual kiss on his lips, then peppered his face with tiny busses. "I just *know* this is right, and I'm throwing caution aside." Her hazel eyes bore into his ocean blues. "I want you—*now!*"

Slipping free, he laughed, grabbed her hand, and headed back into the ballroom. A glance at his Rolex and he grunted. "Too early to leave, darling." He grinned back at her. "We're gonna have to tough it out for at least another thirty or forty minutes. Don't want to ruin a perfect night with a flurry of rumors, no matter how right they may be."

They returned to their table, finished their drinks and ordered refills, then sauntered onto the dance floor for several more tunes.

In an effort to squelch possible gossip (he wasn't sure why he really cared), Alex danced with two other unattached ladies, one possibly old enough to be his mom. She was certainly the grabbier of the pair.

Trudy took some time to interview a few dignitaries for her magazine. That was, after all, supposedly why she was there.

Back together as the lone survivors of their table, he finished his drink, and muttered to her, "I'm gonna leave now. There's a Marriott next door, so I'll register and get a suite, if that works for you."

"Yes, but hurry." She squeezed his hand. "I've never been so turned on."

"Me too." He slipped his cell phone in front of her. "Punch in your cell number, and I'll text you with the room number." He blew her a kiss. "Shouldn't be more than twenty minutes." He fought off the urge to do something more passionate.

"I can hardly wait." She handed back his phone. "Hurry!"

He patted her hand, winked, and headed for the door, accepting congrats by many on the way out. Alex grinned. They didn't know what they were *really* praising him for. His hands stayed in pockets of his loose-fitting pants to obscure the continued bulge there.

Would this really be his first adventure into love? He hoped so.

~ 5 ~

Emma stirred, groaned, and shuddered as the terrifying memory spooled through her mind. She knuckled sandy eyes and pushed upright to stretch before shuffling into the kitchen to retrieve a coke from her fridge, adding a hefty splash of rum. She needed something to cut the edge of lingering panic. *Why can't that bastard leave me alone? Has he done this to other women? I doubt I'm his first.*

She settled at the small desk in the corner of her family room, pulled a yellow, lined pad from the drawer, and began making notes. Would she ever be safe here? Should she move? Whatever she decided, she had the funds, thanks to her very conservative Nana, whose recent death left her with two-thirds of a surprisingly large estate—over a half-million dollars. As the youngest of two granddaughters, Emma had always been her favorite. They'd picnic at the beach when she was little and visited petting zoos and Lion Country Safari.

Sister Charlene never seemed interested in those outings, preferring baking cookies and sewing dresses. Typical of her sibling, Char wasn't jealous that Emma inherited twice what she had. Char and her husband, Larry, made big salaries, she as a doctor and he the VP of a three-store Mercedes dealership, scattered throughout Dade County. Char was happy Emma was secure. Her boutique interior design firm provided enough income to meet daily needs. The inheritance was a lovely cushion.

Hmm. I wonder ...? She slouched in her chair and rubbed her still red eyes. Was the news of her inheritance the reason Brad suddenly reappeared after a nearly two-year absence? Char had warned her—. The trill of her new cell phone snatched Emma from her musing. *Char. It's like she can sense when I need her.* Emma plucked it from the desk.

"Hey, Sis."

"Hi, Em. Thought I'd check on my baby sister. You doing okay at your new place?"

"Not really." A sob leaked out.

"Jeez, Emma, what's wrong?"

"I … I was doing some shopping at the North Miami Beach Mall, and when I left, Brad was waiting for me."

"Brad Barnes?" Char growled out the name. "I thought you were done with him ages ago."

"So did I," now a soft whimper, "but apparently he's not ready to quit."

"So, what happened? Did he try to—?"

"Kidnap me, I think," Emma blurted.

"What! I knew that bastard was bad news."

"Yeah. He grabbed my arms and was dragging me toward an SUV, but I managed to kick him on the knee … hard, and I pulled free and fled back into the mall. Thank God for my TaeKwanDo training."

"Did he follow you, sweetie?" Char's voice was rift with tears.

"I don't know. Pretty pubic place to make a scene, even for him. Anyhow, I hid out for a while, then escaped out the back."

"You think he knows where you live now?"

"I don't know how he could." She dabbed at still teary eyes, the phone on speaker. "I don't see how he'd have my new phone number to run a trace, and I scrapped all my old credit cards and had the GPS removed from my car."

"Okay, but you be careful. That guy might be dangerous, especially with his connections. Thinks he's bulletproof."

"Yeah, I will, and thanks for the boost, Sis. Talking with you has calmed me down."

They disconnected with tossed kisses, and Emma rose, stretched, and moved to the center of the room to begin a TaeKwanDo workout. The regimen had transformed her from soft and feminine to lean and wiry. Anyhow, she'd be ready for him if there were another encounter. She hoped it would be enough

Still, she was scared. Tae Kwon Do or not, she was a 5'4" woman against a much larger, very strong guy.

~ 6 ~

Trudy stepped from the elevator on the eighth floor, her eyes sweeping the length of the lushly carpeted hallway. Apparently, Suite Four was to her right at the far end. She hesitated, wondering if this was the right move? She'd set her mind on snaring Alex, once she realized who he was. She'd done a deep dive into his background before the gala, and found a surprisingly thin social media presence. With the recent mega-sale of his business, he had the bucks to give her the life to which she was currently unaccustomed. She did okay on her own, but just "okay" wasn't her goal. He also needed to be a good guy she could actually fall in love with, and everything she could dig up about the very rich Mr. Jordan seemed to fit him into that niche. The fact that he was ruggedly handsome didn't hurt. Her concern at that moment was that, by rushing into a physical arrangement, she might seem like … well, like what she probably was—a gold-digger.

She sighed, and started down the hallway, justifying her action. While she was after what his wealth could provide her, she wouldn't be doing this if she didn't think she could really love him too. At least, that's what she kept telling herself as she paused at the suite's door and rapped softly.

It opened and Alex reached out, taking her hand, drew her inside, and into an embrace. He kicked the door closed as they continued, rabid lips and tongues exploring each other's. His hands roamed her back and down to her round, firm butt, while her fingers were tangled in his hair. After a few moments, Trudy leaned back, her palms planted on his chest, and panted for breath.

"What?" His heart pummeled his ribs. "Too fast?" His eyes

held hers.

"I … I don't know." She gasped, catching her breath. "I just don't hop in the sack with a guy on the first date," she forced a chuckle, "if you can even call this a date."

"So, why are we here, then?" His grin signaled disbelief of her words.

"Well, because I seem ready to break that previously unbreakable rule." She sighed and stroked his cheek. "I … I don't want you thinking I'm some easy bimbo." Her lips tilted into a tiny smile. "Thers's something … *something—*"

"Magical going on here. Right?" Her face was now cupped between his hands.

Trudy nodded and leaned against him, head on his shoulder. "Yeah. Magical. Like … like …" She trailed off.

"Like this is destiny?" A finger under her chin, he raised her head, their lips inches apart.

She nodded and closed the space for a gentle kiss and a sigh. "Can't fight destiny, can we?"

"Why should we when the rewards seem so perfect?" The next kiss was anything but gentle, and four hands became erotic voyagers. Her fingers were busy with his belt, while his found her back zipper which freely released, all the way to the small of her back. A shrug of shoulders sent the white sequined gown to puddle at her feet, leaving her gloriously bare except for an ivory silk bikini.

Alex cupped a perfect, C-cup breast, a thumb tweaking its nipple which quickly came to attention, and it was soon engulfed by warm lips and a busy tongue. He paused as Trudy pulled his shirt up, and as his arms came free, flung it onto a nearby sofa. A moment later, he stepped out of his pants, and they were locked in a ravenous embrace, both bare now, except for their underwear. The heat of her velvet-smooth skin against him fired electric tingles across his body. Crushed together as they continued to devour each other, one hand was inside her panties, caressing her taut butt. Then a finger slipped into the crease, and ventured down, past her anus, and found the edge of her already soaking pussy.

Trudy gasped and shivered as he stroked those lips, becoming even wetter. Then he scooped up the blonde and staggered to the bedroom, their lips never pausing in the pursuit of pleasure. Alex dropped her onto her feet, sat on the mattress's edge, and peeled down her bikini. She bent over, two gorgeous mounds of flesh dangling in his face as she stripped away his boxers, freeing a massive hard-on.

"Oh, what a gorgeous lollipop." She stooped to take his pulsing dick into her mouth, "I want it."

"Not yet." With both hands on her ass, he lifted her, rotated, and laid her on the bed. On his knees between her legs, his eyes held hers, a pink tongue swiping open lips. "Not before I drink at that sexy fountain." His fingers and lips trailed across her silky skin, licking, tweaking, teasing, until they arrived at her pussy, open and puddled with juices. His tongue tickled its edges and darted in and out, lapping across her bulging clit.

Trudy writhed and moaned, her fingers tangled in his long, yellowish locks. "Oh God. *Oh God."* She panted. "That's so wonderful." Her hips bucked and thrust into his face. "I'm gonna …. I'm gonna c-u-u-m … *now!"* And she did, fluids gushing, with Alex lapping, drinking, thrusting with his tongue, his fingers raking her sides and belly. She continued to thrash, her strong legs crossed over his back.

"Oh, *damn,* that was so intense," she muttered as she finally went slack. Breath finally coming under control, she raised her head, and with her hands cupping his face, drew him up for sloppy kisses. "For a guy who said he'd never had a relationship, that was pretty terrific."

"Never a *true* relationship, but I was far from celibate." He chuckled. "I did what I had time for, and had several pseudo-romantic, adventures." A soft kiss brushed her lips. Enough said. He didn't think she'd like to hear they were escorts, no matter how girlfriend-like they were.

She delivered a devilish grin. "Okay. And, now it's my turn." Pushing up, Trudy shoved Alex onto his back and slithered on top of him, her damp skin and erotic curves igniting electric tingles across his chest. A ravenous kiss enveloped his mouth, tongues engaged in a frantic duel as she wiggled her still wet pussy over his again iron-hard dick. Then a slow descent began, her lips, tongue and long nails teasing and titillating every inch of skin, en route to his raging hard-on. The air filled with his moans and panted breath.

Finally, nestled between his legs, she attacked her "lollypop," tongue swirling up and down the shaft while her fingers played with his "boys."

"So beautiful," she muttered, engulfing the head and shaft, tongue still swirling, teasing the base of the glans, her head bobbing in a slow, sensual rhythm.

"Oh, damn." He arched his pelvis and thrusted to meet her attack. "I can't hold it. I'm gonna cum."

"Do it, Alex," muffled, as she increased suction and speed. "I want it all!"

His body shook as he drove his hips up to meet her, and he exploded as she sucked and gulped, taking all he gave, sucking him dry. He sagged back on the bed, his hands in her hair and voiced a deep sigh. "Holy fuck, that was hot."

She raised her head and let his shrinking organ slip free as a trickle of his release seeped from the corner of her grinning lips. "Yum. I love that." She wiggled up, her firm breasts and erect nipples teasing across his belly and chest, and they kissed. Again, her pussy, open and wet, surrounded his cock. Trudy worked her hips, sliding those moist lips back and forth, and he began to reharden. "Ahh, so nice." A fierce kiss was exchanged. "That first time was so fast because of so much anticipation, but I can see, happily, I can expect more." She kissed him hard again. "Because I really wanna fuck."

"Me too, babe. Nothing in my past experiences felt like this."

Alex groped at the top of the nightstand and plucked up a small rectangular packet. "I stopped at a convenience store on the way over and picked up some condoms."

"Ahh, the consummate gentleman." She chuckled. "No sense in complicating things with a kid this early in our relationship." She took the packet, opened it, and slithered down his body, tits and nipples again grazing his skin, intensifying his ardor.

"So," he was gasping for breath, "this is gonna be a relationship?" He shivered as she slipped the condom over his dick. "Not just a one-time affair?"

"I'm hurt you might think so little of me, Alex." Breathless, she edged up to his waist, rose on her knees, reached back, and engulfed his cock. Tightening her vaginal muscles, she slid back, taking it all, and began to move. "I was falling for you the minute you kissed my fingers when we first met." Head lowered as she began an erotic dance of love, she consumed his mouth with a frantic tongue. "I sense a cosmic connection between us." A gasp, her muscles pulsing around his cock. "God, this is so wonderful." Panting hard. "I'm gonna cum again, you beast." She bit his lip as she increased her pace.

"Oh, geez, me too, gorgeous." Grunting, he thrust deep inside her, "Me, to-o-o." He released with a shudder as they slammed together.

Trudy emitted a passionate snarl and clamped his dick as tightly as she could. Racked by convulsive shudders as he came, she had her own climax, soaking the sheets with gushing fluids. A few final thrusts, and she slumped against him, their sweat-slickened bodies clinging together.

"Wow, wow, wow!" Alex held her tightly, hands stroking her smooth back. "I never expected anything like this." He kissed her ear. "I've been without a real girlfriend for so long …" He trailed off.

"So, does that mean I'm your girlfriend now, Alex?" She arched her neck, their eyes locked.

"I … I don't know." He cupped her face between his hands. "Are you?"

"I hope so." She planted a soft kiss on his lips. "I don't sleep around, but I've known my share of guys, but I've never felt like this." She ran a thumb across his lips, the corners of hers tweaking up. "Kismet, you called it, earlier."

"Yeah, well, I've never felt this way before, either. Of course, I've had little to compare it with, but I can't imagine feeling any stronger than I do right now." He sighed and hugged her. "Finally with some free time, I was hoping to find some real romance. Something more than just physical pleasure." He chuckled softly. "Not that I'm complaining, because tonight's surpassed any fantasies I may have had." He chucked Trudy's chin, raising her head from his shoulder, and kissed her. "I just never expected to be hit by the proverbial lightning bolt, first pass outta the box."

Elbows planted on his shoulders, she raised her head and studied his face, pink-tipped tongue darting across ruby lips. "The lightning bolt! How perfect a simile, Alex. I felt it too, the first time I saw you approach our table. You took my breath away before you even said hello."

"Really? I'm no Adonis, and—"

"You're damned handsome, darling," she interrupted, "but it had nothing to do with looks. Maybe we were lovers in some past life." She shook her head and planted a light kiss on his lips. "Whatever, I knew we were fated to be together. I'm … I'm just happy you seem to feel the same."

"Oh, yeah." He drew her down for a more heated kiss, and their hands began a new adventure. Her pussy again surrounded his hardening dick, and soon they were in the throes of a third venture into passion and pleasure. He fumbled on the nightstand and found the packet of unused condoms, amazed that this succubus could arouse him again so soon.

Exhausted, they slept, locked in each other's arms. Predawn,

Trudy awakened Alex with kisses and feathery touches, and they ventured into another passionate encore of their new love. Sated, they again slept, dreams filled with new expectations. Their lives were changed forever by that one erotic evening, and they each intended to embrace it.

~ 7 ~

Alex stirred, blinked, and raised his head. Trudy lay snuggled next to him, covers cast aside, an arm over his chest and her leg intertwined with his. He knuckled his eyes, and gently disentangled himself. Pushing to sit up against the headboard, he glanced at her as she rolled onto her back, naked and glorious.

She'd awakened him before dawn with gentle kisses and a wandering hand. Amazed that he was once again aroused, he drew her nubile body atop of his as heat filled their kisses. Ten minutes of teasing and exploration of busy fingers and darting tongues culminated with her riding him. Finally, buried deep inside her tight, wet pussy, their mouths engaged in frantic dueling of tongues, he had his fourth orgasm of the night. Still, she surged against him, his cock trapped in her Kegel grip, until she managed another gushing release, and then collapsed against him.

"I can't seem to get enough of you," she murmured. "I've never been like this before." She mewed softly as she slid to the side and drew up the silk sheet, and they drifted back asleep.

Four hours later, she sighed, rolled onto an elbow, and caught his eyes.

"G'morning, lover." She grinned. "Sleep well?"

"Like the proverbial log, once that seraph in my bed let me." He grinned, a hand stroking her cheek and sliding into her silvery hair. He drew her up for a gentle kiss. "That was some evening."

"The night was pretty good, too, wouldn't you say?" She slithered on top of him, the kiss becoming more intense.

Arms circling her back, one hand on her butt, he pressed her close, reveling in her heat. His head drawn back, his tongue sampled the taste of her lips on his, and he sighed. "You've drained me dry, hon." He glanced at the nightstand LED clock. "How about we go downstairs for breakfast. This hotel runs a great Sunday buffet brunch, eggs Benedict and everything."

She nodded and rolled away. "Sounds yummy. There time for a quick shower?"

"Sure." He paused. "I need one too, but I think it best if we do it separately." He chuckled. "I suspect if I joined you in there, it'd be anything but quick."

"Wow." She giggled. "One night together and you've already got me pegged." She plucked her sequined white cocktail dress from the floor and draped it in front of her. "Gonna be a bit overdressed, though."

"What are you, a size six?" He shrugged into his turtleneck and began pulling on his pants."

"Yeah, six works, or even an eight, if I want something loose-fitting."

"Okay. I'll slip down to the concourse shops and pick up something casual while you shower. I suspect they carry a lot of beachy stuff."

"My hero," said as she wrapped her arms around his neck a planted a lingering, busy-tongue kiss.

"Easy, witch, or we may not get to the buffet after all." He studied her face. "Save something for later."

"Okay." She stepped back. "And I do need that shower." She gathered up her bikini undies and headed for the bathroom, as he donned his shoes and left for the shops.

~~~

Trudy braced her hands against the white tiled wall and let the

35

warm water douse her head and rain over her body, sluicing away dried sweat … and the intoxicating odor of sex. A head-shake was followed by a barked chuckle. This adventure into seduction turned out a lot different than she'd expected. Different, but definitely better.

Research into Alex Jordan prior to last night had spawned a plot of conquest. She learned he'd been solely wedded to his business for ten years, and now that he was unencumbered by that bride, she imagined he'd be ripe for the right approach. She knew what that was, and it went flawlessly. He'd need to find another darling after forsaking his first love, and she intended to be right there, first in line to fill that need. Trudy had expensive dreams, and newly minted billionaire, the passionate Mr. Jordan, was just the guy to fulfill those yens.

What surprised her was the intensity of their sex, and the wonderful way he spent time fulfilling her needs. While she was far from a virgin, no one had ever completed her like last night … and that morning. She grinned as she worked shampoo into her hair.

She'd planned on hooking a sugar-daddy, but by God, it felt like she'd landed a real lover. The absolute best of both worlds. Her hair rinsed and doused with the hotels conditioner, she finished bathing and stepped from the shower to towel off. She withdrew a mini-makeup kit from her purse and applied lipstick, a touch of blush, and eyelash enhancer. All small baits to embellish the hook she'd used to snagged him.

A door closing in the suite indicated Alex had returned with their duds for the day. Dry and wearing her white silk bikini, she sauntered into the bedroom and found him laying out an outfit on the bed: tan shorts; a wide, mesh belt; and a flowered, three-button short sleeve blouse. A pair of leather sandals sat on the floor. A straw sun hat lay on the pillow.

"Very nice." She fingered the blouse's material. "You've got excellent taste, and it looks like you thought of everything."

"I try." He scooped her up with one arm and nuzzled her neck, nipped an earlobe, and finally found her lips for a brief, heated kiss. He stepped back, lips tweaked into a grin. "I expect you'll look great in them, but frankly, nothing can beat you standing there, nearly naked." A plastic bag retrieved from the bed, he turned toward the bathroom. "I'd better get in that shower, or we may never leave this room, and I'm hungry."

She laughed as he hurried away. *I'm hungry too, lover, but I'm not sure if it's for food, or that amazing dick in my pussy again.* She shrugged, sighed, and began to dress. She hummed softly as she slipped on the blouse. She'd never felt happier. This was the right guy for so many reasons, and she needed to build a solid relationship based on affection rather than just passion, because she sensed this was going to be an easy man to actually love. That'd be a very happy bonus to all that wealth. She shook her head and chuckled. The whole thing had flipped around for her, and his love had edged into priority one.

"Something funny, Trudy?"

A glance over her shoulder found him standing in the doorway.

"Joy more than humor, Alex." She moved against him, their arms circling each other, and she rested her head on his shoulder. "I came last night seeking an interview from the Entrepreneur of The Year, and whatever happened—the Lightning Bolt, kismet, whatever—I believe I found more ... a lot more." She arched her neck to scan his face. "I know it's not supposed to be so quick, but this feels *real* to me." She arched her eyebrows. "And you, Alex? How does this feel to *you*?"

"Frankly, I don't know." He sighed. "I've never been in love with anything but my business." He cupped her face in his hands and they kissed, then eased back, faces inches apart. "But, this is what I always *thought* it'd feel like, so, yeah, maybe we're in love."

He stepped back, her hands in his. "Anyhow, we're gonna have plenty of time to figure it out, because if it's okay with you, I plan on our spending a lot of time together, and we'll see where it goes."

"More than okay. It's all I hoped for, once we met."

"Great. So let's eat." He finished dressing in his own tan shorts and a green, tie-died tee-shirt, plus a pair of leather sandals.

Hand in hand, they started for the elevator, and the blooming of a passion-filled romance. The sex was better than he'd ever imagined, but there had to be more. They needed to become friends—enjoy each other's company—if it had any chance to last. That would start over a protracted brunch. He hoped for that special connection, because he never expected to find any greater passion, or a more beautiful body to lavish it on.

They entered the elevator, both lost in thought, seeking the same end, but possibly for different reasons.

Time would tell.

~ 8 ~

Emma Logan slowed her Rav4 as she neared Marvin's Deli, along Hollywood's Ocean Drive, and scanned the limited street-side parking. Full, dammit. There was a lot to park in back that many didn't know about, and she headed that way. Circling into the alley, she smiled at finding an open slot behind the trendy restaurant, and she slipped her silver SUV into it, exited the car, and headed for the rear door. She hadn't visited this breakfast and lunch spot since fleeing her rented apartment in North Miami.

Inside, she was inundated by gentle, detectible odors, dominated by cinnamon. José, Marvin's cook, must have just finished a batch of his delicious cinnamon buns. Settled at a booth near the large, plate-glass window, Emma glanced at her watch. Right on time, so Miriam, her bestie from High School, should be along in about ten minutes. That girl was *always* late. A server arrived with a menu and a glass of ice water.

"You alone?" she asked.

"Waiting for a friend. Should be along soon, so you can bring another menu and water."

"Okay." Over her shoulder as she started away, "Corn beef hash is today's special."

Emma nodded, sipped her water, and settled back to await her friend. This would be her first contact with her past in nearly six months, hoping it was finally safe. Brad must surely have moved on by now. Handsome and connected, he was never short of women eager to date him.

She glanced at the entrance, and spied Miriam, sveltely adorned in beige silk slacks and matching short-sleeve blouse, coming through the doorway right on time, ten minutes late.

"Hey, babe," leaning in for a kiss on Emma's cheek, her thick, black hair swirling around her shoulders. "Great to see you, finally. You settled in at your new digs okay?"

"Yeah, it's fine. A bit smaller than North Miami, but it's got all I need, and the building is very nice." Emma perused the menu. "Today's special is corn beef hash, but I think I'm gonna have an omelet and one of those yummy cinnabuns."

Miriam sipped her water and eased back, her eyes holding Emma's. "No Brad sightings, I take it?"

"Think I'd be sitting here with you if he knew where I was?" She shuddered. "He's gotten scarier and scarier, but I hope he's finally moved on to some other poor girl." She sighed. "You know I ditched my I-phone and had the GPS removed from the Toyota. This is the first time I've ventured out to see an old friend since he attacked me at the mall."

They looked up as the server arrived to take their order. Once done, Emma reached out and took Miriam's hand. "You're my best friend, Miry, but I'm not sure even this is safe. That bastard's in tight with the cops, and I don't think he'd hesitate to come after me again if he had the chance."

They paused as their omelets arrived, with two warm cinnabuns nestled together on a separate plate.

"Those smell great," Miriam nibbled on hers. "Yum." Her tongue swiped rosy lips and she licked frosting from her fingers.

"Yeah, cinnamon is a warm, homey odor." Emma took a fork-full of eggs. "I tell clients who are selling their home to heat some up in a small oven before a showing—" she glanced out the window.

"Holy shit!"

"What?" Miriam's head swiveled, and then back to Emma,

whose face had paled, was twisted with fear, eyes as big as quarters."

"There he is! Brad! Double-parking right in front," She snatched up her purse and slid to the end of her seat. "How the Hell? He must have trackers on everyone." She squeezed her friend's hand. "Not your fault, Miry, but I gotta run." She waved at their food. "Can you—?"

"Of course. Just get the hell outta here." She rose. "I'll try to stall him." She gave Emma a quick hug. "Now go!"

Emma nodded, tears coursing across her cheeks as she hurried toward the rear entrance. How lucky she hadn't found a spot in front.

Shit, was nowhere safe anymore?

~ 9 ~

Alex pulled his Lexus sports sedan into his Wellington ranch house's drive and parked to the far right of his three-car garage. Trudy slid her Toyota Camry next to him as he stepped out of his car. He circled the hood of hers and offered a hand as she exited the sedan, looking smashing in teal-green short-shorts and a matching, sleeveless cotton top, unbuttoned well into her delectable cleavage. An arm wrapped around her waist, they shared a brief, intense kiss, mice feet skittering down his spine at the press of her unfettered breast's nipples through his thin tee. Then he leaned back.

"You sure you're ready for this?" Catching his breath, he nodded toward his sprawling house.

"To move in with you?" She planted another quick but fierce kiss on his lips. "Am I ever." She surveyed the street, peppered by mansions with wide lawns and sprawling back yards, many with corrals and horse barns. "I can't wait to begin using the clubs training ring." She grinned at him. "I've already arranged with two owners of open jumpers to exercise their horses." She caressed his cheek. "I'll love it here, but any where'll be perfect, with you there beside me." The second kiss was longer, filled more with love than passion.

"Okay, good." Her hand in his, he returned to his car and reached inside to power the automatic garage door opener. With her wrapped in his arms, they turned toward the door as it started to spool up. "So, I got you a little house warming gift."

Trudy's eyes flared. "Holy crap!" She glanced at him. "You got *that* for me?"

"Seemed appropriate for my new roommate. Like it?"

"Oh, Alex!" Pivoting into his arms for a fiery kiss. "I love it." Another, more protracted meeting of their mouths. "I love *you!*" She twisted free and hurried toward the sleek, silver Jaguar F-Type R75 convertible. "Keys?"

"In the drink holder." He stepped toward her Toyota, which was far enough to one side not to block the Jag's exit. "I'll bring in your things while you take her for a spin, but watch your speed inside the community. They won't hesitate to give tickets." He edged back as Trudy peeled out of the garage, top down, a shout of glee hanging in the winds as she disappeared down the street, his warning falling on deaf ears.

A large suitcase was retrieved from the trunk, and several dresses and outfits, all on hangers, came from the back seat. With the overhead door left open, awaiting her return, he headed for his house's entry. He'd arranged for a groom from the equestrian club to drive out a small U-Haul with the rest of her things. The Jaguar dealer was eager to buy her Toyota, if she wished to sell it. The used car market was still hot, and it would add a nice bump to her personal account. While he planned to buy pretty much anything she wanted, it'd be good for her independence to be able get things on her own. He didn't want her to feel like a kept woman. So far, everything had been on his dime.

Inside, he wheeled her case into the master suite and laid her hangered things across the king-size bed. One of a pair of large, walk-in closets stood empty, awaiting her. He suspected she had much more to fill hers than he had in his. Clothing was never a passion for him. His eyes swept the room, and he shrugged as a small smile tweaked his lips. He expected to spend many passion-filled moments here in the near future. Sex had never been a priority for him while building his business, but it'd become a big part of their relationship.

He'd mused over the fact he'd fallen for pretty much the first attractive woman met after freeing himself from the bondage of running a successful business. Had he rushed into things too quickly, as she seemed to have also done? How much of her love for him was fueled by his wealth? So far, he'd denied her nothing, and in fact, had lavished her with gifts. The Jag was the most recent and most expensive of that list, but while she hadn't asked for it, there had been hints. Buying it for her gave him a sense of pleasure, despite a lingering sense of manipulation.

He sighed. At some point, he might elect to test her, but first he must decide if it really mattered to him. She was gorgeous, passionate, and considerate of his needs. Did he care if she wanted a relationship with the golden ring? He wasn't sure. He shrugged, left the room, and strolled to a guest bedroom which he'd converted to an office for her. He'd encouraged her to retain her position as Event Editor for the magazine. It was something she loved and would occupy her time when he wasn't around. That, and exercising horses for Wellington residents. She loved open jumping and he suspected she longed for her own animal to begin competing with at the many events occurring in that very horsey town. Those beasts, the good ones, didn't come cheap.

Stepping into her new office, he surveyed the room. Her laptop rested in the center of the large, custom oak desk, her executive swivel chair in place behind. A low, oak file cabinet sat below the twin, double-hung windows that offered a view of the expansive back yard. A small stack of *Elite* magazines sat on the side of the momentarily uncluttered desk. While Trudy had spent many hours at his place, she'd never worked from there.

Alex glanced up at the sound of the overhead garage doors closing. Trudy had returned, confirmed by the thump of the inner door from the garage.

"Alex!"

He stepped out and moved to the den. "Here, hon."

"You bastard." She strode toward him and paused, long, tanned legs spread, hands on her hips. Lips curved into a grin belied her words.

"What? You don't like the Jag?" His brow wrinkled.

"I *love* the fucking car. What an unbelievable gift." She moved against him, cupping his face between her hands and planted a kiss on his lips.

"So, what's the problem?" leaning back, studying her hazel eyes.

"I'm pissed I didn't think to buy you something," said snuggled against him, her head nestled against his neck. "This *is* a special day for me … for us … so there's only one other way I have left to thank you." A hand caught the back of his neck and pulled him down for a prolonged, tongue-fencing kiss, while her other fingers trailed down to his crotch and found something growing there.

Alex's heart jitterbugged against his ribs, one hand at the small of her back, the other creeping inside her blouse to tweak eraser-size nipples that stoop proud from her firm, natural breasts.

Trudy's fingers were at his belt, and soon his pants were puddled around his ankles as he released the zipper at the back of her shorts. Those cast aside, he edged back and stripped away her blouse as she yanked his shirt over his head. Pulled back tight against him, his warm skin caressed her velvety body, their mouths locked together with frantic urgency played erotic tag.

"God, I love you!" she panted, "and I especially love that big, hard thing of yours inside my very wet pussy."

"Me too, babe." He swept her up in his arms, lips never parting, and hurried toward his master suite. "I'm too damned hot to take the time to play with you," he whispered in a choked voice.

"That can wait for later, darling." Her arms were locked

around his neck. "Right now, we need to fuck!"

He shoved through the doorway, stumbled to the bed, and perched on the mattress's edge, Trudy on his lap. Still kissing, he managed to strip away her bikini, his fingers finding open, engorged lips puddled with fluids.

She gasped. "Oh, yes-s-s," and slipped onto her feet, and shoved him onto his back. "I need to be on top." Following him onto the bed as he scooched over, she straddled his ankles and leaned forward to trail her luscious tits over his raging hard-on.

Alex groaned and reached for her as she slid up, teasing his body with those erect nipples, until she hung over his crotch, dripping pussy lips stroking back and forth over his pulsing dick.

"You still on the pill?" he gasped.

"Yes, my love," panted softly as she slid back, entrapping his cock in her wet cunt. "We're not ready for babies." Her tight pussy drew a gasp from Alex as she began her slow, deep ride. She leaned forward, continuing to surge and they kissed while his hands played with her teasing breasts.

"Oh, Christ," he muttered, "this is so perfect." A soft gasp as he arched his pelvis to meet her strokes. "You're so perfect, babe. I love you." He snatched the back of her head, and pressed her in for a frantic kiss.

"Oh, yes, my darling," she murmured against his lips. "Fuck me, my love. Fuck me *hard*." And they surged together in their passionate dance, her juices lathing his crotch. "Cum now, baby," hissed between her tight lips. "Cum with me now!" Her pussy pulsed in its wet, velvety grasp of his cock as she arched back and emitted a wail of ecstasy.

Alex thrust up hard and with a wheezed grunt released inside her amid a gush of her fluids, the usual sign of her full-throated orgasm. She collapsed against his sweat-slickened body as they continued to kiss, gently now, with affection rather than passion. They lay, melded together, savoring the contact … and they both dozed off.

Alex awakened twenty minutes later and found Trudy, propped up on her elbows, lightly peppering his face with tiny busses. He grinned, enjoying the heat of her skin against his and the sensual press of her breasts. He lightly caressed her back and butt while returning the kisses.

"My hot lover." She chuckled. "You blow me away." She pushed up to sit across his waist, a hand stroking his cheek. Then she slipped off, stood beside the bed, and grinned. "I'm going for a swim." Fingers trailed across his groin caused a stir there. "We can save that for after." With a giggle, she dangled her perfect boobs over his chest and planted a warm kiss on his lips. A quick turn and she headed for the patio doors that led to the back and his eighty-by-forty pool.

Alex grinned as he sat up. "I'll be right behind you, soon as I find a suit."

"I love when you come up behind me," said with a smiled glance back, "but I'm not gonna wear one. It *is* totally secluded back there."

"Okay. A come-as-you-are party." He slipped off the bed and followed through the sliding doors, arriving as Trudy made a graceful dive into the sparkling blue water. He went after her as they frolicked in the warm water.

Twenty-minutes later, they lay beside each other on padded lounges, holding hands as they dried in the afternoon sun.

Trudy glanced at him and sighed, lips ticking into a soft grin.

"That was a happy sound, darling." He gently squeezed her fingers.

"Ecstatic is a better word, my love." She rolled off her lounge and nestled atop of him. "Our falling in love has offered me a life I always hoped for but never expected." Her kiss was tender. "I'm loved by a kind guy who is also dynamite in the sack, and who offers me luxury and generosity beyond my dreams." The second kiss was filled with more passion. "Everything I could have ever wished for," whispered as she pushed up and grazed her glorious breasts across his face. She shivered as his tongue and fingers teased her nipple erect.

Alex lifted up for a more tongue-active kiss, one hand behind her neck and the other down her belly to already open, very wet pussy lips. A finger slid inside and found her bulging clit, bringing a gasp and shudder.

Trudy edged down his body, teasing and tweaking with fingers and tongue until she reached an already stiff cock. "My favorite lollypop," she muttered, her tongue swirling the head and glans and licking down the shaft. His "boys" cupped in one hand, she swiveled to straddle his head in the classic 69 pose, and they pleasured each other with tongue, lips, and fingers until raging lust became unbearable. A quick one-eighty and she had his throbbing hard-on buried deep inside her as she began a slow, erotic rumba. This was their favorite position, where they could fuck while kissing and teasing with their hands.

One arm around her back, the other behind her head, he drew her down for deep kisses as she clenched his cock, taking it deep inside her with long, slow strokes. Alex rose to meet her thrusts, increasing the pace as he was soaked by her juices. He shuddered, growled, and came hard inside that wet, velvet glove, his orgasm sparking hers, releasing her signature gush of fluids.

Trudy slumped against him, mewing softly as they wound down, their lips now engaged in gentle kisses. "Oh, Alex, you complete me," she whispered in his ear.

"Jesus, you drained me, babe. That was really intense."

"I never thought I could be so much in love, my darling." She raised her head. "You're more than I ever hoped for." A soft kiss and she rolled back onto her lounge.

"Yeah, me too. Who'd of thought I'd find my love so quickly." He sat up. "Anyhow, I'm going in for a shower and maybe a nap." He rose and trailed fingers across her still moist body. "We've got that pickleball match with the Housers at four."

"Okay. I'm just going to wind down a bit out here. Maybe swim a few laps. Then I'll be in for my shower too."

Alex nodded and headed inside.

That evening, Alex reclined in his tilting leather easy chair, reading a novel. Trudy was sprawled across a loveseat, looking delectable in silver silk short-shorts, and a mostly unbuttoned, matching blouse, reading a romance. That afternoon, they'd engaged in three vigorous pickleball games against their neighbors, Jack and Jene Houser, winning two and losing the third at 16 to 14. They'd showered and changed in the locker room, then dined at the country club. It was the weekly menu for all-you-can-eat lamb chops.

He gazed at her over the top of his book, nagging questions spooling through his mind. The ash blond beauty was an exceptional woman, better than him at pickleball, but not his equal at golf. She was a passionate and eager lover, filling his life with glorious sex, and he was especially aroused by her explosive orgasms, a squirter in the erotic vernacular. She fulfilled every man's dream of the perfect lover … and that's what was beginning to bother him.

Continually together, things had settled in … still an erotic-filled adventure, with daily, mind-bending sex around which they patterned their other activities. Was all that passion why he told her he loved her? Recalling their first night together, in retrospect it almost seemed as if she'd come there to seduce him. Had he, a naïve guy who'd never had a real girlfriend, been snared by a succubus? Why would such a beauty throw herself at a modestly attractive guy, who also happened to be a newly minted billionaire? Justin had cautioned him to be careful, but Alex wrote that off as coming from an anti-social nerd.

Alex had lavished her with gifts—diamond jewelry, and the Jag sportscar—and now she was living an elite, country club lifestyle. While 'til now, she'd never actually asked for anything, she'd muttered about being under "blinged" when they attended dinner parties, so fancy jewelry was bought. Then she asked his advice about replacing her Toyota with something more fitting for Wellington, and there was the Jag. That night she had whined over dinner about only exercising neighbors open jumpers, but she had nothing to compete with of her own. An obvious hint.

Alex shook his head and returned to his novel. Trudy treated him with tenderness, affection, and passion, very much like someone in love. He had no doubt she felt love for him, but was that a by-product of reverence for his wealth?

And, did he really love her, or was it her classic beauty and the incredible sex that had swept into a ten-year void? He needed to give it more thought. And maybe a test.

~ 10 ~

Emma darted inside her Rav4 and fired up the engine as she slammed the door. Backed out of the tight parking spot, she peeled off north. A glance in her rearview mirror showed Brad bursting out the back exit of Marvin's just as she swung onto the street, nearly colliding with a delivery van, and raced west, the blast of an angry horn following her. After four blocks hurtling down Hollywood Boulevard, a yellow light run, she slowed, and zig-zagged to the Hollywood Chamber of Commerce parking lot.

Her heart wound down from jackhammering her ribs, and she sucked in two deep breaths. Finally semi-calm, she called her sister.

"Hey, Em," sounding cheery. That wasn't going to last. "I'll bet Miry was glad to see you, huh?"

"Yeah." Her voice cracked. "It was going great … until Brad showed up."

"Shit. Again?" Angst charged her sister's voice. "Did he—?"

"No. Luckily, I parked in back of Marvin's, so I got outta there in a flash, but he was hot on my heels." A soft groan. "Damn, Char, that fucker's not giving up. What am I gonna do?"

"The only thing that's safe now. Get out of town."

"Yeah? How do I do that? He's gonna find me before I get home and pack, and—"

"You're not going home." A slight pause. "How are you fixed for cash right now?"

"Got six-hundred in my wallet 'cause I was gonna do some shopping after lunching with Miry."

"Good. Leave your car there. Larry and I'll pick it up this

evening. Key under the mat."

"Then what? Walk? To where?"

"No. Call an Uber and go to one of the Fort Lauderdale airport motels." She sighed. "I've got to consult on a surgery at two, then I'll go to your place, fill a suitcase with some basic things, and meet you there later."

"And then?" Tears sluiced across her cheeks. "Where am I gonna go and still be safe?"

"I got an idea about that." All business now. "I've a friend with contacts to women's shelters. You definitely qualify as a battered woman, fearing for your life. I'll locate someplace even that monster can't find you."

"A shelter? Jeez."

"I know it sounds scary, but you'll have a lot of company, and there's going to be plenty to keep you busy. It's the best option now, until we can figure out something else."

"Okay. I guess I've got little choice. I'll give it a go." She sighed and shook her head. "I'll call you once I've found a spot."

"Good. Talk to you later. And stay vigilant."

"You bet!" And they disconnected.

Emma made the call, and ten minutes later she was settled on a second-row captain's seat in a Honda Odessey minivan, en route to a Days Inn near Fort Lauderdale International Airport. Tears again leaked from the corners of her emerald eyes. She wondered about the life she was about to abandon: her family, her friends, her business … all deserted as she fled for her life. A soft groan welled up as she blotted her tears. Arms folded across her breast, she eased back and closed her eyes.

Thirty minutes later, she entered her second-floor room from the motel's outside balcony. With no baggage to handle, she double-locked the door and settled on an armchair near the window, awaiting her sister bearing clothing and plans for her future … whatever that may be. She whimpered, trying to visualize her new future, but nothing pleasant occurred to her.

~ 11 ~

A hand at the small of her back, Alex guided Trudy between tables as they followed their waiter to a booth near the back of Morgan's Steak House. The posh ambiance and delectable odors of roasting meat did little to ease his tension. Would tonight be the time it all comes out? Everything depended on Trudy.

Arriving, she slid into the C-shaped booth, her powder blue, silk cocktail dress he bought for her last week at Saks, inching up to expose a firm, tanned thigh. As usual, she looked smashing in the strapless dress with a plunging neckline, adorned with the diamond choker and matching earrings he'd also given her. Scootching in, she patted the seat next to her, a sexy smile twitching her lips. "Right here, nice and close, darling, so I can warm you up."

He sighed and relaxed his jaw, pretty sure what she wanted to "warm him up" for. He hoped he was wrong. "Enjoy the concert?" He unfolded the napkin. "Rimsky-Korsakov's *Capriccio Español* and *Scheherazade* are two of my favorites."

"Oh, yeah." She patted his thigh. "That *Capriccio* really turned me on. Such an exciting melody."

"I love how that composer often seems to have beautiful violin solos in his pieces. It created the voice of *Scheherazade*, talking to the emir at the start of each movement." He sipped from his water goblet.

"I never was much into classical music until I met you, Alex. It's really stirring." His head was drawn over for a tender kiss. "I love you."

He held back the expected reply. "Yeah. I always loved it, even as a kid." He picked up a menu. "See something you'd like tonight?" An arm circled her shoulder, snugging her against him, offsetting his lack of response. "Their twenty-ounce porterhouse is a signature dish here."

"Sounds like too much food for me." Trudy squeezed his thigh, stroking toward his crotch.

"Behave, girl," he chuckled, blocking the advance, "and pick something to eat."

She grinned at him, then glanced at the menu. "The filet seems more my size, with baked potato and asparagus. Okay?"

"Swell." A waiter arrived, pen and pad at the ready. "Let's order." Alex looked at their server. "We'll start with a good California Shiraz. I'll leave the choice to you, but something mid-priced." A nod toward Trudy. "She'll have the eight-ounce filet, medium-rare, a baked potato …" The order was placed and the man left to bring the wine.

Alex turned to his lover and covered her hand with his. "So, I'm glad you enjoyed the concert."

"It was *perfect*, darling." She inched around to better face him. "Everything about you … us … is perfect." His head cupped between her hands, another kiss, this one more fused with passion, was delivered. Their faces now inches apart, a pink tongue swiped ruby lips. "I can't imagine anything better in my life." Hazel eyes bore into his blues, the sense of her words a clear declaration.

Alex kissed her and stroked her cheek, not willing to commit. "It does seem great, doesn't it?" The waiter arrived with their wine. *Just in the nick of time.* Alex tasted the sample and nodded. "It's fine."

Drinks poured, they clinked glasses, both smiling, and fell into silent thought, enjoying the nearness of each other. Then the food came, and conversation was again delayed until the arrival of their key lime pie desserts.

Trudy toyed with her classic dessert, pushing it around the plate and taking tiny nibbles as she studied Alex from the corners of her eyes. How to approach this, and was now the best time to discuss both? She desperately wanted to marry this wonderful guy and cement this life style she immersed herself in over the past nearly half-year. That she really loved him was a happy bonus. And he seemed to love her. The wonderful sex was like a narcotic, and she believed he'd become addicted, and *she'd* never been so orgasmic. His lovely, very large cock was a definite bonus.

She pivoted on her seat and shoved the pie away. Time for pitch one. She'd intended to get off the pill too. Becoming a father should be all the hook she needed for pitch two ... marriage. She'd be as surprised as he, wondering how the hell birth control had failed.

"This has been a wonderful day and evening, my love.'" One of his hands gathered in both of hers. "Do you mind if we head home now, though."

"Certainly." He waived at the server and signaled for the check. Glancing back at Trudy, he said, "You feeling okay?"

"Oh, yes, nothing's wrong, I just want to hit the sack early tonight." She gathered her jeweled Lieber handbag. "I'm prepping the O'Brady's open horse for that Grand Prix next week, and I need the rest. Very challenging fences." She sighed. "Wish it was my animal I was training. I really love the sport."

Alex cocked an eyebrow. "Yeah, you've mentioned that before." He slid out of the booth and pulled her up and into his arms. "You were researching jumpers, weren't you?"

A chuckle. "Yep, caught red-handed. I found the perfect gelding, right here in Wellington, but I can't afford him." Perfect lead in. She withdrew a folded paper from her bag and handed it to him. This was going right to script. She'd fuck his brains out, and he'd buy her anything.

Alex scanned the one-page registry for a seventeen-hands German Warmblood with champion bloodlines. "Pricey animal, Trud. A quarter-million?" He handed back the paper and escorted her toward the exit. "So, you'd like me to buy him for you, is that it?"

"Only if you want to, darling," hugging his arm. "It *would* be so perfect, but I promise you a wonderful reward for tonight, whether you buy the horse or not." She pulled him to a stop, wrapped her arms around his neck, and delivered a fiery kiss. "My love for you isn't dependent on a horse," whispered breathily into his ear. *But it would seal the deal.* They looked up as the valet delivered his Lexus.

Seated inside, Trudy's arm stretched across the center console, her fingers lightly stroking his inner thigh. Silence mostly draped them like a heavy quilt during the forty-minute drive to Wellington. Her eyes caught his sidewise glance, and she murmured, "I love you more than words can ever say." A pink tongue swiping moist lips suggested she'd planned a demonstration of that love once they got home. Every stop would be pulled to get that gorgeous roan gelding. And she loved the sex as much as he, and that big cock made it perfect.

They entered the house arm in arm, and once inside, Trudy grabbed a hand and tugged him toward the bedroom.

"C'mon, lover. I'm so horny. We need to fuck, *now!*" A glance over her shoulder. "Quick, unzip me."

She's a damned succubus. He released the zipper, and she stepped out of her dress, nude now except for her bikini undies, as they stormed into the master suite. Alex hauled her to stop when they reached the bed and spun her to him. He shrugged out of his sports coat while she opened his belt and shoved down his pants. Both of her wrists snatched in his hands, he stilled her actions, his eyes holding hers. "We need to talk first." The sight of that erotic body made what he intended really hard.

"No, darling." Her hands freed, she grabbed his shirt, hauled it over his head and cast it aside. "We need to fuck first. Glorious, passionate sex." Her lips were on his in a tongue-dueling attack. "I need to ravish you, and you're gonna shove that beautiful, big thing in me, and I'm gonna soak you when I cum." Another fiery kiss. "And *then* we can talk."

Her hand crept inside his boxers, and no surprise, he was already hard. Despite his best intentions, he couldn't resist her, and he knew that was her plan. She'd have her way with him, and he'd love it … and then he'd be strong. He hoped. He stepped out of his slacks, puddled at his feet, and stripped away her bikini, then crushed her flaming body against his, setting his whole being afire. They tumbled onto the bed, Trudy on top, and she began trailing her lips, tongue and fingers down his body, nipples of firm boobs teasing his skin.

As she reached his rigid dick, caressing and licking it, he shuddered and clenched his jaw. *This isn't right. Not now. Not anymore!* Alex curled up, grasped her head between his hands, and drew her alongside his body.

"What, baby. I'm just getting started." Her wide, hazel eyes studied his.

"I know, Trudy, and I love our sex … and maybe that's the problem."

"I don't understand." Propped on an elbow beside him, fingers still teasing his dick. "How can our great sex be a problem, Alex?"

"Because you use it to melt me down so I'll buy you that

horse." He sighed and ran a hand through her short hair. "Just like I bought you the Jag, the jewelry, the fancy duds."

"I … I never asked you for those other things, darling. You did it—"

"I know. Never directly. But this whole thing has happened so fast. Terrific sex the very first night we met. I've been thinking. It's almost like you planned to seduce me."

"Alex!" She pushed up, eyes flared, and sat next to him. "I never—"

"Okay, maybe that's a stretch, but you knew I was relatively inexperienced …" He slid up against the headboard. "You're a wonderful, intelligent woman … gorgeous, and beyond my dreams in the sack, but I've come to realize none of this would have happened if I were some poor schlub with a mundane office job, making 50K a year." He stroked her cheek. "You want—no, deserve—the finer things in life, and I've been providing them for you because I thought I loved you."

"You thought …?" Tears pooled in her eyes. "You've *said* you loved me. I thought we were headed for marriage, but …"

"Frankly, it's occurred to me. But I've realized that while I *do* like you, there has to be more than terrific sex … and buying you expensive toys." He sighed again, slipped off the bed, and started to dress. "I'm drawing the line at the horse." She sat, arms crossed across her breasts, tiny rivulets trailing across her cheeks, eyes big as quarters. "True love doesn't come with dollar signs. I'm really sorry it's come to this, but I realize I *don't* love you. At least not yet, and I'm done buying your love, if it ever even really existed."

"Oh, Alex! Don't say that. After everything we've—"

"Okay. Maybe that was a bit harsh," turning toward her. "I'm really new to this whole relationship thing. But these are the facts … how I feel, and it's not fair to give you hopes for things that aren't going to happen." He finished dressing. "We need a clean break. Luckily, your condo hasn't sold yet, so you can move back there tomorrow." He retrieved her dress from the floor and tossed it to her. "You can spend the night in here, and pack up what you'll need for the next few days. I'll sleep in a guest room tonight."

He turned toward the door. "I'll get your things packed up and delivered to you in the next few days." He paused in the opening and regarded her, crying softly, the sheet modestly draped across her magnificent figure. Jaw clenched, he fought down a groan. *Gotta stay strong.* "I'm sorry to be so abrupt, Trudy, but I learned in business that unpleasant things need to be dealt with swiftly, and I'm sure this has transformed from something idyllic in your mind, to something horrible. I just don't know any way to make it easier." He shrugged. "As I said, I like you, but I've come to realize I don't *love* you. All the wonderful sex clouded my judgement, and I'm apparently very inexperienced at this romance stuff." He pivoted and left the room, closing the door behind him. Her soft keening followed him down the hallway.

Alex ground his teeth and shook his head. He hated himself for what just happened, but he knew of no other way to handle this. But, it was a good, very expensive lesson learned. How can he find real love not tainted by his wealth? He needed a plan. He was tired now. Like Scarlet, he'd think about it tomorrow. A new day.

~ 12 ~

The last box taped up, Alex set it with two others by his front door. Manuel rattled through the entrance with his two-wheel dolly and paused, his eyes sweeping from the three cartons to Alex.

"These are the last, *Señor*?"

"Yes, that's everything." Alex patted the man on the back. "You have the address?"

"*Sí,* and I am to call her *un media hora* away. Miss D'Angelo, she is expecting me, no?"

"Yes, I talked to her this morning." He peeked out the door at the U-Haul. "You have room for everything?"

"*Sí, sí,* I have it all." He slid the tongue of his dolly under the bottom box as Alex handed him an envelope.

"Here's your payment, Manuel. There's enough there to cover your time to help her unload and organize everything." He gripped the man's shoulder. "I know you have to get back to the show arena to help set up for the coming grand prix, but please spend as much time with her as she needs."

"Of course, *Señor*. You are very generous. I will do all that is needed." He tilted the final three cases onto the dolly's wheel and exited down the walk to his waiting rental van that Alex had provided for this trip.

Alex hung in the doorway and watched him finish loading Trudy's things and drive off. He sighed as he reentered his house and slouched on a leather armchair in his den. The finale to their affair, and though he had few regrets, somehow he felt hollow. A soft chuckle bubbled up. He certainly would miss their mind-blowing sex. With little experience, other than high-paid escorts, he wondered what he might expect from whomever his next lover might be.

That would be his next project—finding a woman who could love him for himself, and not his money. Rising, he strode for his office. The obvious thing was a change of venue, where, hopefully, he might be unrecognized. He settled at his desk and fired up his laptop. Need he go as far as Miami? Maybe just Ft. Lauderdale? His fingers attacked the computer's keys as he began his research.

An hour later, he'd formulated the bones of a plan. First, he needed a modest car, and he'd found and bought a four-year-old blue Dodge Charger through *AutoTrader*. The money was wired, and it would be delivered tomorrow.

Throughout his business life, he'd never been a fancy dresser, so he had plenty of worn jeans and wrinkled cargo pants, and a good supply of polo shirts. No problem dressing for the part. Comfortable, scuffed leather loafers had been his everyday footwear. So, his toned-down persona was set.

Back on the laptop, he surfed the Ft. Lauderdale social scene, looking for modest gatherings. The Dania Beach Boat Club drew his attention. He'd loved to fish as a kid, and his Uncle Carl had taken him bottom fishing several times over the middle reef in his Boston Whaler, so joining that club may have a dual value. Anyway, it'd be a start.

Next he found his way onto some sort of Dark Web and located an ID forger. Despite being fifty miles south of his usual stamping grounds, the name Alex Jordan may still be recognized. He'd made a lot of the newspapers with his company's sale. He settled on an alias, Alex Penny, and arranged for a driver's license, Social Security card, and phony auto insurance IDs, along with a few others, just to lend credibility. He'd open a checking account in that name with a local Wells Fargo when he got on site. A new

VISA card with a $10,000 credit line was arranged online with little trouble.

Membership was arranged at the boat club, and an annual fee paid, the first charge on his new VISA. They had a monthly cocktail party scheduled for the following weekend, so he had plenty of time to get fully established as a new local.

His final act was to research apartment rentals and find something modest, maybe two-bedroom/one bath, in the area. Hopefully something furnished, but if not, there were several local thrift stores in the area that should have all he needed. He'd probably return to Wellington most nights, if he didn't have company. He'd decide all that as he went.

Now, how to present himself to his new acquaintances? After some thought, he settled on that he was a new arrival working for a local tech firm with a modest, recent inheritance that would tide him over for a while until he got established.

Easing back, hands clasped across his belly, Alex surveyed his work and smiled. He'd put together a pretty good package. Once the Dodge arrived he'd venture south and survey what he'd arranged, and visit several apartments he'd make appointments to see. Two or three days at the most to get everything set up. He'd start with the boat club's monthly get-together, and then see what other opportunities there were to meet a *real* woman and maybe find romance. This time he wouldn't rush in just because of great sex.

He rubbed his eyes and sighed. Great sex would be nice, though. Were there women out there just a hot as Trudy who might do it out of love? He hoped so.

~ 13 ~

Emma stirred at screeching of a car stopping outside on the Motels driveway. Peering down, she gasped. Brad's black Audi A6, parked in front of the office.

Emma lurched to her feet, snatched up her purse, and cracked open the door for a peek. As her stalker hurried into the motel office, Emma slipped out the door and raced to the end of the row, circling to the rear balcony that accessed the rooms on that side. Down those stairs two at a time, she ran past parked cars and into a rear lot of the next building.

How did he find me again so quickly? Probably my damned VISA card. She tried to pay cash, but they required a credit card for a security deposit. Brad must be hooked into all the cop's surveillance systems, with cohorts ready to report if they flagged her. Dammit! What now? She worked her way through rear parking lots and back yards for two blocks before she chanced making it to the street. This was the airport area, so she hoped to find a taxi.

Six nervous minutes later, her eyes constantly scanning the area for that black Audi, she was safely inside a Checkered Cabs minivan.

"Where to, lady?"

"You know any motels nearby that accept cash?" *Probably a hookers' hangout.* She gave a wry chuckle.

"Sure." He peeked at her. "Gotta say, ya don't look the type, though." He shrugged. "No offence intended. Ya gotta do what ya gotta do ta make it in this fucking world."

"It's not like that." She smiled, in spite of her straits. "I've lost my credit card, and I'm waiting for someone to bring me another." Sounded lame, but she really didn't care what he thought.

"Okay." He began to drive. "I know just the spot. The least grubby of the lot, but it's a couple miles from the airport."

"Sounds good to me." She settled back and closed her eyes.

Forty-minutes later, Emma was once more in a room, the Apex Inn, and had called Char to let her know the change of location. The clerk's eyebrow arched when she asked to pay for the night, rather than an hour or two. He studied her and shrugged. She wasn't dolled up like a hooker, so maybe—? He gladly accepted her seventy buck and gave her the key.

Emma again settled on a not-so-clean stuffed armchair and tried to tune out the grunts and moans coming from the next room. That was soon over, and she heard them exit. Peace at last. At least for the moment.

She'd talked to her sister, who'd just finished up at Memorial Hospital and was on her way to Emma's place to collect necessary things. They'd meet about four. And then what, she wondered again? Char had a plan. No surprise there. Her big sis always seemed on top of whatever was going on, always in control. A good feature for a cardiac surgeon. Emma had never been that organized, but she'd always been the "creative" one in the family, and her interior design business was a logical extension of that. Two different peas from the same pod, but it had worked for them. No siblings were closer or more loving than they. Thank God, under the current circumstances.

Emma dozed in the chair, no sugar plums dancing in her dreams. Instead, it was Brad, choking the life from her as he fucked her with a giant dick. She writhed and moaned, but managed to still sleep. Rest she would need for the coming days.

Charlene Hamlin let herself into Emma's apartment just before three p.m. She'd stopped by her husband's office to pick up $9,000 in cash he'd retrieved from their bank. They'd replace it later from Emma's account, which held just under a half-million in a premium Fidelity money-market account, earning about 5%. Char would need about twenty minutes to pack a small suitcase with basic clothing and necessities for travel. Emma would buy what else she needed when she arrived. Thanks to her friend, Nancy, Char had found the perfect place, just north of Chicago. A battered women's refuge that provided both protection and activities to keep their charges busy and involved with living. Larry was calling to register her there, a place Emma would thrive at, but Char would surely miss her. Visits, and even phone calls, would be off the table because they could lead Brad to his victim.

She was about to slip Emma's laptop into the case after removing her location app, but changed her mind, unsure if Brad could still trace it. Cyber experts could do amazing things. Her sister could buy a new one after she arrived, and see that it was air-gapped, with no cyber connections. She downloaded all Emma's personal files onto a thumb drive before wiping the hard drive, then shouldered her purse and closed the suitcase, ready to leave. She jerked to a stop by a rattle at the door. Some scrapping at the lock and it blew open, Brad Barnes standing in the opening.

"What the hell are you doing here, you bastard?" Char snarled.

"Looking for your little sis, Char." He strode in, his eyes sweeping the room. "Long time, no see, babe." He perused her. "You're looking pretty hot, too."

"Emma's not here, and you shouldn't be. Get the hell outta here." She unsnapped the clasp on her purse.

His eyes settled on the suitcase by her feet. "Packing for Emma, huh? Where d'ya think she can go that I can't find her?"

He moved closer, eyes narrowed.

"You'll never know. She wants nothing to do with you." She slipped her right hand into her bag. "Go find some other poor woman who likes to be slapped around. It's going to come back to haunt you one day."

"Yeah, sez you." He stood a foot in front of her. "Tell me where she is and I won't hurt you … much." His grin was evil, his handsome face distorted by hate, as he snatched her by both upper arms, squeezing hard.

"Oww, that hurt, you nut."

"That's the idea, Doc." He breathed an evil chuckle. "A little pain is good for the soul." One hand raised, prepared to deliver a slap. "So, where the fuck is she? I got plans for us."

"Your plans won't mean much, if I put a few 9mm slugs in you, will they?" Her eyes bored into his.

His downward glance found a small S & W pistol pressed against his lower chest. "You gonna shoot a Miami ADA, ya dumb bitch? They'll have your ass—"

"I think not when I show them the bruises you've just made on my arms, you asshole." She pressed hard against him. "And my bruised cheek when I'll slap myself with your dead hand and get some skin under your nails for the CSI boys. Even your cop buddies won't touch me, and besides, you won't be around to see it."

"You tough enough to do that, bitch?" He stepped back and squinted, appraising her.

"You bet your shriveled balls, I am, tough guy. Bullies like you are easy." She gestured him toward a chair. "Sit."

He snarled but complied, eyes riveted on the gun. Char never took her eyes off him as she found the ever-present roll of duct tape in Emma's cabinet. She forced Brad to bind his right wrist to the chair's arm, and left ankle to its leg. She then felt safe to secure his other arm and leg the same way.

"I know you'll figure how to get loose pretty quickly, but I'll be long gone." She strode to Emma's kitchen and retrieved a sharp paring knife. Paused in front of Brad, she rested the short blade on his throat, next to his carotid artery. "Maybe a little flick there, and let you bleed out. Save other poor girls the misery of thinking you're some kinda catch."

His eyes flared. "You wouldn't … No way to call that self-defense."

"Yeah." She sighed and withdrew the knife. "And I'm pledged to save lives, not take them, even from assholes like you." She pivoted toward the door. "Forget about Emma, Brad. She'll be long gone to places you'll never finds her. Move on, asshole."

And with the suitcase in hand, the pistol back in her purse, she was out the door, en route to her sister and her new future. On the way, she plunged the small blade into three of his tires. That ought to keep him stranded a while longer.

~ 14 ~

Alex, now in the persona of Alex Penny, exited I-95 at Griffin Road and followed instructions from his Android phone's GPS, spying the small harbor off the Cut Off Canal, just to his south. Once in the parking lot, the clubhouse was easily located, popular music wafting out from through open windows. The Fort Lauderdale Boat Club's monthly cocktail party was in full flow. He parked his newly acquired Dodge Charger in an open slot, killed the engine, and lingered for a moment.

A call last week was all he needed to acquire a year's membership, and he'd learned of the coming cocktail party, just four days hence. He'd opted to pick up his membership card tonight at the sign-in table.

A sigh, and he exited the van, uncertain what to expect. This was his first stab at meeting a woman after the messy breakup with Trudy, and he hoped to avoid a repeat of that circumstance. Whatever woman he may or may not meet, the relationship must be built on personalities, not wealth. For anyone concerned, he was an everyday guy, making a modest income as the new tech nerd at a local internet firm.

Inside, he registered and picked up his ID card. About sixty people, more men than women, and mostly middle-age, milled around the floor, a few dancing to piped-in music. Dress was modest to scruffy-casual, so his khaki cargo pants and Guy Harvy white t-shirt, with his signature frolicking blue marlin on the back, fit right in. He spotted a cash bar and ordered a vodka and tonic. Drink in hand, he edged to one side and scanned the room. Mostly little cliques of people, standing in small bunches or seated at tables. Alex reminded himself, he'd developed few social skills as he built his business. Steeling his nerve, he approached a pod of three men and two women. Two turned toward him offering noncommittal smiles.

"Hi." His hand offered. "I'm Alex Penny, newly minted member."

"Bill." His hand shook.

"Charles." Also shook.

"Miguel." With a nod.

"Nancy." Dead pan.

"Anne." The only really welcoming smile. "You a boater, or a fisherman?"

"No boat yet." He chuckled. "Just moving into the area. Loved to fish as a kid, but too busy lately, and probably outta reach right now."

"No one should ever be too busy to fish," Anne said, her sky-blue eyes regarding him over the rim of her cocktail,

"Geez, Anne. Just met the guy and you're already promoting a trip." Bill turned to Alex. "Anne captains a charter boat."

"Interesting." Alex grinned. "I pictured that guy as scruffy and bearded." He studied the blonde's compact, 5'6" frame, sporting a khaki short-sleeve, buttoned shirt and tan cargo shorts that displayed a pair of well-shaped, tan legs. Modest boobs, attractive face with a pug nose, and classic bow-shaped lips. "You certainly aren't that."

Soft laughter from the group.

"Don't let her looks fool ya," Charles added. "She's all business on her boat."

"I bet," Alex mused. "I used to bottom fish with an uncle, and worked as mate for two summers during high school on a charter boat outta Miami."

"Well, if you get back into it," handing him a card, "I'm available."

He nodded, pocketed the card, and wondered what else she might be available for. He hung with the group for ten minutes, discussion ranging from boating, to football, to politics. That's when he decided to move on. A glance back found Anne, gesturing with a flowing hand, the antics of a recent tail-walking sailfish caught by one of her clients.

Alex circulated around the room, getting comfortable with meeting people on a social level again. He danced with Deena, a willowy brunette, but felt no chemistry when all she could talk about was her pushy boss, who wanted her to spend her day on the job actually doing her work.

Next he tried Terry, a tall, washed-out blonde who'd apparently had more than one too many and kept stepping on his toes. Disappointed he retired to a table and nursed his second drink as he scanned the room. This might turn out to be a bust, but it was only his first move. Then he noticed Anne, the boat captain, sitting with two girls.

What the Hell. He finished his drink and strolled over to her. The music was a country love song he didn't recognize.

"Hey, Captain." He grinned. "Care to dance?" He nodded at the open floor. "They're finally playing something my speed."

Her face lit up with a warm smile, and she offered her hand. "Why not?"

He drew her to her feet, led her to an open space, and spun her into his arms."

"Whoo. Pretty good move for a computer nerd." Her head arched back, she grinned.

"Well, I try." He snugged her close, and she rested her head on his shoulder. Her body was warm and firm against his, and a familiar stirring began in his crotch. He pursed his lips and willed it away. He wasn't going to rush into something again. He hoped he learned his lesson. They continued the dance in silence and stayed there for a second tune before returning to her table. She paused.

"Thanks, that was nice … for a change."

"What?" His brow wrinkled.

"Most of these guys tend to get a bit grabby." A small kiss to his cheek. "You were different, which was sweet." She settled on her chair. "Call me if you want to try some offshore fishing. It'll be peak season for the next month or so."

"Will do, and I also enjoyed the dance." He kissed her hand and left. No sign she wanted him to call for anything other than a fishing charter, which was disappointing. Circulating the room, Alex found nothing more of interest. A glance at his watch signaled it was time to go. He'd made an evening appointment to see a rental apartment, not far from there. If he were going to be committed to finding a woman who knew nothing of his wealth, he needed a local base of operation. He waved goodbye and headed for the door.

~ 15 ~

Alex paused at the exit. His eyes swept across his newly rented furnished apartment, and he gave a satisfied nod. The living room sported a brown cloth sofa, two faux-leather armchairs, coffee table, and a dining area with four chairs at a glass-top table, and a four-door storage cabinet. A fifty-inch TV hung on the wall opposite the sofa. The small eat-in kitchen was off to the right with a three-seat breakfast counter, and the hallway at the left led to two bedrooms with a shared bath. The smaller one would work as a home office or den. Not very fancy, but he *was* a "working stiff."

Now he was off to a nearby Target to buy bed linens and some towel, and then he'd cruise a couple of upscale bars on Las Olas that Internet searches showed were regular after-work watering holes for local office workers. While he was seeking girlfriend material, he wouldn't pass up a romp of casual sex. Trudy had whetted his appetite for that. But he knew he was no lothario, so conquests may not prove easy without the lure of his wealth. It would be an interesting challenge.

A sigh and a shrug, and he exited, locking the door, then hurried down two flights to the under-building parking area where his newly acquired, four-year-old Dodge Charger awaited in his one reserved spot. A glance at his Timex—the Rolex stayed in Wellington—showed he had time for his shopping before joining the evening happy hour crowd. His affair with Trudy hadn't really taught him much about meeting women. She'd done all the heavy lifting, but despite probably being a so-called nerd, he wasn't that shy … he hoped. He'd survived at the boat club cocktail party, and had met one appealing woman—Anne Parsons. She'd seemed more interested in him as a customer than a date, so he'd leave her in reserve in case he struck out now.

Alex beeped the Dodge's alarm, slipped inside, and fired up the engine. He ordered his thoughts while the a/c cooled and dried the air. *I'm Alex Penny now. Gotta keep myself centered on that, and hope I can find a real woman who appreciates him, despite his average circumstances.* With a nod, he backed up and exited the building, determined to build a new life.

He chuckled. Totally opposite direction of most guy's goals—poorer, not richer.

~~~

Alex backed into a curbside spot on Las Olas Blvd. and hesitated, staring at the blue neon sign: Gulfstream Bar & Grill. His earlier visit to Ray's Place proved unproductive in finding a woman of interest. Seated at the bar, he'd nursed a Coor's Lite for an hour as he scanned the influx of office workers, mostly white and Hispanic young to middle-age office types, but the only three who ignited a stir of interest were clearly already attached to a partner.

Casual conversation with a guy on the next stool brought the recommendation of the joint where he was now parked. A glance at his watch and he shrugged. Time had snuck past the usual happy hour, but the worst that might happen was he'd drink another Coors. He exited his Dodge and strode toward the entry. *Alex Penny's first night on the hunt.* He snickered softly and pushed through the doorway, determined not to let impatience push him into another error with a greedy woman.

Dimly lit, he needed a moment for his eyes to adjust. A long mahogany bar near the rear stretched across more than half the room. Small tables for four filled the rest of the space, many still occupied … definitely an office worker crowd. Apparently, happy hour ran longer here. He stepped to the bar and slid onto a stool next to a willowy but pleasantly buxom Latina who was talking to a chunky blond babe, wearing thick-lensed glasses.

"What's yer pleasure, handsome?" a female barista asked.

"You sure you're talking to me?" He swiveled on his stool and shot her a grin.

"Sure, compared to a lot of guys I see in here, you're a knockout." She smiled back and placed a paper napkin on the bar top.

"Well, thanks." She was a pert, washed-out blonde, nicely filling out a logoed T-shirt, but he was hoping for something more upscale. "Coors Lite, in a glass." He scanned the room. "Still pretty busy happy hour, huh?"

"Yeah." She poured his beer from a can. "But it's Friday. TGIF, ya know, so no one's in a hurry to head home."

The dusky-skinned Latina next to him turned from her friend, picked up what looked to be a martini, and glanced at Alex, who drew in a sharp breath. Her raven hair, straight and silky, hung well below her shoulders. Almond-shaped hazel eyes bordered a small, straight nose, above full, bow-shaped lips, all delectably centered on a classic, heart-shaped face. A slender figure with curvy hips implied a blended European heritage.

He tipped his glass toward her. "Hi. I'm Alex Penny."

She nodded. "Camilla," and sipped her drink. "Haven't seen you here before."

"Yeah. Just took a new job in Fort Lauderdale. Tech security for a financial company." He arched his eyebrows. "You?"

"Executive assistant for an attorney at Burns, Samuel, and Leverstein."

"Sounds important."

"Mostly boring. We do mainly contract law." She chuckled and turned to face him, the other woman now ignored. "But it pays well, and there are plenty of perks." She was sleek in tailored black slacks and a short-sleeve silk blouse that did little to hide the jut of firm, young tits. "So, you're a techy, huh?" She laid her hand on his knee. "You don't look like a nerd." Hazel eyes lingered on his as she sipped hcr martini.

Alex chuckled and dropped his hand on hers. "Thanks ... I think. Seems like I've got a knack for cyber stuff, but I try to live a normal life." He took a swig of his Coors. "I like sports ... playing and watching ... and I hope to have a normal social life after work ... whatever that is." Someone shoved coins in an old-style juke box, nestled in a far corner, and Neil Daimond was soon crooning "Hello Again," one of his love songs.

"Ha, a golden oldie." Jordon rose, Camilla's hand in his. "Someone waxing nostalgic." He drew her from her perch. "Wanna dance?" nodding at the small open floor space, where one couple was already swaying together.

"Best offer I've had today." She laid her drink on the bar and trailed him to the floor, "and the night's still young."

Alex spun her in a circle and drew her lithe body into his arms. A smirk creased his lips as he silently thanked Trudy for drawing out his sexuality. Prior to their affair, he'd been way too shy for any of this. Camilla pressed close, her head rested on his shoulder as they swayed around the floor.

Cheek-to-cheek, he whispered in her ear. "You smell delicious, Camilla."

"Thanks. It's Black Orchid. You're not too bad, yourself. Musk?"

He nodded. "I bet you taste even better," said with a muted chuckle, as he was beginning to stir from her contact, amazed at how easily he was aroused, post Trudy. His right hand at the small of the woman's back, Camilla's body molded even more closely. She couldn't miss his growing erection, teasing her abdomen.

"Oh, Alex," the lobe of his ear sucked between moist lips,

"you're such a *naughty* boy."

"Can't help it, babe. You're the first woman to excite me since I moved into the area." No need for her to know this was his first night there. "I'm swamped by some instinctive connection I can't explain." He arched his neck, their eyes locked. "I sense you feel it too."

"Yeah." Her cupid's bow lips tilted into a smile. "Animal instinct." She wiggled her pelvis against his growing hard-on, "and that *very* intriguing thing." The song ended, and they eased apart. "How 'bout you buy me dinner and we get better acquainted." A glance at the bar. "They serve a great burger and crunchy sweet potato fries."

"Perfect." Her hand in his, he strode to the bar and they ordered, then moved to a small booth in a far corner. As Camilla turned to slip onto the bench, she snaked an arm around his neck, and they savored a heated, tongue-dancing kiss.

"You're such a horny beast, Alex." She chuckled, slid onto the bench, and patted the seat next to her. "I love it, 'cause I'm your mirror image." A pink tongue swiped ruby lips.

Alex perched beside her, his arm circled her shoulder and drew her in for a sensual kiss. Soon hands voyaged into tentative exploration and teasing, and he was now rock hard under the feathery touch of busy fingers. His roamers eventually found their way inside her waist-band, venturing down to very wet and open lips, drawing breathy pants.

"Those fucking burgers better get here in a hurry," she muttered. "I can barely wait for dessert." She shoved his hand away. "You live close by?" she gasped.

"Yeah. Just moved in today." He kissed her. "Gonna help me christen the bedroom?"

"You bet, darling." She stroked his crotch. "This is something a girl like me could never pass up." She gave a small squeeze through his pants. "Wow!"

~ 16 ~

Emma lurched awake at a rap on her room's door. A peek through the curtains assured it was Char. She released a pent-up breath she didn't realize she'd been holding, removed the chair she'd wedged under the knob for extra security, and unlocked the door.

Char stepped in, set a small suitcase on the floor, and folded her weeping sister into her arms. She rubbed her kid sister's back, murmuring softly in her ear, just as if calming a skittish colt. They shuffled inside, and a well-placed kick swung the door shut. After the well of tears dried, the sisters eased apart, Char gripping Emma's shoulder at arm's length. "Jesus, hon, what a mess." She glanced at the shabby room with its tattered bedspread and threadbare chair. "This place is a real palace, huh?"

"Yeah." The corners of Emma's lips tilted into a shadow of a smile, the first in hours. "Like what I've done with it?" turning and waving her hand. She glanced back at her bleached-blond sister, clad in fitted navy blue gaberdine slacks and a blue-striped, matching blouse. No matter what the disaster, Charlene Hamlin always looked cool and ready to rumble. Piercing blue eyes and an unmessable pixie cut withstood any challenge.

Emma swiped away tears, perched on the edge of her mattress, and motioned Char into the chair. "So, any problems getting my stuff? And you're sure you weren't followed?"

"Some, and yes, in that order." She sighed. "Brad burst in to your apartment just as I was about to leave."

"What?" Emma gestured at darkening bruises on her sister's

biceps. "Did he hurt you?"

"Tried to. Thought he could force me to tell him where you were." She chuckled, reached into her purse, and withdrew her small, 9mm handgun. "My little Bodyguard here stopped that in a hurry."

"You *shot* him?" Emma's eyes flared.

"Didn't have to." She replaced the weapon. "The threat was sufficient. Bullies are rarely brave, and he's no exception. I used some of your duct tape to bind him to a chair, then punched holes in three of his tires on the way out. No way he coulda followed me, and I'm sure he was alone."

"Couldn't you get in trouble for that, Char? Isn't that assault? He *is* an ADA, and—"

"I doubt it. How could he explain what he was doing in your apartment. I had a right to be there, but he was trespassing. Anyway," she reached into her purse and withdrew an envelope, "I've got $9,000 here, and I've packed some essentials," nodding at the suitcase. "I left your laptop, in case his tech buddies could find a way to trace it. You can buy a new one when you arrive at the shelter."

"You've already arranged that?"

Emma's sister nodded.

"You're efficiency personified, Sis." Emma shook her head grinning. "So, where is this refuge you've booked for me? And, how will I get there?"

"Highland Park, Illinois. It's an upscale northern Chicago suburb." She pulled a small sheath of papers from her purse. "I printed some info from their website." She chuckled. "I even used the library's computer for that so there's no trail to follow from mine, in case that bastard gets clever. And you'll travel via bus. You can use cash for the ticket, so there'll be no digital record of the sale." She removed a small, Android flip-phone from her purse.

"I used this burner phone I bought earlier, again so there's no trace back to you." She handed it Emma. "It's a basic phone, with no smart features that might get hacked. Use it sparingly, but Brad can never trace it."

"Jeez, Sis, you're a regular CIA spook." Emma took the envelope and phone. "How did you manage all this in one day?" She waved the envelope of cash. "And, can you afford this?"

"Yeah, thanks to Nana, but I'll get it back from your Fidelity account. I'll just need your signature here," another paper from her copious purse, "to authorize me as a user." She handed Emma the paper and a pen. "I'll funnel you cash as you need it, using UPS to a local shop. I found one in Evanston, about twelve miles south of your new digs. That distance will be another buffer from him finding you."

Char glanced at her watch and rose. "C'mon, baby, it's time to go. There's an eight p.m. Greyhound leaving from Fort Lauderdale. You'll have to change in Memphis, and overnight there, and I think there'll be two nights on the buses, but it's the only safe way to go, other than buying a car and driving yourself ... and a single young woman on the road isn't safe."

"Which reminds me," Emma pushed to her feet, "what about my Rav4?"

"You left the keys under the floor mat?"

Emma nodded.

"Larry and I will pick it up tonight. Where's the title?"

"In the glove box, with the registration and insurance papers. Why?"

"We'll have to sell it, I guess. Too easy for him to trace, so we can't get it to you. The shelter has shuttle service available at to take you any place local, and you can use a cab, if necessary." She handed the suitcase handle to Emma, who began rolling it toward the door. "Uber's probably out because I think they only accept credit cards, but you'll manage. I don't want you to buy a car there, because Brad may be able to trace a registration, once you get it insured." Char's eyes swept the room. "Got everything, hon?"

"Yeah, I didn't come with much." They exited onto the outer, second-floor walkway. "That sonofabitch has really screwed up my life." Salty rivulets again traced across round cheeks. "I was happy again, until this shit."

Char nodded and circled her shoulder with an arm, thinking of the old lemon/lemonade saw. But number one was to keep her baby sister safe.

No need to check out, since it was a cash deal. A minute later, Emma was settled in Char's Lexus 350 sedan, heading toward the downtown bus station, and a new life.

Suburban Chicago. *Wonder what that's like.* She'd never been there.

~ 17 ~

Alex slipped the Dodge into his apartment's assigned spot, killed the engine, and turned to Camilla, whose hand had been teasing his crotch all during the heated rush from the bar. They'd choked down their burgers and fries with lots of interspersed kisses and fondling, then hurried to his car for the short trip to his new digs. No question this gorgeous Latina creature was hot for his cock, and his wandering fingers, while in the booth, discovered a very wet and obviously welcoming pussy.

He leaned over and planted a heated kiss, one hand caressing a firm tit and tweaking its nipple, then pulled back and opened his door.

"C'mon, gorgeous. Let's get inside so we can do this properly."

"Properly?" She chuckled and exited his sedan. "I'm looking for *improperly,* buster. I expect to be ravished, 'cause that's what I'm planning for you." She circled the front, and he swung her into a fierce embrace, their mouths fused, their hands erotic roamers.

Breaking free, her hand in his, he hurried toward the exit. "Two floors up."

"I'll race ya." Camilla charged through the doorway and leapt up the stairs, two at a time. "C'mon, slow poke." She glanced over her shoulder. "I'm on fire."

Alex had snatched the Target bag of bedding from the Dodge and hurried after her. He snickered, as eager to get naked as she seemed to be. Probably little chance to make the bed before they got busy. At the second floor landing he found Camilla, hands on curved hips, her eyes sweeping up and down the hallway.

"Which apartment?"

"206," starting up the hall, fishing out his key. "Follow me." A moment later, the door opened and she darted inside, then spun to face him as he kicked it closed.

"Christ, I'm horny." She flung herself against him, arms around his neck, their mouths welded with tongue-fencing kisses. Alex's hands found her butt, and he hoisted her as her legs circled his waist so tightly he couldn't work fingers inside her blouse to play with a pair of firm, unfettered B-cups. Fused together with frantic passion, they stumbled into the bedroom and perched on the edge of his unmade mattress.

Camilla slipped free, stood, and snatched at his shirt, yanking it over his head as he unzipped the back of her slacks. A quick shimmy and they puddled at her feet as she stripped away her blouse. One backward step, arms raised, wrists crossed with finger interlocked, she did a slow pirouette. "Like it?" Clad only in black panties, she was Erotica personified. A narrow waist separated luscious, curved hips and a firm, round butt from a flat belly and those lovely tits. As she finished her spin, she shed the panties. A grin split her wide mouth, a pink tongue darting across full, red lips.

Alex was out of his pants and boxers, and his eyes feasted on her other lips, open and wet. "You're fucking gorgeous and you know it, witch." He snatched her wrist, drew her in, and spun her onto her back across the bed. "I wanna feast on that lovely, flowing well." He slipped between her spread legs, his raging hardon hovering above that pulsing pussy, and attacked her breasts, licking, sucking, and tweaking very erect nipples.

"Oh, *yes*," she muttered. "That's *so* wonderful." Fingers of one hand fluttered across his cock, teasing the head and shaft. Her thumb wiped away seeping pre-cum, and she brought it to her mouth, sucking it clean.

Alex worked his way across her ribs and down her belly, his mouth venturing across damp skin, sucking, licking, and teasing on its way to the final target. Arrived, his tongue grazed those swollen lips as it darted in and out of the wet pool, tweaking an engorged and very large clit. Camilla quivered and shook at his attack, moaning, fingers clutching the mattress.

"Oh, God, oh, God, I'm gonna cum." Back arched, she bucked and squirmed, "I'm gonna … oh, *shit!*" She snatched at his hair and thrashed back and forth, projecting a feral moan. With a finger inside her, he felt the pulsing tightening of her cunt. Alex continued to work her, both finger and tongue as she surged into a protracted orgasm. Her body eventually relaxed and went slack, and their breathing spiraled back to normal.

"Jesus, Alex." She hauled him atop of her, his still very hard cock pressed into her belly, and they kissed. "That was fucking intense, baby." She chuckled. "Never had anyone play my fiddle so well, you beast." A hand slid down and found what she sought. "Now, it's my turn." She shoved him over onto his back and lay beside him, propped up on an elbow as fingers trailed across his damp skin. As they settled on that beautiful, hard thing between his legs, she scootched down and began a maddening tongue tease, licking the shaft, sucking his balls, and especially teasing around the head and glans.

Camilla then straddled his belly, her still very wet lips cushioning his cock, as her nipples tweaked his chest, and they shared a passionate kiss.

"Now," she whispered in his ear, "I want that big boy inside me."

"I've got condoms." He reached toward his night stand.

"Shhh." She kissed him again, adjusted her hips, and drew him inside. "I'm on the pill."

He shuddered at the tight, wet grip of her cunt, and she began to pulse and squeeze with Kegel trained muscles. They continued to kiss, tongues on a frantic journey, as she surged against him. "Oh, God, your cock is so beautiful," she groaned. "I'm gonna cum again. Cum with me, baby. Cum *now* ..." Camilla shuddered and quickened her pace, and her pulsing orgasm fired his as he thrust against her.

"Oh, fuck," Alex muttered as he emptied inside her, while she continued to buck against him with another protracted release. Finished finally, they collapsed together with soft kisses and gentle hands as they wound down. He thought of Trudy and her soaking orgasms. Camilla oozed fluids, but wasn't a gusher. *A lot easier on the bedding.*

His new lover slid off him, a smile tilting her lips. "The second and third of many to come, darling." She rolled onto her side, bodies warm against each other, red polished nails lightly patrolling his skin. "I'm just getting started, if you're up for it."

"Damned right. I'm glad you wanna stay, because I'm not done with you either. It's been a long time since I've had anything so wonderful as this," he lied, then sat up. "So, how about we make the bed." He rose, drew her to her feet for a passionate kiss, and then grabbed the Target bag and emptied it on the mattress. Once made, they slid onto the crisp sheets, snuggled together, and napped.

The night was young, and while temporarily sated, Camilla and Alex were far from finished. The woman bordered on nymphomania, and she made it plain she was there for the sex, which was okay by him as he sought a replacement for the glorious fulfillment he'd shared with Trudy. If Camilla wasn't real love material, he was okay with great sex. What guy wouldn't be?

They enjoyed three more heated adventures on Fridays over the next weeks, pure glorious sex, filled with both passion and tenderness. Each time, Camilla spent night, and they'd breakfast together in the morning. Usually, after waffles or pancakes, they returned to his bed for one last romp of the day. Alex was never shown her life out of work ... or bed. Was this purely sex, as she claimed, or it would move into something like love? The first woman he'd found after freeing himself from the chains of his business, was incredible, loving, a glorious sex machine. But love required something more. At least Camilla wasn't with him because of his wealth. If anything, she probably thought he was a paycheck-to-paycheck kind of guy. Maybe he was just her sex toy. *Nice.*

So, he'd enjoy the great screwing while sorting that out, but he suspected this might prove to be short term. Regardless, he intended to see Camilla never lacked for fulfillment.

He certainly wasn't getting short-changed on that, either.

~ 17 ~

Camilla arched back, hands planted on Alex's shoulders, his erupting dick gripped firmly in her pulsing pussy, as she shuddered, moaned, and squeezed his cock dry with practiced skill, as her own orgasm wound down. Slitted hazel eyes regarded him, then, still panting, she snuggled down, their damp skin still flushed from the heat of their sex, and kissed the crook of his neck.

"That was one hell of a fuck, babe," Alex murmured. "Those pussy muscles are amazing. How d'ya do that?"

"Practice, sweetheart. Lota practice. When I fuck a guy, I want him to remember me." She chuckled. "Working, isn't it?"

"Oh, yeah. You're the best." He kissed her ear then rolled to his side, Camilla still in his arms. "But—and don't hear this as a complaint—but, we've been doing this for a while, and so far pretty much all we do is screw all night." Alex caught her chin with his fingers, easing their heads apart. "Are we heading for a relationship, or am I just your sex toy?" He loved the fucking, but realized he was seeking more.

An elbow planted, she tilted up, and the other hand caressed his cheek. "You're a great guy, Alex, a handsome, premium 'sex toy,' as you called it, but I never led you to believe this was anything more than a casual fling. Maybe we coulda had something more, except for one thing."

"Which is?" He scooched up to sit, back braced against the headboard. He suspected early on what was coming.

"Advice from Momma. 'You're a catch, *chica*,' she'd say. 'Just as easy to fall in love with *un hombre rico,* as *un pobre.*' So,

--" Camilla swiveled onto her butt and took his hands in hers, "while I love what we have together, you're obviously," a hand swept across the room, "no *hombre rico*." She leaned in and kissed him, as fingers trailed down his chest to his cock. "Í love our time together, baby, but if this isn't enough for you—" gently teasing him erect again "if you're looking for more, I think we've gotta consider moving on."

Alex sighed. "Yeah, I suppose," He pushed her down and straddled her waist, his lips beginning a teasing trail from her mouth to her erect nipples, "but not before we finish what you started here." Sliding down, his mouth and fingers continued to venture into places he'd learned in their times together, really lit her fire. Finally, settling at an open, already very wet pussy, he began to dine.

Ninety minutes later, they'd completed two heated and frantic encores, followed by showers, and Camilla dressing. With their affair ending, he'd asked her not to stay the night, and she agreed a clean break was best. They lingered at the door, hugging and kissing.

"This is tough, babe, but ya gotta go," Alex said. "I loved our fling, but like you said, it was purely sex. Really great sex too, but we're both looking for something more." He stepped back, cupping her face between his hands. "I don't check an important box for you, and frankly, that fact taints for me what we might have had otherwise." He opened his door. "Best we make a clean break now, before things get more complicated."

Camilla sighed, leaned in to kiss his cheek, and shrugged. "You're right, Alex, but it doesn't make this any easier." A quick squeeze of his hands, and she slipped away.

Alex watched her sway down the hall toward the stairs, and

licked his lips, then closed the door. *Such a delicious babe.* He shook his head, a small grin tweaking his lips. Lucky for him she didn't know she'd found exactly whom she was looking for. This was his second venture into love that became based almost entirely on great sex. He was making up for ten lost years, but that wasn't going to cut it. The next time, he wanted a woman with some depth of character. One who loved good sex, but had other things on her mind. Camilla might have been that, had they spent time really learning about each other, but that was never her intent. Oh, well.

He settled at his kitchen counter and popped a Carona, his thoughts drifting to the lovely boat captain, Anne Parsons. He had her card somewhere. Maybe it was time to charter her for an offshore trip. Luckily, he had the cash for such expensive endeavors, thanks to a "modest inheritance" he claimed. She said it was still peak season for sailfish. He chugged the rest of his beer and rose to look for her number.

If nothing developed romantically, he'd at least get in some good fishing.

~ 18 ~

Emma's eyes fluttered open at the hiss of airbrakes as the Greyhound bus slid to a stop at the Highland Park Metra Station. She yawned, stretched, then pushed into the aisle and retrieved from the overhead rack her backpack she'd purchased in Memphis. She exited the bus, the pack slung over a shoulder, and scanned the street. She'd called the shelter from their stop in Chicago and was told to look for a brown Chrysler Town & Country minivan on arrival. Nothing in sight, so she shrugged and strode to where the bus driver was offloading luggage and found her small, wheeled suitcase.

"Miss Logan?"

She spun, arms instinctively raised in a defensive position, but it was just a fifty-something, average, white-haired guy with a small beard, looking quite harmless.

"I'm Robert," offering a warm smile, "here to bring you to the NSBW shelter. You're safe now." He glanced at her small suitcase. "Everyone calls me Bobby."

Emma nodded. "The North Shore Battered Women's Shelter. Right." She offered a hand which he shook. "Sorry about being jumpy. This is all kinda new to me."

"No worries." He grinned and took control of her luggage. "Every woman at the shelter has been through similar situations. I'm in no way downplaying that, but we're used to it." He signaled her to follow. "I'm parked in back." A glance over his shoulder as she trailed him. "I'm the guy who'll get you around the local area, once you're settled in. We've got about a fifteen-minute ride."

She was soon settled in the second-row seat of a brown Dodge Grand Caravan, traveling west on Clavey Road, away from downtown Highland Park. Residential areas soon disappeared, and the road cut through fields and wooded areas.

"The shelter was built on a five-acre plot, outside of metropolitan Highland Park." Bobby glanced at her in his mirror. "The land was donated by a trust fund set up by the son of the widow, Marcia Bauer, who was stalked and eventually murdered by an ex whom she eventually rejected, realizing he was after her money. He'd begun physically abusing her." He paused as he stopped at a crossroad and turned north. "Almost there. Anyway, he became a stalker … and then her killer."

"So sad." Emma scanned the passing countryside. "That's a very generous donation." She leaned forward to be better heard. "She was wealthy, then?"

"The widow? Yeah. Inherited a half-billion, mostly in stock from her deceased husband's half-ownership of a medical device company." He turned into a long, tree-lined drive. "Unfortunately, she underestimated her stalker's zeal, or maybe she'd have hired protection."

They continued down a long, curved lane. "So, her son set up that trust in her honor and funds the shelter when necessary. We try to keep costs down for our women, 'cause many don't come from means, and some become long-term residents." They entered an oblong, circular drive, and Emma spied her new home at the end.

"Wow. Pretty neat." She hitched forward for a better view of the two-story, Victorian motif, stone block building.

"Yeah. For some of these women, their stalkers and abusers are never caught or punished. No one is ever forced to leave for lack of funds." He glanced over his shoulder as he stopped at the stoop to a double-door front entrance. "I hope you have better luck, but I think you'll find a better life here than you may have anticipated." He exited and opened the sliding door for her, offering a hand for balance at the large step down. "Every effort is made to make this place feel like home." He retrieved her bag from the rear. "C'mon, I'll introduce you to Madge."

Emma followed him up the two stairs and through the doors, entering what would pass for the lobby of a deluxe, boutique hotel. A short, gray-haired woman, probably in the fifties, stepped around a desk and hurried toward them, her face split by a broad smile. Her hair, piled into a tight bun at the back of her head, and her simple, gray frock, ignited visions of Emma's beloved Nana.

"Miss Logan." She offered a hand in welcome. "Happy to see Bobby found you. I'm Madge Stine, the manager here."

"Thanks, and please call me Emma." She patted the man on the shoulder. "Bobby took good care of me and filled me in a bit on the background here." She sighed, hands in the pockets of her slacks. "First time in a while I can relax a bit."

"Good. And of course, call me Madge. We're family here." She took Emma's hand. "So, come with me to the office and I'll get you organized." She nodded at the man. "Bobby'll take your things to your new room while we talk."

Madge strode across thick, beige carpeting toward a door at the rear of the lobby. Emma's eyes swept the room as she followed. Plush sofas, armchairs, coffee tables, a large TV along one wall, bordered by shelves replete with books and video CD's … a well-stocked reading and movie supply. Two women were in chairs, engrossed in books, and a third at a small desk, tapping at a desktop computer. All very homey.

Madge pushed through the doorway and gestured Emma into an upholstered chair in front of an early English, walnut executive desk. The woman settled on a leather chair and drew a folder in front of her. "I've got most of your details here, forwarded by Mr. Hamlin." She glanced up. "Your brother-in-law?"

Emma nodded. "My sister, Char, arranged it, but Larry made

all the contacts from his office, so Brad ... my nemesis ... couldn't trace it."

"Good idea. Many of these stalkers are quite clever ... and remorseless." She closed the file and settled back. "So, here's the deal. We have eight rooms for our girls, but with you now, only six occupied. The kitchen is open for you to make your own breakfasts and lunches, but we serve a sit-down dinner five nights a week." She passed Emma a packet of papers. "Building and grounds layout in there, plus schedules and most anything else you might need to know. We have a tennis court and two pickleball courts out back."

"Wow, I never expected something like this."

"Yes. Well, we're probably one of a kind for this type of facility. Luckily, well-funded and in a lovely community." She hitched around in her chair. "Anyhow, two of our residents, Carrie and Trisha, are quite good at both racket sports, so if that's your thing, you have company. Bobby's always available as a fourth, if you need one." She opened the folder and withdrew a floorplan. "There's a two-lane lap pool at the far end," pointing at the schematic, and a small gym here, with a Peloton, a treadmill, a rowing machine, and some weights, plus room for a mat or two for floor work, if you're into any of that." Madge sat back. "We strongly recommend our girls stay fit and strong. The endorphin release is healthy, and you never know when fitness and strength may save your life."

"For sure," the corners of Emma's lips tilted up. "TaeKwanDo training already may have saved mine."

"Nice. Anyway, here are the rules ... and they *are* rules, because any error by one resident can endanger all." Madge's eyes held Emma's. "You're not prisoners here. You can go to town to shop, see a movie, or whatever. Bobby will drive you. But absolutely no credit cards or smart phones, and avoid social media like the plague. That includes other's taking photos where you may be seen. More than one stalked woman has died because someone else posted a photo with her in the background." She rose and stepped around the desk. "One more thing. Every woman here does jobs inside … usually helping in the kitchen or housekeeping. Nothing's assigned, so you get to volunteer from day to day. There's a signup sheet." She paused and studied Emma. "Being useful and having responsibilities makes for a healthier lifestyle. We also want you to have an active social life. Just do it carefully. Now, let me introduce you to your new 'sisters.'"

Emma sat on the very comfortable easy-chair in her new room … a small suite, actually. Whoever designed this place pulled out all the stops to see that the women who needed to be there felt like they were home. The problem was, this wasn't home. It was more like a luxurious purgatory. She missed her sister and her friends, and can she ever have another relationship with a man, hiding out here, far from a real life? How in the Hell might that happen? She had no idea. Bottled tension seeped through the cracks of the wall she'd erected. She curled up on the bed, her well of tears overflowing, and began to sob, her head stuffed into the pillow to keep the sound down.

Ninety minutes later, she lurched from a drugged-like sleep, jarred by a repetitive gong, then a soft rap at the door.

"Dinner time, Emma," called softly by Sandra, one of her new "sisters." "Prime rib, tonight."

"Coming." Emma struggled to sit up on the edge of the bed and knuckled her eyes, then rose and went to her bathroom to wash her face. Time to begin making the best she could of her new life. She was no quitter, and this was going to be a lot better than constantly worrying Brad would show up. Making lemonade from lemons, her Nana always said.

She could do this. She exited the room and headed for the dining room, and the first night for a new Emma Logan … survivor.

~ 19 ~

Alex glanced at the card on his desk, then punched in the number, answered on the third ring.

"Anne Parsons." A clear, bright voice, tinged with a touch of huskiness.

"Hi, Anne. Alex Penney here."

"Who? Do I know—?"

"We met at the yacht club social last month." He hesitated. "The new guy in town."

"Oh, yeah. A good dancer, as I remember … and a fisherman."

"Right, and that's why I'm calling. You said you do offshore charters?"

"I do. Interested in a booking?" No personal chit-chat. All business. Alex wasn't really disappointed. No reason she'd have any other interest in him at that moment.

"Yeah. When are you available? I'm pretty flexible."

"I actually have a cancellation for a morning half-day tomorrow, if that works for you."

"Half-day, huh?" He'd hoped for more time with her. "No full days?"

"Rarely. I get $500 for a four-hour half, but on a morning charter, if you can be aboard by seven a.m., you'll get five hours: seven 'til noon. That's usually plenty for a newbie."

"Okay, I'll take it. And I'm not a 'newbie,' as you put it." He chuckled. "Haven't fished offshore in a dozen years, but I worked two summers during college as a second mate on a big, Miami-based charter boat. Got pretty good at making baits and rigging tackle." He paused, but she didn't comment. "So, where are you docked?"

"I moor at a private home, so I pick up clients behind the 15Th Street Fishery. It's a Fort Lauderdale restaurant located, strangle enough, on 15Th Street." Her turn to chuckle.

"Swell. So, I'll be there tomorrow before seven. What do I bring?"

"Sandwiches or snacks, if you want them. I provide water. If you want beer, I only allow two aboard, and no hard liquor."

"Don't want any drunken sailors, huh?"

"Not on my boat." A brief pause. "And no bananas."

Alex laughed. "You believe in that old saw that they bring bad luck?"

"Not sure believe is the right term." Humor in her voice. "but it never hurts to err on the safe side. Anyway, see ya tomorrow, bright and early." A brief pause. "This number you called from, if I need to contact you?"

"Yeah. It's my cell. So, until tomorrow. I'm really excited to get out there again. It's been way too long."

"Great. I'm driving a thirty-seven-foot Pursuit with triple Yamaha outboards, named HoneyBun."

"Gotcha. Cute name. See you then."

He pocketed his phone. This babe really piqued his interest. All business. Efficient and to the point, but friendly. How friendly would have to be seen. He'd enjoy a bit of wooing, if that's what it took. Something different from his first two affairs. New parameters this time, as his wealth would play no part in any interest Anne Parsons develop in him.

And if they don't hook up? Well, at least he'd get in some

fishing. Offshore action was seldom fast, but always exciting when it happened.

Alex found his way around the sprawling restaurant, perched on the shores of the Intracoastal, and stepped onto a long, planked dock. They apparently solicited traffic from the water as well as from land. Six-forty-five, and there was the slick, thirty-seven-foot fly-bridge, open-fisherman, moored against white rubber bumpers alongside the pier. The shapely, blond captain was in the cockpit, organizing rods. A squatty, broad-shoulder Hispanic man was at the rear at the fish box, working on baits. Obviously, her mate. No one worked a boat that size by themselves. He stepped alongside.

"Permission to come aboard, Captain?"

Anne looked up and smiled. "Welcome aboard, Alex." She offered a hand for balance as he stepped onto the covered gunwale and dropped lightly onto the cockpit deck.

Alex caught her startling blue eyes and smiled. This babe looked hot, clad in khaki cargo shorts and a short-sleeve, buttoned shirt, blond hair and capped by a peaked hat with a draped neck cover at the rear. Nothing about her duds concealed her compact figure and the jut of modest, firm breasts. He clucked to himself at his stirring crotch. It would be great if when he found love, the woman would be as sensual as Trudy and Camilla, but he'd realized sex would eventually become less important in a relationship than character and companionship. He'd learned what an aphrodisiac sex could become, and he wasn't going to rush it his time.

He scanned the cockpit. "Anything I can do to help?" He glanced at the mate. "I got pretty good at rigging baits when I worked two summers on a charter boat during high school. I think I mentioned that at the cocktail party."

"I remember, but Mauricio can handle it. Park yourself on one of the fighting chairs, and we'll be underway in a few."

"Okay." He hoisted a small lunch box. "Got a cooler for this? Some yogurt cups and fruit." He shook the box. "No bananas, though."

Anne nodded. "Aft, against the port gunwale. Ice for any fish we keep."

Jason stepped to a cooler and put the box inside. "What'll we expect to catch, Cap?"

She chuckled. "Call me Anne, please." She climbed onto the raised helm. "Bonito, blackfin tuna, maybe a dolphin or two, and certainly a shot at sails." She glanced at palms shimmering in the breeze. "This nor' easterly wind usually brings in loads of billfish."

"Sounds like a blast." He settled on a gimbaled fighting chair. "Let's go get 'em."

"You bet." She watched her mate cast off the lines, then accelerated slowly down the Intercoastal toward the Lake Mable Cut and access to the Gulfstream.

Alex relaxed in the chair, eager for action—both fishing and, possibly, romance. A contented sigh. He enjoyed this new, uncomplicated life as Alex Penny.

~ 20 ~

Alex pawed through papers littering his small desk and found the business card. He flicked it against his thumb, momentarily unsure, then shrugged and punched in the number on his new Android phone, answered on the third ring.

"Anne Parsons."

"Hi, Anne. It's Alex Penney."

"Who?"

"Alex. We met at the boat club party last month." He paused. "We danced."

"Oh, Alex." A soft chuckle. "Yes. A good dancer too, as I remember."

"Yeah. A required gym class in high school." He paused. "Anyway, you said you run offshore charters, and I'm interested in a trip. Sailfishing still hot?"

"Yep. The current northeasterly winds really bring in the billfish." Sounded like she was leafing through a book. "Yeah. Just checked and I got a cancellation for the morning half-day tomorrow. That work for you?"

"Yes, I'm free, but I was hoping for a full day."

"Rarely happens. I charge five-hundred for four hours, but on a morning trip, if you're aboard by seven, we make it five hours." A soft chuckle. "Lots of guys can't handle more, with a northly wind running. That bucks the Stream and can push up some heavy chop."

"I can take choppy seas," he said. "Or think I can, anyhow. You probably don't remember, but I told you I worked as second mate on a big charter boat summers during high school. I'm no newbie."

"Yeah, I do remember that." A short pause. "So, tomorrow morning then?"

"Okay." It would be a start. "Where are you berthed."

"Private dockage. I pick up clients at the wharf behind 15th Street Fishery, which, not surprisingly, is located on the Intracoastal at the end of NE 15th Street. I run a thirty-seven-foot Pursuit with triple Yamaha 250's. Called *HoneyBun*." All business now. "I supply water, and of course, all the bait and tackle. You bring any snacks you want. No hard liquor, but two beers are okay. No bananas, though."

Alex laughed. "You actually subscribe to that bad luck superstition?"

"I play all the odds. Why not? So, seven a.m.?"

"Yep. Looking forward to an exciting day." Goodbye's said, they disconnected.

Alex leaned back, hands clasped behind his head, and ran images of Anne Parsons through his head. She was attractive and fit. Maybe his first shot at a woman who might fall for him, and not his money. And if they didn't click, this fishing promised to be exciting, He rose and prepared for an early departure. He wanted to get the full five hours, and see where it led.

Alex exited his Dodge Charger in the 15th Street Fishery's parking lot toting a backpack and small lunchbox. *I like being Alex Penney now. Gotta immerse myself in his character.* He circled the south end of the sprawling, nautical-theme restaurant and spied the Intracoastal and a wharf behind the building. As he stepped onto the planked structure, he saw a gleaming white boat, secured against the dock, three big Yamaha outboards gurgling at idol. Twenty-foot outriggers stretched back from the center cockpit's roof, which was also lined with six fishing rods, secured in rod holders at its rear edge. He was surprised there was no flybridge, a staple of most offshore sportfishermen.

A glance at his watch showed 6:45 a.m. He was early. As he approached, he noted a burly Hispanic guy at the transom fish box making baits, and Anne Parsons stood by one of the two swivel fishing chairs in the aft cockpit, setting out trolling rods. He strode to the edge of the wharf.

"Permission to come aboard, Captain." A smile ticked at his lips as he saluted.

"Ah, Alex." Her eyes, blue as the Gulfstream, caught his, and she grinned. "Of course. Welcome aboard." She held out a hand to offer balance as he stepped on the covered gunwale and dropped lightly onto the deck. She nodded toward the bow. "You can stow your things in the forward hatch."

"Right. I've got some Yoplait yogurt and a beer in here." He hoisted the lunchbox. "Got a cooler?"

"Sure. That deck box, port side, aft. That's where we keep fresh bait and anything edible we catch that you wanna keep."

Alex nodded and stepped to the box, and found it layered with a bed of crushed ice. He slipped his things into a corner and closed the hatch. He paused beside the mate and watched him prepare finger mullet and ballyhoo, then turned to Anne.

"You don't use live bait for sails, Anne?"

"Yeah, when they're scarce. But with this northeasterly running, small mullet and 'hoos are just as effective, and a lot less hassle."

"So," he ran a hand over the conventional trolling rod she'd placed in a starboard rod holder, "catching a sail is likely today?"

"Yep. Maybe even two or three." She stepped to the port side to place another rod.

"What else?" He watched as she set two sturdy spinning rods in aft rod holders.

"Always bonito, and a good chance for a blackfin tuna this time of year. And kingfish, dolphin, and wahoo are always possible." She moved to the transom. "You ready, Chico?"

"*Sí, Capitán.* Six baits ready, and bonito strips for the flatline jigs."

"Okay." She turned to the shaded center console helm. "Cast off, and let's go fishing." Moments later they were cruising south on the Intracoastal Waterway, heading for Port Everglades, an outlet to the Atlantic. Alex lingered beside Anne as she steered the boat.

"No flybridge?" He glanced up. "The boats I worked on as a kid all had them."

"Yeah. The height makes seeing what's going on around our baits easier. It's the one disadvantage of this baby, but I make it work, and Chico's got binoculars for eyes. He rarely misses anything."

"Still," he looked at her, "it's gotta be a competitive disadvantage."

"Well, it's all I could afford to finance." She surveyed their wake as they entered the inlet. "Sure, I'd love to have a nice diesel Hatteras 48 with a big, comfortable bridge and a roomy cabin, but this is a lot faster boat, and we catch plenty of fish." She chuckled. "I promise, you won't be disappointed."

Alex nodded and grabbed a siderail as they surged into the wavier Atlantic. He studied the woman from the corners of his eyes. Competent, attractive, and so far, very nice to be with. He'd take his time and see where it leads.

The *Honeybun* idled into a mooring at the wharf against white bumpers, already in place. Chico leaped off the transom with a stern tiedown, and Alex stepped ashore from the bow, similarly equipped, and the men secured the boat to dock cleats. Anne hopped onto the planking and turned to her new client.

"Enjoy the morning, Alex?" Her grin forecasted what she knew was the answer.

"You bet, Annie." He took her hand. "You're a hell of a good captain. One nice sail released, and another shook off, plus those three blackfin were great on the spinning rods."

"Yeah," turning to inspect the boat as Chico washed it down. "They're great fighters, and Chico's fileted one for you to take home. Cook it just like ahi tuna."

"Thanks." He fished a wad of bills from his back pocket. "Here's your fee, plus a little something extra to show I appreciated a good trip." He turned as the mate approached with his backpack and lunch box. "You make good baits, Chico." Alex handed him a twenty. "And I appreciate you letting me hook my own fish." He patted the man's shoulder. "Next time, if you'll let me, I'll show you how I rig a swimming ballyhoo. It can be a killer."

"Next time, huh?" Anne said, sporting a wide grin. "So, I've got you hooked, have I? Sure you can afford it on your salary?"

"Yeah." *Hooked more ways than you know.* "I got a small inheritance from my grandma with explicit instructions to spend it having fun." The story Alex created in case he wanted something special. And that *was* both the woman and the fishing. "I enjoyed the fishing, *and* the company. You're a hell of an interesting woman, Annie." Their eyes locked.

"You're not so bad either, Alex ... both as a fisherman and company."

"Glad you think so." He hesitated, unaccountably nervous. "So, maybe we can do an afternoon trip, and then I could buy you dinner." He held his breath.

"Dinner, huh?" A small smile danced on her lips, and she took his hand. "Yeah, I think I'd like that." She glanced at her boat, then back at him. "I've got an afternoon open next Tuesday, if that works for you."

"Sure. My schedule is flexible, so I can arrange the time." *As if I've got anything else to do with my days.*

"Okay. It's a date. Tuesday, same place," nodding at the wharf, "before one p.m."

"Great. I'm looking forward to it." He was enjoying the warmth of her hand on his.

"Me too." A small squeeze of his fingers, and she dropped his hand and turned to her boat. "Now I gotta get ready for my next party. See ya then."

With nothing else to say, Alex left, heading for his Dodge, his heart doing a small tumbling act in his chest. He sensed this was going to work out, and for a change, it wouldn't be about his money.

He drove off, full of expectations.

~ 21 ~

"Thanks, Bobby." Emma stepped out of the minivan. "I'm gonna browse around and buy a few things at Walmart, or wherever." She scanned Highland Park's main street. "Where should I meet you?"

"There's some shaded benches in front of the library. What time?"

"Let's say one p.m. Gives me time to get acclimated to my new neighborhood. I'll probably grab a sandwich from that deli I see up the street." She peeked at her watch. It was an hour later in Florida. "And I've gotta make a call. There a pay phone around somewhere?"

"Yep," gesturing up the street. "Both Morrie's Deli and Walmart." He touched her arm. "Need any coins."

"Nope. Gonna do it collect." Emma turned to leave, but Bobby caught her arm.

"Be careful, Emma. Your stalker may have family phones tapped. From what you told me, he could have the clout."

"I know." She smiled and patted his hand. "It's a distant cousin who shouldn't be on his radar. She'll relay any messages to my sister."

"Okay, that should work." He opened the driver-side door of the van. "I've got some errands to run and shopping to do for Madge, so I'll see you in about three hours." He paused. "Probably not a problem today, but remember, don't get in any photos, even as background."

"Right." She pulled her sunhat lower over her eyes. "I'm incognito," and gave a small chuckle.

The man nodded as he entered the Dodge. "Can't be too

careful," he called as he shut the door.

Emma nodded and started up the street. Walmart was a block off the main avenue, so she'd start there with a call to Sally, and then do some shopping. She needed more clothes, makeup, and a new laptop. The shelter had a desktop available, but she'd only use that to go on the Internet. With more time on her hands now, she'd decided to begin the novel that had been rummaging around in her head.

Sally, a mom of two and a classic homemaker, answered on the second ring. "A collect call from Princess Layla (from play acting as kids). Will you accept the charges?

"Yes." Sally chuckled. "Put it through." A click came over the line, then …

"Sally?"

"Yeah, Em … I mean Princess." A silent pause "How are you doing, cuz?"

"Well, I'm alive … and apparently safe here … at least for now."

"Glad to hear it, and so will Char. We've been worried."

"I know." A soft sigh. "Gotta keep contact limited, I'm told. Even cautioned not to be in any photos, even as background. Social media can be a killer … literally."

"How're your new digs?" Sally asked. "Char said they looked pretty nice on the web."

"Oh, it's quite lovely, and the people are super. I have a mini-suite, the meals are yummy, and there's lots to do to keep one occupied." Emma sighed again. "One of my new 'sisters' has been here six years. She's afraid to go home because her stalker is still there."

"Jeez, six years? You'd think the louse woulda given up. She didn't try to relocate?"

"Yeah, twice, and the bum still tracked her down. I hope Brad moves on quicker than that. I can't imagine ..." She trailed off. "So, please call Char and let her know I'm okay."

"Will do." Sally rose and started to pace. "I talked to her two days ago. She's got another money package to send you. Some UPS store in a nearby town."

"Evanston. It's about twelve miles south. They've got a car I can borrow to drive down and get it. Post a note on your Facebook page, 'The sun still rises in the east,' so I know it's been sent, and 'A lovely sunset,' when you're advised it's arrived. I can monitor the web from a library computer."

"That's probably safe, huh?" Sally paused.

"Yeah, because I'll just read it, but won't post anything. Any idea of when?"

"A day or two." She glanced at a wall calendar. "Char's already got the cash." She chuckled. "This is real spy stuff, huh. Like games we played as kids."

"Yeah." A soft groan. "But this is no game. Anyway, I gotta go. Got some shopping to do. I'll check Facebook, starting tomorrow ... and thanks. Sally Crisp to the rescue, just like the old days." Emma gave strained laughs as they disconnected.

Emma hung up the phone and sagged against the wall, just outside Walmart. Her sister and cousin were doing all they could to keep her safe, and she'd landed in what otherwise might be a very nice place. It *was* a nice place, but somewhere she didn't want to be. Friends and family were missed, and that wasn't going to get better any time soon.

Pushing away from the wall, she straightened her shoulders and grabbed an empty cart. Time to make the best of what she had. Walmart probably had everything she needed, including the laptop. One-stop shopping. She shook her head and began strolling the aisles of the huge store.

Emma sat on a bench, shaded by a towering elm tree, just outside the Highland Park main library, lost in thought, a half-dozen packages strewn around her feet. Snatched from her musing by a horn's beep, she glanced at her Casio. One p.m., on the dot, and there was Bobby, coming from his double-parked van to help with her purchases. Time to return to her new home and finish settling in. Perched on the passenger seat, she closed her eyes and struggled for positive thoughts. She *was* safe, and that's what she needed to concentrate on. But for how long? She sighed, opting for the glass half-full.

~ 22 ~

Feet braced against the swell as *Honeybun* entered the Port Everglades inlet, Alex leaned against a fighting chair an inhaled the mixed aroma of salt air and fresh-caught fish. This fourth afternoon trip had been their best and especially rewarding since Anne had allowed him to act as his own mate. Making baits, handling the rods, hooking up three out of three sailfish hits ... all fond memories of his carefree high school days. Besides the billfish, he'd caught three dolphin, including a fifteen-pound bull, a blast on the spinning rods. A twenty-five-pound cobia, taken on an outrigger mullet was a real tussle, and they'd finished the day with four amberjacks pulled off a man-made reef. All were released unharmed except for a nice cow dolphin which he'd already fileted on the way in. Yum.

He glanced over his shoulder at Anne, managing the boat at its helm. Her bare, strong legs and firm ass, well displayed by her tight, khaki cargo shorts, brought a twinge in his pants. Tonight would be the night, he was pretty sure. They'd dined four days ago at the 15th Street Fishery—as they would again this evening—and engaged in some protracted kissing with a bit of touchy-feely while in the lot by his car. He liked that they hadn't rushed into things, as he'd done in the past, but he hoped to bring it all the way in tonight.

Now in the quieter Intracoastal, Alex plucked the last two rods from gunwale rod holders and stowed them in the overhead holders at the rear of the cockpit's roof. This brought him right behind the woman, and he pressed his body against hers, arms circling her waist. Cheek-to-cheek, he spoke softly. "Oh captain, my captain, you run a pretty mean ship, babe." A soft kiss on her cheek, and she giggled and rubbed her buns into his crotch.

"You're not so bad yourself, bub, especially for a techy nerd." She glanced at him, luscious lips parted into a saucy smile, and seemed unsurprised when they were kissed. She sighed, still smiling. "You're a lot more than I expected in many ways, Alex. Too bad the day has to end."

"But it doesn't. I'm still buying you dinner," He tighten his grip, drawing her closer. "And it doesn't have to end there either." He kissed her ear. "We can finish at my place with some dessert." Nuzzling her neck, he said "I promise it will be very sweet."

Anne laughed, one hand catching the side of his face, pressing it against hers. "We'll see how dinner goes. I do believe I'm ready for that dessert with you, though." She shimmied free and pointed ahead. "Thar she blows, mate. Get ready to tend the bow line." She idled the boat and eased it toward the restaurant's wharf. "We'll tie up at the far end, so not to interfere with other arrivals."

Alex nodded and went about deploying two white foam-filled bumpers along the port side, then moved to the bow with a tie-down rope. The boat slipped smoothly onto its spot, and a moment later it was securely moored. After a quick inspection, they went ashore.

"Why don't you go to the bar and order us drinks while I give my baby a quick wash-down." Anne surveyed the boat. "Shouldn't be more than ten minutes, and I'll join you." Long fingers caressed his cheek. "I'm looking forward to dinner again tonight … and maybe that dessert later that you promised." She winked.

Alex drew her in for a brief, tongue-teasing kiss, then stepped back, her hands in his. "Can't wait," as he turned and entered the not yet busy restaurant. The usual dinner crowd wouldn't begin arriving for another hour. He was rife with anticipation for the evening's eventual progress.

Anne nestled close to him on the booth's bench, hips in contact, as she doodled with the remnants of her tasty key lime pie. She studied Alex from the corner of her eye, a saucy smile tickling her lips. "That was delicious," she murmured.

"Yeah," his arm circled her shoulders, snugging her closer, as the other hand cupped her chin, their eyes locked, "but I had another, more exciting dessert in mind … at my place."

"Your place, huh?" emitting a soft chuckle. "That's my option?"

"Unless you have something else in mind, Cap'n." Their lips met in a soft, slow, teasing kiss. "I really like you, Anne … a lot … and hope you feel the same."

"Oh, yeah." Her hand at the back of his neck, this kiss was more intense, with busy tongues. They pulled back, faces inches apart. "Much to my surprise," breathlessly, "you're much more than I ever expected." His hand in hers, she scooted to the end of the bench, drawing him after her. "I've never felt so … so *comfortable* with a guy as I do with you." She pushed to her feet. "Let's go."

"Your boat?"

"I can moor it here for now. The manager's my cousin." She grinned, her face flushed. "Even overnight, if I want. They've got full-time security on the dock." She chuckled. "And if you're really good at the dessert you promised, well, I can pick her up in the morning."

Alex rose and gathered the woman against him for a more protracted kiss. Pelvises pressed together, he began to harden.

"Oh, my!" She arched back and wiggled against what was growing there. "I think I'm *really* gonna enjoy that dessert."

Alex threw cash on the table with plenty enough for a decent tip, and hand-in-hand, they hurried for the parking lot. The fifteen-minute drive to his new apartment was spiced by teasing fingers. Her engorged pussy lips were open and wet, and his cock was iron hard by the time he'd parked his Charger. Fired by the release of previously restrained lust, a mad dash was made for the stairs, taken two-at-a-time.

They burst through the door and kicked it closed behind them. Alex spun her against him, and hands on her taut ass, he hoisted her up for a sloppy kiss, her arms crossed behind his neck. She locked her legs around his waist and wiggled down so her undulating pussy teased his cock.

"Damn, you're a big boy, Alex." She dropped to her feet and was quickly out of her shorts, while he shed his chinos. Anne shoved down his boxers and dropped to her knee, long, ruby-nailed fingers fluttering along his hardon and cupping his balls. "My god, I could cum just playing with that." She licked away the ooze of pre-cum. "Yum." Her shirt went over her head, revealing unfettered, perky B's, nipples fully erect, and she lay back on the carpet. "I need that inside me, *now*." Legs spread, her fingers trailed over her open, very wet pussy and an engorged clit. "Fuck me, Alex. Fuck me hard!"

"So much for foreplay," he panted as he straddled her, sliding his cock back and forth between those very wet lips.

"We'll save that for the second round," the words hissed between drawn lips. "Do it now!"

"Birth control?" He'd inched back, the head of his dick easing into her opening.

"On the pill," she growled and arched her pelvis, squealing softly as she drew him inside.

Alex gasped. She was so tight. Pulsing slowly, he worked his cock deep inside as she thrust her hips against him. Arms straddling her head, he lowered himself as she tore his shirt away. Her skin was silky and damp with sweat, the contact igniting fire throughout his body. A hand behind her head, they kissed, nibbled and nipped, while her fingers ran tracks across his back as they pulsed together, the carnal dance of love.

"Jesus, you're so tight, babe." He grimaced, fighting to hold off. "I'm gonna cum … too damned fast. Too damned—"

"Oh, yeah. Me too, darling." Hissed between gritted teeth. "Yeah, yeah. Right *now*." She crushed him against her, legs and arms locking him down, her soaking cunt quivering with her release as he also came with a gush and a groan. They continued to move against each other, the surge of her pussy draining him, and they sighed, tension from their heat drained away.

Alex slid down a bit, withdrawing from her. He rolled onto his back, pulling Anne atop of him, and they continued to kiss, more gently now that passion was slaked.

"God," he cupped her face between his hands, "I knew you were special when we first met, but this … Geez, it exceeded my wildest expectations." He planted gentle kisses on each eye.

"Well, you turned out to be a lot more than just a good fishing buddy, that's for sure." She rolled into a sit. "I don't sleep around, but I'm not a prude, either." Fingers trailed lightly over his now slack organ. "But I've never encountered anything like *this* before." Leaning back in for a kiss, she said, "I hope you're not a one-shot wonder, Alex, because, if you're up for it, I'll stay the night, and we can do this again, this time with the foreplay you said we missed."

"My thoughts exactly." He rose and drew her up. "I'll pour us drinks, and we can head for the bedroom." He kissed the tip of her nose. "Scotch okay? Don't have the makings for a martini."

She nodded, and with arms around the other, they moved to the kitchen for the drinks. They'd spend the night making love, and she could hardly wait. That big dick was an aphrodisiac, but she also really liked this guy. They seemed to have so much in common. But she needed to know more about him, if she were to allow herself to fall in love. Research could wait, though. Tonight she planned to slake long-dormant passion. Tomorrow, she'd see what she could learn about Mr. Alex Penney.

~ 23 ~

Brad Barnes stepped through the doorway of North Miami Police, and his eyes swept the detectives' room. He nodded, spying Dominic Rosa studying a file at his desk in the bullpen. He wound his way across the floor and perched on the edge of a utilitarian, blue metal desk.

"Hot on a case, Detective?"

Rosa glanced up and lay the file down. "Mr. hotshot Assistant DA." He leaned back. "What can I do ya for?"

"Tell me you found my missing person of interest."

"Emma Logan?" He shook his head. "So far, no joy." He sorted through several folders and opened one. "Got an out APB to all the airports, trains, car rentals, her credit cards, and phone." He retrieved a slip from the file. "The latter turned up at a Goodwill store, here in North Miami. Wiped clean of everything but Apples basic programs. Not a ping on anything else, except for that one airport motel at Fort Lauderdale International." He closed the file and lay it aside. "I presume you missed her there?"

"Yeah, someone else using her card," he lied, not willing to admit failure.

"Well, as of now, she's a ghost. What's the deal with her anyhow? I don't remember ever seeing you so worked up over one missing witness, or whatever she is." He studied Barnes. "Must be a pretty big deal."

"Actually about a cold case I was working. Kinda sensitive, so

I can't say much other than I need to find Miss Logan, ASAP." He pushed off the desk. "So, keep all the feelers working, 24/7, and hit me up the minute anything pops. Any time, day or night. Okay?"

"You got it, Brad. I put it near the top of techs list, since you seemed pretty hot about it." He also rose. "We still on for racquetball tomorrow?"

"Yeah. You're a real glutton for punishment, Dom. Four p.m., at the Y." Barnes grinned. "Bring cash."

"Yeah, yeah, but I've been practicing. I'm gonna beat you one of these days."

They shook hands, and Barnes left. *Where the fuck did Emma disappear to. That bitch sister did it.* He pictured that little .380 pressed against his breastbone, and the look in Charlene Hamlin's eyes. He shuddered, sure she would have shot him without a blink, if he'd given her a good reason.

Emma was going to pay for *that* too, once he found her. He licked parched lips. He was eager for that. Meanwhile, he'd found a cute little nurse from Doctor's Hospital to play with. She hadn't learned yet what was coming for her, but soon. They had a date tomorrow, and some sex was definitely on the menu.

But she wasn't Emma. That's who he lusted for.

~ 24 ~

Alex swiveled toward Anne on his stool, seated at the 15th Street Fishery's bar, and clinked her martini glass with his tumbler of Scotch.

"To our best day ever." They'd just settled in from their third trip after becoming lovers. "Two outta three for a Grand Slam."

She chuckled and nodded. "Just one kingfish short, but the top dolphin in the KWD tournament, plus your forty-two-pound wahoo in the running is pretty exceptional."

"Thanks to my terrific, and very sexy, captain." He sipped the amber fluid. "What a pair of heart-thumping strikes."

Anne giggled. "When that dolphin tore up fifty feet of foam hitting the outrigger mullet, I thought it might be a marlin. Really got my adrenalin going." She tasted her own drink. "Fifty-six-pounds is the second largest ever taken on my boat."

Alex nodded. "And that wahoo, bounding through the air to smash that ballyhoo, wasn't chopped liver. That leap musta covered thirty feet." He arced his hand with a swoop, emulating the vault. "And what a run! Musta taken six-hundred-yards in a blink."

"Yeah. With their speed, they can really fly. Some say they can hit 70 mph" She giggled. "Maybe that's why they call 'em *wahoo*."

"Two really gorgeous fish." He drained his drink. "Ya know, I'm almost too pumped to eat." He touched her hand, eyes locked. "Why don't we skip dinner and go to my place to really celebrate?" His tongue swiped sun-parched lips. "These last couple of weeks with you have been amazing, and I'd like to see where it's going."

"Music to my ears." Her eyes glistened, white teeth bared by a face-splitting smile. Fingers caressed his tanned cheek. "I've never felt so connected to guy like I do with you."

He kissed the back of her hand, slid off his barstool, and tossed some bills on the counter. "Me too, so let's go."

Arm in arm, the strode for the door, just fifteen minutes from a voyage into ecstasy.

With Anne in his arms, their lips locked in a frantic kiss, Alex burst through the doorway of his apartment and kicked it shut. Locked together, they lumbered toward his bedroom, their tongues still dueling, her fingers busy with the buttons of his shirt. Kicking off his Sperry boat shoes, he plopped onto the edge of his mattress, his blond lover on his lap, one hand inside her open top, tweaking an erect nipple.

Anne moaned, her breath coming in short gasps, as she peeled away his shirt. She slithered onto the bed and began peppering his cheek, ear, and neck with wet kisses while she shimmied out of her shorts, taking her bikini undies with them. Then she was busy with his belt, and soon his cargo pants were gone. On her knees now, bedside, her short-nailed fingers teased his turgid dick as she leaned over and swirled the head and glans with her tongue.

"God, I love this big thing," she whispered and began licking up and down the shaft, taking time to tease and suck his balls.

Alex's hand cupped the sides of her face, and he grunted as she took the head again into her mouth, slowly bobbing up and down, her tongue continually swirling. "Christ, baby, You're so … oh, shit, I'm gonna cum." Arms braced beside him on the bed, he arched his pelvis to meet her busy mouth.

"Do it, Alex," slurred by a mouthful of rigid cock. "Give it to me. Give it—" Cut off as he grunted and erupted in a massive orgasm. Anne took it all and choked down the fluid, sucking and licking him clean while still in her mouth. Finished finally, he slipped free of her lips. He grasped her upper arms and drew her atop of him, lying back on the bed, both panting as they wound down.

"Damn, that was terrific." He bound her to him and kissed her neck.

"A special reward for my champion fisherman." She snuggled tighter into his moist body.

"Yeah?" Rolling over, Alex lay her on her back, legs dangling over the mattress's edge, and straddled her. "Now it's my turn to reward the best, and definitely most beautiful captain plying South Florida waters." He roamed slowly down, his lips and tongue lingering with each breast, and especially her large, rigid nipples. Her breath tiny gasps, his mouth ventured across her belly as fingers kept up a teasing dance, finally arriving at a neatly trimmed forest of blonde hair.

On his knees, he spread her legs as he teased past open, very wet lips and her engorged clit, and licked and sucked inner thighs, his hands busy venturers from her belly to her ankles, all accompanied by soft moans and muttered "yeses." After a maddening delay, his tongue flicked at the edge of those quivering lips, then a dip into the growing pool of her pussy, and up to the pleading pleasure button. Five minutes of licking, teasing, and sucking brought a wailing, body-shaking orgasm, her fingers tangled in his long hair as she shuddered to completion. Not the gushing O of Trudy, or even Camilla, but wet and intense.

Alex slid onto the bed beside her and drew her still quaking body in for a warm snuggle. Her legs tangled with his, Anne arched her neck and delivered a passionate kiss.

"That was fucking fantastic, darling." She breathed a long sigh. "I can't imagine anything more intense." She nestled her face into the crook of his neck, their sweat moistened bodies pressed together.

Alex chuckled, his hands running up and down her taut body. "The evening's still young, my love, and we haven't actually fucked yet, so who knows." They giggled. "Right now, I need a short nap to rest up for the coming trials."

"Copy that, lover." They slithered the rest of the way onto the bed, drew the sheet up, and slept, snug in each other's arms.

As she dozed off, Anne thought of the research she'd done before deciding to take this all the way. She knew Alex was falling in love with her, and why not? The sex was great, he was a hell of good fisherman, and with what else she'd learned, the perfect mate she'd sought. Everything needed for her to profess love for him too. Not a real chore to make that work

Anne lay on her side, elbow planted on the bed, her head rested on her hand. She studied Alex as fingers of her other hand tripped lightly down his chest, nudging him from sleep. A pink tongue slid across uptilted lips and she sighed, replaying her intense arousal as that big, thick cock plumbed her tight, wet pussy, once last evening, and again in the early morning. Never before had she come so hard … and so often. Couldn't be more perfect … an actually loveable guy who could fill all her other needs.

Moisture seeped from her again flowering pussy. Teeth gritted, she shook her head and tamped down her rising passion. Other things were on the table this morning, and they needed her very best efforts if she were to succeed. This was everything she'd ever dreamed of.

Eyes slitted, Alex rolled onto his side and grinned. "G'morning, gorgeous," glancing at the digital clock on his nightstand: eight-forty. "Slept in, didn't we, after a busy night." He chuckled, cupped the back of her head with a hand, and pulled her down for an extended kiss. He stilled her prowling hand. "Not sure

I've got another romp in me this morning, though, baby."

"Oh, no. I wasn't … I was just enjoying touching you, Alex." She shimmied back and leaned against the headboard, the sheet pooling in her lap, her firm, upthrust tits a delectable sight.

He joined her, his fingers intertwined with hers. "Breakfast?" He smiled. "I fry a mean bacon and eggs." His grin echoed her chuckle and a nod.

"Scrambled, please, and crisp bacon, if you can." She slipped out of bed and donned an old, khaki shirt he'd lent her. "Any toast?"

"Whole wheat, and I've got both butter and cream cheese." Exiting the other side of his queen-size bed, Alex slipped into his boxers and pulled a polo shirt over his head. Barefoot, he padded toward the door. "And I've got raspberry jam, if you like."

Anne was close behind. "Sounds perfect. I'll make coffee." In the kitchen she found a can of Folger's in the cupboard. "You like it bold, right?"

"Stronger the better for me, but suit your own taste, darling." A carton of eggs, a pack of bacon, and a stick of butter were retrieved from the fridge. At his cooktop, he paused, turned, and studied the woman, busy charging the coffee pot.

Anne glanced at him and grinned. "What?"

He shrugged and held out a hand to her. "I'm enjoying being domestic with you." He drew her over for a quick kiss, then returned to the stove, setting a skillet on a burner, and adding six slices of thick bacon. "This is our first time house-making." He chuckled. "It's nice."

"Agreed," said over her shoulder. "Feels kinda natural." She pressed the BREW button. *After a nice, homey breakfast will be the perfect time.* She peeked at him from the corner of her eye. *I hope I've hooked him well enough that outing the truth makes us stronger together.*

Alex shoved his empty plate aside, leaned back, a small smile ticking at his lips. "Hated my cooking, huh?" nodding at her plate, scraped clean.

"Perfectly done eggs and bacon. Really tasty cooked in the bacon fat." She took his hand. "Don't know why I should be surprised." She paused and studied his eyes. "You're the best fisherman I've had on my boat, so it's no surprise if you excel at everything."

"Well, thanks." A blush infused his cheeks. "Always loved it, and you're a pretty great captain too."

"Nice of you to say." *What the hell. Here we go.* "We're a pretty good team, Alex. On the boat, in bed for sure, and everywhere in-between." Fingers caressed his cheek, and she drew him in for a lingering kiss. "Could be I'm falling in love."

"Could be, me too." Another kiss, and they sat back, eyes locked.

"We should team up, enter some tournaments. Kick butt." She grinned and sat back. "We could really compete with the big guys if I had a better boat … flybridge and real fighting cockpit." She paused. "Actually, I found the perfect one, a six-year-old Viking 48, fully rigged: fly-bridge, riggers, live-well, and a really nice cabin and galley."

"A Viking, huh? That aughta cost a pretty penny."

"He's asking nine-fifty K, but he seems pretty eager. He might go as low as nine for a cash sale. And with a better boat, we can have a ball." Her eyes held his as she reached for a hand. "Perfect for weekend trips to Bimini or the Keys."

"Can you afford that, Anne?" He eased back. "Do you have clients for those kinds of overnight trips?" Their eyes still locked. "Even if you get a good price for your Pursuit—"

"There's a guy pestering me to buy the boat. He's offered four-hundred, cash. I might get more if I advertised it, but who knows how long that'd take, and the Viking might be gone by then."

"So, where are you gonna get a half-mil? I've heard boat loans have literally dried up, even with a big downpayment."

She paused. *Here we go.* "I was hoping my lover would want to be my partner, instead of my customer." Both his hands were in hers. "We could fish together every day, and fuck the charter business." She hitched forward, the neckline of the oversize shirt billowing open, right on cue. "We could fish tournaments all over the place. What could be more exciting than doing what you love with a person you adore?"

"With me? How d'ya expect to pay for *that* on my salary? Where the hell would I come up with so much bread?"

She took a breath and reached for her most seductive smile. "C'mon, Alex. It's a drop in the bucket for you."

"Huh? What are you—?"

"Look. I've fallen for you, so I did a deep Internet dive." She dug up her most earnest and adoring smile. *He's mine. I just gotta sell it.* "Wanted to be sure what I was letting myself in for." Her fingers caressed his cheek. "Anyhow, when I couldn't fine much on-line history on you, I ran your photo with facial rec program my brother got from a cop friend." She sighed. "Y'know, to keep me safe from weirdos. I've run into a few of those." A soft snort. "And wow, to my surprise, up popped Alex Jordan, billionaire entrepreneur." She gently squeezed his hand, still in hers. "I don't know why you've created this deception, but—"

He drew back, groaned softly, and plumbed her eyes. "So, you'd like me to buy a bigger boat and finance our fun and games." He shook his head and sighed. "Actually, I created an alias exactly because of this."

"This? What d'ya mean, darling?"

"I hoped to find love that's not tied to a golden ring, Anne." His glanced away. "It's a lot easier to love a rich guy than a mid-American wage-earner, isn't it?" He studied her. "When did you find out who I really was?"

"Hey," her eyes flared, "that's not fair. I ran the program last week, but I'd already fallen in love with you. That's why I did the search. You're the guy of my dreams, whether Alex Penny or Alex

Jordan.

"Yeah, so you say."

"Oh, Alex! No, please ..." Her eyes, flared and pooling, searched his.

"I'm ... I'm sorry. I didn't mean to sound cruel, but I gotta think about this." He rose. "We're gonna need some time apart while I sort this out, Anne." He stood at arms-length, both hands or her shoulders. "I thought I was falling in love with you too, babe, but I've been burned before. I need some time to work this out." He cupped her chin and sighed. "Just give me a few days to digest everything, okay?"

"Please, Alex. Please know I love you, money or not." She stoked his cheek and tiny rivulets trickled across her cheeks. "I'm so sorry if—"

"Nothing to be sorry about, Anne. You did what you needed to protect yourself. You just found something I would have told you later, once I was sure our relationship was based on love, and not a love of money." *And last week was the first time you said, "I love you." Not a coincidence, I think,*

"Alex! I never—"

"I know, I know," turning toward the bedroom. "Let's dress and I'll take you to your boat." He looked at his watch. "It's Wednesday. I promise to have it all settled by the end of the week." A shudder skipped down his spine at the sounds of Anne sobbing while they dressed. He hated hurting her, but this unexpected turn of events was already souring him.

They rode back to the 15th Street Fishery in silence, except for soft whimpers from the woman. Alex gritted his teeth. He needed alone time, with no outside pressure from her, to see if this was his future, or time to move on. He shrugged, already suspecting the answer, and it weigh heavily on his heart, because he *was* falling in love with a pretty exceptional woman. How much of her love was fired by his wealth? That was a question for which there was no clear answer ... a judgement call he'd have to make, but memory of Trudy would certainly be an influence.

He wondered how he could avoid this trap a third time, already gearing up in his mind to move on. Was there nowhere he could go and not be recognized. That question nagged him as he drove away from the restaurant. A peek in his rearview mirror showed Anne, on the curb, staring after him.

Damn, can I ever find true love, without the taint of my wealth? And should that even matter, if in fact I really am in love, and not just in heat.

Something to ponder.

~ 25 ~

Alex sprawled on the only easy chair in his apartment, legs atop of an ottoman, as he mulled the events of the day. A head shake and grunt expressed his dismay at the turn of events. The idea someone would recognize him was always a worry, but to have the woman he was falling for actually search him out was a stunner ... but should it have been? It was totally reasonable that in this age of loonies, a woman would be careful whom she committed herself to.

So, now what? Anne was beautiful, bright, talented, and fun. What every guy sought. Had she found her professed love for him before or *after* she learned who he really was? And, was he falling for her because of who she was as a person, or because she was sending all the right signals? A question he'd never know the answer to. One thing was sure, though ... buying that Viking sportfisherman for her wouldn't have hurt.

Alex massaged his eyes, then rose and began meandering around his den, arms folded, wrestling with this conundrum: did he love Anne enough to accept she may be there more for the money than for true love? He paused and stroked his chin. Or did he actually love her at all? His brow wrinkled. *Love? Do I really even know what that is? Certainly more than great sex, I guess.* A shrug, followed by a sigh, got him moving again. This was still a world where he had little past experience.

He'd thought he loved Trudy, but once he understood the primary reason she claimed to love him ... the golden ring ... he realized he was mostly hooked on the incredible sex. Sex was why he began his relationship with Camilla, but they broke it off because it would never be anything more, she not knowing he was exactly whom she sought.

He'd taken it more slowly with Anne, but their eventual sex was also pretty terrific. He chuckled. After ten years semi-celibate except for paid romance with Gulia, had he become addicted? He slumped back onto his chair and stretched, coming to a resolve. Next time he'd build a relationship based on true love, not wealth. He'd have no problem with casual sex as long as the understanding was two people enjoying mutual satisfaction.

Alex jerked upright and realized he'd made a decision. If he was considering a next time, that meant he *was* finished with Anne. Thinking back, he never had a sense that their relationship was anything more than physical to her until she learned he was mega-rich. Somehow, he needed to create a persona totally different from who he was. The problem was, how to do that? And where could he pull that off?

He lurched to his feet and strode to the kitchen. Lunch and a nap to clear his mind, and he'd tackle a new Alex who was foolproof. An every day Joe who some woman would love because of who he seemed, avoiding this not-so-new problem again. Someone totally different and … he paused at the fridge … somewhere far away from South Florida. He nodded. With his business sold, no reason to stay here anyhow.

~ 26 ~

Emma stacked plates in the cupboard, closed the door, and surveyed the kitchen. The rest of the volunteer staff was gone until prep-time for dinner, so she had the afternoon off. Another of the women was scheduled for the evening kitchen work, but Emma also opted to serve the evening meal. She, like most of the other five girls, needed to keep busy.

That night would be a celebration, as news that the violent stalker of one of her new "sisters," Ruth, had been convicted of first-degree murder of the woman he'd moved on with after Ruth disappeared. She was preparing to return to Omaha and resume her life. The other five women voiced their pleasure for her ... and their jealousy.

Emma returned to her rooms to acquire her new, air-gapped laptop, with no Internet connection, and her spiral notebook. Back in the lobby's lounge, she set up at a small table and called up the outline of the novel she'd begun. She'd attended an online writer's conference while in Hallandale and learned the value of a chapter-by-chapter outline. It was a fluid thing, where chapters could be added or deleted, or even rearranged as the story developed. She'd envisioned a love story, complicated by a nasty stalker, so she had plenty of real-life data to draw from ... except for the love part. She hoped that would come someday, but not likely for the near future.

Sitting back, Emma rubbed her eyes with the heels of her palms, brushing away tiny droplets that formed there. A sigh, and she gritted her teeth. This was her life now and for the near future. Nowhere to go until Brad was out of the picture. A twinge of guilt ticked at her brain at the thought of him going the way of Ruth's stalker. *How do I wish that calamity on another innocent woman— killed by a stalker?* She chuckled quietly at another thought. *I could always hire a hitman. I doubt anyone would lament Brad's passing.* That thought was quickly cast aside with a head shake. That's not Emma Logan, no matter how desperate things got.

Another sigh, and she returned her attention to the outline on her computer. A third of the story envisioned: a budding romance, ended by growing physical and psychological abuse; then the breakup, followed by stalking and fear for her heroine's, Carlene's life. All a reflection of Emma's existence. She'd just outlined three chapters dealing with Carlene's flight to safety, imagining something very different from what Emma did. But, what next? Well, she was going to live "what next," so maybe that would give her ideas.

Ruth was finally getting to go home … after *seven years* in hiding. *Seven Years! How do you do that without going crazy?* With a lot of help from others, she supposed. That's what this place was all about … keeping hope alive and her safe.

She prayed it would be enough.

~ 27 ~

Alex slouched at his desk at his Wellington estate, and stared at the page resting atop it's oak surface. *What the fuck am I doing here?* The real question was, what was he really seeking? Love and someone to share his life with, or an uncomplicated existence where love might just happen? Chasing love had pushed him into phony situations … for both the woman and *him*. Straightening, he plucked up a pen and drew the white paper closer. The pen tapped his chin as he mulled the conundrum, and suddenly, he saw the answer.

Justin and he slaved ten years to build their biotech dream, and during that time, he'd cast aside any and all other aspirations. His share in that effort had brought him nearly a billion dollars, a sum still growing from the surge in value of the stock he'd received. Now was the time to return to his roots and be Alex Jordan, the man, not the billionaire. Rekindled by his affair with Anne, his love of fishing and the outdoors was what he'd seek. But how and where? Some place far away where there was no chance anyone might recognize him. No more confusing great sex with love, either. If he met someone special, he resolved to go slow, and be sure the connection was for who he was and not for what he was worth. Where could that happen?

Mexico or Canada were the obvious choices, and their southern neighbor seemed the better answer, primarily for the saltwater fishing he loved. There was a lot to do before he could leave. He'd listed his Wellington mansion with a realtor specializing in high-end properties, and it sold in a bidding war three days later. His Lexus is500 sedan went just as quickly on AutoTrader, and he bought a five-year-old Dodge Ram 4 x 4 crew-cab pickup there, which seemed more appropriate for who he'd planned to become. It was arriving tomorrow.

He'd attended the monthly gun show at the South Florida Fairgrounds and acquired an almost new Glock 40, two extra mags, and five boxes of .40 caliber ammo. The dealer promised to expedite the background check. The disadvantage of Mexico was the cartels and crime, and he didn't intend to be an easy victim, if it came to that. He'd set aside two days to visit a nearby gun-range to get acquainted with the pistol.

Alex slouched in his chair and knuckled his eyes. Just two more tasks before he began packing up: an offshore account for backup funds, should he need it in his new environs; and a fresh identity—a totally new slate, with no strings that might lead back to him. He would disappear and become an every-day Joe, someone working for an honest living, trying to survive on his earnings in his new endeavor, whatever that might be, but the money would be there if needed.

If Alex Weaver, the name he'd settled on, couldn't cut it after a year or two, Alex Jordan could always reappear. He hoped he'd find what he was seeking, and that included a woman who loved a working man, but if not, little would be lost. He'd still be young and rich, and able to live whatever life he sought.

Rising, he moved to the kitchen to microwave a frozen pizza for dinner. There was a prepared salad from Publix in the frig, and two Coronas on ice. After dinner, he'd pack a duffel bag with his very best rendition of a common man's clothing. Goodwill was scheduled to come the next morning and take everything else. He'd pick up his pistol in two days and should receive his new ID via

FedEx in three.

During dinner he fielded a call from his realtor asking if the buyer could take residence in a week. The daughter wants to get her two open jumpers there ASAP, as she intended to compete in the Winter show jumping season, and his house and stables, which he never used, were ideal.

Perfect timing, because the newly minted Alex Weaver would be on the road by then, en route to Arizona's border with Mexico. He was going to look for a place to live, somewhere on the Pacific coast, along the Sea of Cortez, or possibly even further south.

Some place where they never heard of Alex Jordan.

~ 28 ~

Brad Barnes pulled into a visitor's spot in front of the Hallandale Beach Arms condo, killed the engine of his Audi, and paused, eyeing the building. *So, this is where she moved. That damned double-murder trial occupied so much of my time, this is my first chance to get away since the bitch escaped me from that deli.* His investigator needed three days to dig up the address after Brad had used a "person of interest" excuse, saying it was an old case he was looking into in his spare time, as a favor to a friend. He got curious looks, but no one dared ask questions. A little fear from his staff was how he liked it.

He grumbled as he stepped from his sedan and into the glare of the midday sun, unusually muggy for that time of year. Mopping his already damp brow, he strode toward the entry, not expecting to learn a forwarding address, but maybe someone knew more than they were aware of. Brad was good at getting to those kinds of facts. Stepping through the glass entry doors, he spied the sign he sought: MANAGEMENT. Inside, he discovered a small, four-desk office with two staff present. A slim, silver-haired guy, tapping away at a desktop computer, glanced up as Brad approached,

"May I help you?" his eyebrows arched,

"I hope so." Brad dialed up his best smile and flashed his ID. "I'm Brad Barnes from the Miami DA's office. We're looking for Emma Logan." He waved his hand. "She's in no trouble, but may be a witness to something that went down in North Miami."

"Oh, sorry. She moved aways. Kind of sudden, actually." He eased back, hands folded over his stomach. "She was on a month-to-month lease, so no problem at our end, other than we lost a nice tenant."

"I see." Brad rubbed his chin. "Did she leave a forwarding address? Maybe to collect her security deposit, if there were one?"

"I don't believe so, but let me check." The man leaned forward and began to tap at his computer. "Ah, here." He scanned the monitor. "Yes, we *did* have a deposit, but no forwarding. Been … let's see … ten days, and actually her sister came to close her account. Ms. Logan just left without so much as a word or a goodbye." He looked at Brad. "Kind of strange, actually." He sat back. "Anything else I can help you with?"

"I guess not." Brad proffered his card. "Just advise me if you should hear from her, or get any information where she may have moved. As I said, she's not in trouble with the law, but it is important that I have an opportunity to talk with her."

"Of course." He took the card and wedged its end under the border of his desk blotter. "Good luck with your search."

Brad nodded, turned to leave, then paused, pivoting back. "Did she have any friends here? Someone else who may know something?"

The man shrugged. "Not to my knowledge. Ms. Logan kept very much to herself." A finger stroked the crease of his nose. "Her sister seemed to be her only visitor. Have you asked her?"

"No, but I will," he lied. He had no interest in tangling with that bitch again unless he was sure it would pay off. *Charlene Hamlin surely knows Emma's whereabouts, but short of torture, she not gonna to give that up.* Brad strode through the door and returned to his car, his lips twisted into a snarl. Maybe, if Emma never surfaced, he *would* take it out on that bleached blond bitch. Teach her who's boss, and give her a good fucking, too. He sighed and shook his head, knowing that would never happen. Too much risk, especially with her packing that nasty little .380, but the vision lingered as he drove off.

Gotta be patient. Emma's going to show up sometime, and I'm not about to quit looking ... no matter how long it takes. Meanwhile, things were progressing with his new babe. A good fucker, too. Couple more dates, and he'd begin the "program."

He licked lips at the thought, then snarled as a vision of Emma crept into his mind. He wanted that hot, fucking little redhead more than anyone and wasn't going to quit until he had his hooks into her again.

He fidgeted on the car's seat as he became hard at the thought.

~ 29 ~

Anne Parson's glared at her cell phone, then disconnected from the repetitive AI voice, droning "Sorry, that number is no longer in service." *What the hell happened to Alex?* It was a new cell phone he'd apparently activated when he began his charade as Alex Penney. A paper plucked from her desk, she scanned her notes. Maybe his house phone, which she'd discovered with her research into Alex Jordan. That number dialed, she heard the same musical beeps, followed by the same message, "not in service." Had something happened to him?

Anne slumped in her chair and rubbed her eyes. She desperately wanted to alter Alex's perception of her. Apologize for sounding like a gold-digger, and emphasize she'd fallen for him as Alex Penney, *not* Alex Jordan. Claim she'd only researched his background because guys had hurt her in the past, and she wanted to be sure she wasn't putting her heart out there to be stomped on again. It was a believable half-truth, and while she really did like him … and the great sex … a lot, his wealth had sealed the deal. A practical woman, she'd make "love" work, to be with a guy like him.

Sighing, she dug in a drawer for her phone book. Unlike many in the modern tech world, she kept things like contacts on paper, not some electronic app. The sought number found, she dialed, answered quickly by a brisk female voice: "Carlyle and Simms."

"Hi. This is Anne Parsons. Is Wilton available?"

"Oh, hi Miss Parsons. Yes, I believe he just got off the phone.

How's fishing?"

"Best sailfishing of the season right now. Thought maybe Wilton might want to make time for a trip before things cool off."

"Could be. He's just between cases at the moment. I'll connect you."

Anne waited for her client, a criminal defense lawyer, to come on the phone. A guy who kept rigorous contacts with anyone influential in Palm Beach County, he'd know if anything happened to Alex. He came on the phone.

"How's my favorite charter boat captain? Prospecting for business, are you?"

"Well, with this northeast wind, the sails are hitting, and we took a fifty-four-pound dolphin and a nice wahoo last week. I had a no-show for today and tomorrow from someone up your way. Thought you may be interested." Playing in cool.

"I am. Tomorrow at seven?"

"Yeah, I guess it's open, since I haven't heard from Alex Jordan." Fingers crossed.

"Ah, the newly minted billionaire. I'm surprised he stiffed you with no notice. Doesn't seem like him."

"That's how I felt. Actually, I'm a bit worried. We've fished together several times the last month, and he's the guy who caught the dolphin and wahoo. He's always been prompt and ready to fish." A pause. "You haven't heard of anything bad happening to him, have you?"

"Other than selling his firm and retiring at twenty-eight? No, not really." He cleared his throat. "Well, there was an affair that ended somewhat badly, I've heard."

"An affair?" She swallowed, unsure of her reaction.

"Yes, with a Thursday D'Angelo. They were going hot and heavy, and I understand she'd moved in with him. The rumor was they would marry, but it suddenly ended with a thud." He tsked. "Gorgeous woman, but I suspect she was after his money, and he figured that out and dumped her." He paused. "I'm blathering on. It's not like me to gossip, but since you think he's disappeared—"

"It's probably nothing, Winny. Just he seemed like a nice guy, and I was worried." Anne swallowed and tried to sound calm. "Anyhow, she ya tomorrow, bright and early. Bring plenty of sunscreen. It's been hot out there." She disconnected.

So, he had a run in with another gold-digger, and I stupidly chased him off. The old saw, "Fool me once, shame on you ..." And that's how Alex sees me ... looking for the golden ring. Not far wrong, actually, but he'd be an easy guy to dock her heart with. *Best damned fisherman I've ever had in my boat. We coulda had a ball together.* She sighed and scratched her head. *It's early. Maybe I'll run up to his house and see what I can find.*

Three hours later, Anne re-entered her apartment and flopped on the bed. It took over an hour to find Alex's mansion in Wellington, and when she arrived, she'd discovered a new family in the process of moving in. They confirmed they'd just bought the estate from Mr. Jordan, whom they never met. He was gone when they arrived, and the house was sold, fully furnished.

Alex Jordan had seemingly vanished without a trace.

"Shit," she snarled, tears forming in her ocean-blue eyes. *The guy of a lifetime and pushy me, I screwed it up.*

"Alex, come back." She sniffled. "I'll love you for you. I'll sign any kind of pre-nup or contract you want. I just wanna be with you." Murmured softly into her pillow. Her alarm was already set for her early morning trip. She chuckled despite her angst. Winny was forty years her senior, married, with three kids. Didn't stop him from making a pass at her, but she wasn't about to become "the other woman," especially for someone old enough to be her father.

Finally, her well of tears empty, she slept.

~ 30 ~

The mid-morning sun crept well above the horizon, shimmering brightly in the cloudless, robin-egg-blue sky. A normal, hot day in the desert. Alex slipped his Dodge Ram crew-cab pickup to the curb, shifted into PARK, and left the engine idling as he peered ahead at the Nogales US border crossing into Mexico. Retrieving his document billfold from the glove box, he pawed through his new ID papers. He flipped open the passport for Alex Weaver. A photo-shopped pic by the forger added the two-week beard he now sported, and it looked pretty accurate. Faked driver license and Social Security card were in his wallet, along with a legit auto insurance ID. He sighed and glanced at the short line of vehicles awaiting clearance to exit the USA. Mexican customs and immigration would be on the other side of the border.

The passport slid into a shirt breast pocket, he nodded. "I'm Alex Weaver," he muttered. "Alex Jordan is gone." *For now, anyhow. Time to embrace my new life.* He checked that the hidden compartment under his seat where he'd stashed his Glock and ammo was undetectable, then shifted into gear and entered the cue of cars and trucks, just another *gringo*, headed south … sightseeing and doing some fishing. Used trolling and spinning rods he'd bought on Ebay lay on the back seat.

Forty-minutes later, Alex Weaver drove away from Mexican Border Security, passport stamped and travel approved. Easy-peasy. A glance at his map (the old Dodge lacked a screen to display Wayz) and headed for Federal Highway 15 which would take him along the mainland Pacific coast of the Sea of Cortez.

Alex hadn't decided on a final destination, and would allow instinct to pick that for him. Certainly nothing north of Mazatlán, which nestled at the western mouth of the Sea of Cortez. Cabo San Lucas lay across the gulf at the tip of Baja California, a popular resort spot, but not somewhere that beckoned him, despite the great fishing. Too likely to run into a vacationing acquaintance there. He'd loitered down Highway 15, his Glock 40 now tucked under his seat, just "in-case," and see where that led him.

Mazatlán was a two-day drive. He paused along the way for a view of the narrow sea dividing the mainland from the skinny peninsula, Baja California. Rippled waters glittering like a blue blanket of tiny diamonds in the early morning sunlight. He sighed and drove on, not yet ready to stop.

He arrived in Mazatlán mid-afternoon and cruised through town and along the beach, studded with numerous fancy resorts, uncertain what to do next. Definitely a tourist location. Lots of small hostels and inns too, but somehow he didn't feel the vibe. Tooling past the marina, he spotted several sportfishing charter boats flying little blue billfish flags from their outriggers—a good day fishing. Probably for sailfish, as it was low season for striped marlin.

That's why most people came to Mazatlán—the fishing, but despite Alex's love for the sport, he was drawn by sites farther south. Puerto Vallarta was the next major port. Another leisurely two-day drive. If not there, then Ixtapa. He wanted someplace between there and Acapulco.

Back on the road, he paused at a beachfront café for lunch, and was on the road again by 2:00 p.m. He had no schedule, a thing that ruled his life for ten years as he built his business, so many impromptu stops were made along the way. Despite his planning, he was uncertain of exactly what he was looking for.

Maybe he'd find it, whatever *it* was, in Puerto Vallarta.

Alex yawned, felt for his tumbler of black coffee, luke-warm now, and glanced at his watch. Four p.m. Another hour to Ixtapa. Puerto Vallarta had no lure for him, so he'd continued south. Sipping the strong Colombian brew, he was happy he'd brought his portable propane tw0-burner stove. He'd stopped three hours ago for a rest and picnic lunch of two peanut butter slathered bananas and his final cup of Greek Yogurt. He'd brewed a full pot of java using the last of the three jugs of spring water he'd brought from the States. A slow introduction to local water to attempt to avoid a "touristas" bowel might work, but for now it was to be all bottled.

Ixtapa/Zihuantanejo were the last major cities before Acapulco, and he didn't want to go that far south, especially since that once glorious vacation spot now seemed riddled with crime. Alex concentrated on the road and staying awake. It'd been a 1300-mile trek from the U.S. border, and he was ready to call it quits. Time to find a place to land and start his new life.

An hour later, he cruised along the wide avenue between the seashore and the looming mountains. He spied a marina and pulled in to scout it out. Ixtapa was a sportfishing destination, and many charter boats lined the pier, ranging from a basic thirty-foot lapstrake sea-skiff to a well-equipped, forty-eight-foot Hatteras. A dozen, twenty-five-foot pangas—native open, outboard-driven boats, usually with one fighting chair, short outriggers, and a canvas canopy—bobbed at mooring buoys scattered across the bay. Several of the boats flew billfish flags from their outriggers, heralding a successful day's fishing.

A stroll along the pier brough Alex to a Mexican, probably one of the panga captains, fileting two modest cow dolphins at a cleaning table. He paused and watched the man's dexterous knife work.

"Hola," he said. *"Habla Inglese?"*

The man glanced up, nodded, and returned to his task.

"Nice fish for the table. Had a good day?"

"Si, no p*ez vela* (sailfish), but some nice d*orado*," gesturing at the dolphin. "Then we fish the *playa* (beach) and catch *dos pez gallo* (2 roosterfish). "You fish?" He gestured at the bay. *"Mi launcha* very nice. Two-hundred-fifty US for *media dia."*

"Yeah, I love it, but just arrived. Maybe another day." He extended a hand. "I'm Alex."

"Ricardo," his hands wiped on a rag and then taken. He handed Alex a slip of paper, a hand-printed business card. "Is good fishing now. Many *gallo* on beach."

"Thanks. I will call, once I get settled." With a wave, he turned toward shore and his truck. *Roosterfish, huh? I heard they're great fighters and good jumpers.* His gaze swept the hotels, nestled at the foot of the mountains close to the water, and the nearby *mercado.*

"This is gonna be the spot," murmured softly. *My new life.* He lingered in the truck, engine idling and a/c cooling and drying the air, as he considered his next move. So far, he'd been playing this venture "by ear," with no concrete agenda. Time to alter that.

Find somewhere with a good bed for the night, and tomorrow explore my options. I suppose there must be realtors here. Number one is to get a place to live. He drove from the lot and began cruising around the city center, seeking restaurants, real estate offices, and lawyers. He needed both of the latter if he were to become a resident.

Three hours later, he'd eaten at a small restaurant in the city, found a cozy, in-town inn with reasonable room prices, and settled in for the night. Tired from a long day, he turned in at ten and slept soundly, visions of leaping striped marlin filling his head. For the first time in a year, beautiful women and hot sex didn't visit his dreams.

~ 31 ~

Fifteen days passed in a whirlwind of activity. Working with Dulce, a slim, attractive blonde realtor, Alex spent two days scouring Ixtapá and its connecting town, Zihuantanejo, which was more of a resort spot. Both were replete with upscale hotels, mostly snuggled on the edge of a mountain along the vast beaches, but Ixtapá seemed more a town of the locals. On the third day, they'd located a small, adobe house needing repair, north of the Ixtapá, nestled at the foot of the slope and close to the beach.

"The owner has died, and his son, who lives in Mexico City, wants a quick sale so he can get home. Want to make him a low-ball offer?"

Alex did, and the offer was quickly accepted. A day was spent surveying the house's needs and getting supplies. *I can do most of this myself. 'Bout time I do some physical labor.* He only needed an electrician to replace the antiquated fuse box with a breaker panel, increasing the total service to one-hundred amps. He spent more bucks than an Alex Weaver should be able to afford, but this was a one-time thing, and while he wanted a simpler life, he didn't want to live like a monk.

Then he went fishing with Ricardo and caught and released two nice roosterfish, a dozen mackerel (some of which he kept for meals), and a few small bonito. He eyed the blue, offshore waters, picturing marlin, sailfish, and dolphin, but while those were in season, they were for another day.

By the end of the second week, his new little abode had shaped up into a comfortable home—open to ocean breezes except for his single bedroom, in which he installed a window a/c. Still not a monk.

Then he booked a second morning trip with Ricardo, this time going offshore, seeking sailfish and dorado, catching a nice bull dorado of about twenty-pounds, and a few cow dorado but no billfish. Filets for the top freezer in his new fridge.

Alex spent the next two days seeking a boat of his own. *I love this fishing, and I need something to fill my time in this new life. Maybe I'll even become a charter captain.* Fiberglass hulls were rare in the area, so he found a sound, twenty-six-foot lapstrake open skiff. The owner had lost his outboard motor to theft and couldn't afford a new, or even used one. Alex found a four-year-old, 200 h.p Yamaha and got the engine to a repair shop for full servicing and mounting on his sea skiff. He ordered new canvas for the folding sunshade and a lightly used set of fifteen-foot aluminums outriggers he found at a resale boat shop. His craft was shaping up nicely, and he was eager to go. He christened her *Pegasus.*

House repairs finally finished and new boat setup in the works, he ventured one evening to the bar at a luxury resort, Cala de Mar, eager to meet locals ... probably staff ... to polish up his Spanish. He already had a grasp of the language, as many of his workers in West Palm Beach had been Latinos, mostly Cuban.

The hotel's lounge was peppered with Happy Hour clientele, both locals and guests. He slid onto a stool at the bar and was greeted by an attractive, honey-skinned barista.

"*Ola,*" he said. "*Una Corona, por favor.*"

She chuckled. "Not bad for a *gringo,* but we speak English here." She withdrew the beer from a cooler, popped the cap, and poured it into a tilted glass to minimize foam.

"I figured." He sipped the amber liquid. "But I just moved here, and I'm working on my Spanish." He proffered his hand.

"I'm Alex Weaver."

Hand shaken, she wiped the bar with a cloth. "Okay." She caught his eyes, her's mahogany brown. "I'm Chiquita, and I've heard every wisecrack." She chuckled. "No, I don't sell bananas."

A laugh bubbled out of Alex. "I get it. Anyhow, let's converse from here on in Spanish, and see how I do." He took a larger taste of his beer.

"Okay." She folded the rag. *"En dónde vives?"*

"Una casa, al norte, circa de la playa." A house to the north, near the beach.

"Muy bien." She smiled, and continued the conversation in Spanish, in between serving a few others at the bar.

Alex found he spoke the language easier than he understood it. He had to slow her typical Latina pace, but eventually got the hang of it. After a half-hour of give-and-take, the lounge began to fill, and the seat next to him was taken by an American guest.

He introduced himself to Harvey Meyers, a lanky, deeply tanned Texan, in his sixties, visiting with his mistress (oil money?), who was still "dolling herself up" in their suite.

"You doing any fishing?" Alex asked.

"Most every day. That Hatteras 48 at the end of the dock."

"Yeah," Alex nodded, "I know it. You were flying three flags today." He was working on his second *cerveza.* "Pricey boat, I suspect."

"Yep, but y'all git what ya pay for. Good captain and mate." He took a swig of scotch. "Three sails and a bunch of dorado, and Cindy fought somthin' fer an hour that we never saw. Cap'n thought it was a big yellowfin." He grunted. "Tough bastards."

"For sure." Alex signaled Chiquita for another beer.

Harvey looked up and nudged Alex. "Ah, and the princess arrives."

Alex swiveled on the stool and spied a raven-hair, tall beauty in a slinky, skin-tight red sheath that barely extended below her pussy, strutting into the room on four-inch stilettos. Apparent manmade boobs, barely hid behind a deeply cleaved front. The ultimate Other Woman.

Cindy waved, a small smile tickling her lips, cobalt-blue eyes sparkling behind bulked-up lashes and heavy mascara. Harvey gathered her to him, and arm around her waist, and she smeared his cheek with a lipsticked kiss.

"Hi, babe." He nodded at Alex, made the introduction, then turned to her. "Martini?"

"What else?" She patted his red-stained cheek. "Shaken, not stirred, just like James Bond. So," she turned to Alex, "you here alone?" She brushed a hand across his cheek. "I like the blond beard. Kinda sexy."

He nodded. "Good to know," and chuckled. "Anyhow, I'm working on it. Actually, just moved down here. Love the fishing and the climate, so I'm planning on staying. Maybe set up my own charter service," turning to Harvey, "for your next visit."

"I'll remember that, sport." He took Cindy's hand. "Well, time for dinner, babe."

"Swell. I'm starved." And they headed for the elegant dining room.

Alex swiveled back to the bar and nursed his beer. Chiquita was too busy with a burgeoning crowd to partake in much conversation, so he waved at her and tossed cash on the bar to cover his drinks. He wanted to check on his boat's progress. In the morning, he planned to visit a small estuary he'd seen where he thought he might find schools of silver mullet. He'd been practicing with a cast net he'd bought, and planned on catching a supply to use as bait when fishing offshore. He had silvery bonito belly from fish he'd caught with Ricardo … great strip baits for use behind feathered jigs, or skipped on the surface from the 'riggers.

He learned *Pegasus* would be ready to go by mid-morning. Back in his *casa*, he rigged and inspected his tackle. Tomorrow he'd begin fishing, and once he learned the local secrets, he'd become a charter captain. He'd checked requirements and picked up necessary licensing paperwork from the local courthouse.

Captain Alex Weaver, professional fisherman. His now full, neatly-trimmed, yellow beard, leaner physique, and deeply tanned skin should make him anonymous to anyone who knew Alex Jordan.

Captain Alex Weaver sounded great. A home-cooked dinner of baked dolphin, a yam, and green beans, completed his evening. He crawled into bed and turned on his small T.V. for local news, and more practice with his Spanish. He was becoming adept.

Then he slept, pleased with the new life he'd created—at least for now.

~ 32 ~

Two Years Later

Emma sprawled across her unmade bed, face buried in her pillow, blubbering softly.

Two damned years here and nothing's changed. She rolled over and knuckled away tears, knowing things could have been a lot worse. People there were great, and the other women were a strong support group, as they all fully understood what she was going through. But, contact with family and friends back home wasn't going to happen. She'd only talked to Char three times in the last 26 months, all collect calls from payphones, usually from Evanston. The train there once or twice a month took forty minutes, and she'd go to audit classes at Northwestern ... usually history, finance, or civics ... because she couldn't chance signing up for one. She didn't know how penetrating Brad's reach was, and was cautioned not to chance it.

Now Trisha, her main pickleball and tennis buddy, was leaving. Her stalker was still out there, but her family had created a fictional life for her in Seattle, including a complete new identity. They'd sent her a new driver license, social security card, and credit card. The only thing missing was a passport, and she didn't plan on leaving the country, Her long, natural blond hair was already pixie-cut and dyed jet black, and she was about to replace her glasses with brown-tinted contacts. The shelter had cash payment arrangements with several doctors, and everything was done off-book.

Emma squiggled off the bed and took a shower before dinner.

A celebration party was planned for Trisha, as she was leaving in the morning, traveling to the West Coast via Greyhound.

"I've got mixed feelings about this, girls," she'd said. "I'm gonna be happy to return to some sort of normalcy," soft applause from the women, "but I'm gonna miss my sisters." She'd looked at Emma. "I hope I can find as worthy an on-court opponent as you, out there, Em."

"You'll do fine, Trish," Emma said, giving a hug, "but now my only opponent is gonna be Bobby."

"You three girls," Trisha's eyes found Ruth's, "should learn pickleball, at least. With a little practice, anyone can do it. It's be good for all of you."

Murmured ascents had filled the room, and Sandra had later asked Emma to show her the game.

Well, we'll see, Emma thought, remembering that afternoon. *I'd thought I could get set up somewhere, like Trisha, but Char felt Brad had too many resources and might track me down.* Dressed for the party, she started down to the dining room. *Think I'll call sis and see if we can figure something out.* She strode into the shelter's main lounge and spied tables of shrimp, oysters on the half-shell, and sparkling wine. All the residents pitched in to make it a good party, but the only woman there really happy was Trisha. The others struggled not to show their jealousy.

The next morning, Bobby drove Emma into Highland Park with Trisha. She'd see her friend off, and then call Char. The women hugged and wished each other luck as Trisha climbed the steps of the 10:30 a.m. bus. They waved as it departed, and Emma turned to Bobby.

"I need about an hour or so, if that's okay?" A sweater was donned in face of the cooling, fall weather.

"Sure. I got a few things to pick up for Madge, and I want to look for a couple of books. Noon, in front of the library?"

"Perfect. I gotta get a new pair of sneakers, and I want to call my sister. Then I may come in to look for a good novel, too."

"Okay." He studied her. "The call safe? You usually do it from Evanston."

"Yeah, I'm pretty sure. I'll call my cousin, Sally, and she connects me with Char in a three-way." She shrugged. "Even if Brad's got some way of monitoring Char's phone, he'll only see a call from her favorite cousin. They talk all the time."

"Good, but stay alert. There's a busload of people in from the city for the afternoon concert at Ravinia, and they're cruising downtown. Don't end up on social media."

"Roger that, my captain." She grinned and patted his shoulder. Madge had a real gem in Bobby. Noon on a Saturday in Miami was quickly approaching, and she expected Sally would be making lunch for her tribe, so she headed for the nearest payphone. The call made and charges were accepted.

"Hey, Em," Sally sounding cheerful, "how are you?"

"Safe but miserable, Sal," tears in her voice. "I mean, this place is great. Couldn't be nicer, considering what it's here for, and really nice people." A soft whimper. "But I miss my family and friends. It's been twenty-six months!" She sighed. "I guess I really shouldn't complain. One girl's been here over 4 years."

"Damn, I can't imagine that. Hang on a minute," a short pause, "I'm hooking up Char on a three-way." Followed by a few clicks and the buzz of a ringing phone.

"Hello?"

"Char, it's Sally. I'm connecting Emma on a three-way." A soft click, and then …

"Emma? You there?" Charlene's voice tinged by angst. "Anything wrong?"

"Hey, Sis. No, I'm okay. Just lonely as hell for family. Despite how upscale this shelter is, it's not home."

"Yeah, I get that, but it's not safe to come back. That bastard's still out there." She paused. "Don't get your hopes up on this, Sis, but it's occurred to me that you may not be the first girl he's done this to. I hired a PI to quietly investigate Brad, and we *have* learned that two women he's dated over the last ten years had vanished right around when they broke up. Don't know if anyone's been looking for them, so maybe it's just coincidence, but ..." she trailed off.

"We don't believe in coincidences, do we?"

"A good cop doesn't, I hear. Neither does the P.I." Char sighed. "Anyhow, none of this helps at the moment. I don't know what else to do."

"Me either. One of the women here is moving somewhere far away, and she's got a new identity, much like witness protection, I guess." Emma moaned. "Even if we could do that, I don't wanna start new without you guys in my life."

"Okay. You know what I'm thinking? With winter coming, maybe we can meet on a vacation somewhere, far away and warm,. How about Mexico?"

"Jeez, I'd love that. It's already starting to get cold up here. You think it's safe?"

"Probably. I'll see what I can set up. You can buy an airline ticket with cash at a travel agency, and you've got that alias VISA card, but I'd use it sparingly. No way to avoid using your name on the ticket and passport when you check in, though." A pause. "Not sure it's safe. May be somewhere else—"

"I'll chance it, Char. Mexico is a long way away. I really need a break."

"Well," Char hesitated, "if we're gonna do this, I'll send more cash and let you know what I've arranged. Okay?"

"Better than okay." Emma's voice light and eager for the first time in months. "Nobody's got a better sister than me. Can you get away ... maybe for two weeks?"

"Yeah, I've accumulated over four weeks of unused vacation time. Late November work for you?"

"You bet! That's only a month, but I can hardly wait." She took a breath. "What about Bob and Judy? Mom available to sit for two weeks?"

"You kidding? She'll love it. Last time we were away, she had her bridge buddies play at our house." The three women giggled.

"I'll post the signal words on the Internet," Sally pitched in, "soon as the money's sent, and again after I get notice it's arrived. The Evanston UPS store, right?

"Yep. That'll work," Emma said with a gleeful chuckle.

"Okay. You guys better end this now. We've been on too long." Sally grunted. "I wish I could join you, but no way I can get away. Anyhow, it's better you have uninterrupted time together, after all these months."

"Okay. 'Bye, Char. Can't wait to see you guys."

"Me, too, Sis. Meantime, stay careful." Followed by a click.

"Okay, Sal. Thanks for the help. Sorry we can't talk more."

"Me, too, Em. Take care, and I hope everything goes well. I'm jealous." A chuckle, and then the disconnect tone.

Emma hung up the phone, leaned against the kiosk, and suddenly found it hard to breathe. She replayed their conversation, especially the part about investigating Brad. It *had* occurred to her she might not be his first victim. What happened to those other two women? Could he have used them, then killed them. Jesus, what a monster.

She pushed away and glanced at her watch. Less than an hour to finish her shopping, and maybe find a good book at the library. She strode off, a smile dancing across her lips for the first time in many months. A cool, fresh-smelling breeze ruffled her hair, and she paused, following cotton ball clouds skittering across the bluest sky she'd ever seen. A fast, little tap-dance was executed around a street light pole, and she giggled, then glanced around, embarrassed that someone might be watching. She chuckled, glad no one was in view, and headed out to shop.

She loved her sister and her great hubby, Larry. Mexico, huh? They catch sailfish there, remembering the trips as a kid with Dad out of Miami. That'd be fun, and a new memory to hang on to.

~ 33 ~

The sea-skiff slipped alongside the Ixtapá wharf and Alex snatched a piling to hold her steady against two scarred rubber bumpers. The Marchand brothers jumped off, each with a mooring line, securing the boat as Alex killed the engine before also stepping ashore. The squawk of a flock of greedy gulls swirling above drew a chuckle as he turned to his passengers. He nodded up at the birds.

"Our welcoming committee, hoping for scraps." He checked the lines to see they were secure. "A good day, huh, guys?"

"The best, Alex." Tim handed him six Benjamins. "Something extra for such a great captain."

"Thanks. Always appreciated." The folded bills went into a pocket. "So, proof you don't have to spend a fortune on a big, fancy boat," nodding up the dock where the large sportfishermen were berthed, "to catch a lot of fish."

"Fer sure," Rafe Marchand shook his hand. "We coulda afforded it, but liked the idea of fishing with a fellow *gringo*." He chuckled. "Couldn't have had more fun." He turned to his brother. "Do it again tomorrow, bro?"

Tim nodded. "How about it, Alex. You free?"

Long caramel-colored hair swirled with a head shake. "Sorry guys, booked." He scratched his beard with sun-darkened fingers. "Day after is open, though."

"You got it, Cap," Rafe said. "Maybe we'll get that marlin next time."

"Yeah. Kinda strange he trailed that mullet but wouldn't eat." He looked at his boat. "You want marlin, I can set up the eighty-pound, and we'll catch a small bonito for live bait. If there's a blue or black marlin around, they'll eat that." He clapped Rafe on the back. "But I thought you wanted *gallo* on the fly. Casting this time, not trolling."

"Yeah, well, as far as our buddies back home are concerned, we both caught roosterfish on the fly." He chuckled. "No need to admit we weren't casting."

"Whatever," Alex stepped aboard *Pegasus* and began a washdown. "Let me know your pleasure, and I'll be ready for you. Seven-thirty, right here, and remember, no bananas, and three beers max, each. I'll have plenty of bottled water." He waved as they strolled off the pier, then began organizing his tackle. All the rods, lures, hooks, and the portable cooler came home with him. While theft wasn't a major problem in Ixtapá, no sense in tempting fate.

He chuckled, appreciating that most tourists left him with nice tips. Afterall, he was a struggling fisherman, trying to make ends meet. And it was working. After he got set up using some of his wealth two years ago to buy his *casa* and outfit the boat, he had managed to live on what he made. It took him back to the early days with Justin, struggling to get their dream on track. His work ethic stood by him now, and he enjoyed the challenge.

His thirtieth birthday was just around the corner, and he needed a woman to share it with. He'd developed a relationship, based on good times and sex, with both Dulce, the real estate agent who found him his little house, and Chiquita, the sexy little barista at Cala de Mar Resort. They expected a fun evening, and then some great sex, and neither seemed to aspire for anything more … which suited him fine. At least, no one down here was after his money.

He sighed. Probably ask Dulce, which would lead to a quieter, more intellectual date … and he loved her multi-orgasmic adventures in bed. A night with Chiquita always proved hectic … fun, but hectic, and she was a lot more aggressive in the sack. They'd troll the local cantinas, dance, listen to Mariachi bands, and he'd splurge on lobsters. Maybe he'd even order a small chocolate mousse cake from the little French pastry shop. Thirty only came around once.

He sighed again. Too bad he hadn't found a life partner, but he came to Ixtapa to avoid the wrong kinds of entanglements. He realized if that were to happen, he might have to hook up with a tourist. A nice, everyday babe who could find a rugged workingman interesting enough to fall in love. If she ever appeared, and loved him for him, he wasn't tied to Mexico. He could live anywhere, and plenty of visitors were from Europe: Spain, France, and Germany, mostly. Someone he could settle down with and raise a family, before it got too late.

Well, *Que sera, sera,* as Doris Day sang it. What will be, will be. One thing for sure, he wasn't gonna rush into another affair. Been there, done that ... twice, so next time he'd better get it right. Meanwhile, he'd shower, wash the salt out of his hair, and drop in on Chiquita at Call de Mar for a drink, and maybe a little fun later. The birthday bash was in four days, on Saturday, so he needed to see if Dulce was free first. Nothing to keep him from a pre-birthday party tonight with the hot little barista, though.

He grinned. Thirty was a woman's prime, but he was far from over the hill, and had become a much more consummate lover over the past three years. Giving a woman pleasure was at least as important to him now, as receiving it.

All his tackle and the cooler stowed in the bed of his Dodge Ram, he started for home. No late night out, because he had full day charters for the next two days, and he needed some rest. Visions of that black marlin trailing the split mullet filled his mind. A good three-hundred-pounds, for sure. Two or three hours of exciting, hard work on his eighty-pound tackle. That's what this was all about.

He loved the new life he'd created over the last two-plus years. He'd lost fifteen pounds and become leanly muscled, healthier than he'd ever been. Now, all he needed was the right woman to lavish his new person onto. Somewhere out there, he'd find true love.

~ 34 ~

The trill of dance music led Alex into the Cala de Mar Hotel's lounge just shy of six p.m. Chiquita still lingered behind the crowded bar, busily tending to a foursome of male guests, serving two pitchers of beer. Germans, from the sound of their clamor. He waved, and she replied with a smile and nod toward the end of the bar. Alex moved down there and settled on a stool.

Chiquita arrived a few minutes later, toting his usual, a Corona beer. "*Hola, mi corazóne*," said as she leaned over for a kiss. "I'm off a bit late today," reverting to English, as Alex's Spanish no longer needed practice. "Just swamped with a tour group of Huns," she chuckled and glanced down the bar. "I'll get Maria caught up with the rush." She reached over and caressed his cheek. "Fifteen minutes okay?"

"Sure. We got no schedule." He caught her hand and kissed its back. "Found a new Mariachi group over in Zihuantanejo, *Los Caballeros.* Heard they're pretty good."

"Sounds fun." She snatched a look at new arrivals, filling three tables, then back at Alex. "You had a full day charter today, you said."

"Yeah. Second day with the brothers from K.C. Didn't get them their marlin, but they both caught *gallo,* actually fly-casting this time. They were really hyped." His eyebrows arched. "Why'd ya ask?"

She grinned and patted his hand. "Just wanted to be sure my handsome stud wasn't going to be too tired for a proper party after we're done bar-hopping." She edged toward the growing clamor for service.

"Never too pooped for what you bring to my bed, you sexy imp." His tongue darted across his lips as he watched her lovely ass sway as she moved off.

"*Bueno*," said over her shoulder with a thrown kiss. "I'm itching for a visit from the big boy you bring to the party." She giggled as she joined Maria and began serving drinks.

Alex sucked in a breath, his heart beginning a small rumba at the vision of that buxom little hottie, straddled across his waist, squeezing his rigid cock as she drained him. He sighed. The sex was super, but that's all it was, for both of them. That was their deal. They'd discovered very little else in common, other than music and dancing. Their time together was purely animal gratification, something both craved, but he knew it would never develop into anything else.

He shook his head and sipped his beer. Both Chiquita and Dulce, his realtor turned lover, were in their relationships, if you could even call them that, for pleasure, and only that. Pleased he'd found two sweet and passionate women for that purpose, with no real commitments, he was also saddened that he hadn't found true love. To be fair, he hadn't looked for it that hard, either, having been burned twice while still in South Florida. They were hard lessons, but he believed he could now separate carnal need from the reality of actual love, if and when he found that. A woman who loved him for *him,* and not his money. Wealth no one in southwestern Mexico knew anything about.

Meanwhile, he eagerly anticipated the carnal adventure hot little Chiquita would provide that evening. It was his pre-thirty birthday party gift to himself.

Tires crunched on the gravel drive as he slipped his Dodge under the protective canopy next to his little *casa*. He swiveled to kiss Chiquita, leaning across the pickup's center console, her fingers successfully busy at his crotch. She'd teased up a massive hardon.

"C'mon, you vixen," disengaging her hand. "We can do this better inside."

"You bet." She snickered. "But we gotta pass up all your usual, very tantalizing foreplay, *mi amor*." A heated, tongue-dancing kiss devoured his mouth. "My pussy's so hot, I'll cum without that *tipo grande* inside me right away." She slipped out her door and grabbed his hand.

"Nothing wrong with that, *Cara*." Tight against him, they traded sloppy kisses, his hands busy with D breasts, bulging inside her T-shirt. "Knowing you, it will be only the first of many, and driving you wild is a real turn on for me."

"You never seem to need any extra incentive, *mi corazón*." She squeezed his erection, grabbed his arm, and headed for the house. "*Vámonos.*" They hustled through the front door and charged for the bedroom, she shedding her shirt and stepping from her from her flowered, full Spanish skirt en route.

He peeled off his polo and reached for his belt as she spun at the beds edge, and thrust down his jeans. Grasping his arms, she flopped onto the bed, pulled him after her, threw him onto his back, and wriggled to perch across his thighs, casting off her bra. Alex always marveled at the lack of sag of such a glorious set of tits. His fingers caressed them, tweaking their erect nipples as she ripped away his boxers and lowered those magnificent mounds of flesh to encompass his dick, slowly stroking back and forth.

"Oh, shit," he murmured, and reached up for a heated kiss. "You ready?" he panted.

"Past ready," her voice breathy as she raised to her knees and swallowed his pulsing cock into her greedy and very wet pussy. "Ahhh." A soft sigh. "Squeezed into its favorite garage," and she began to move.

Alex arched his neck, seeking her lips as his pelvis rose to meet her thrusts, and they developed a now familiar rhythm. He ached to bury his face between her magnificent boobs, but she was so much shorter, he could never reach. The tongue-dueling kisses were a strong second choice, however, and his hands went where his face could not.

After nearly two years sporadically together, this dance of love was more slow than frenetic as they savored exquisite pleasure, honed to a sensual art. Chiquita rose and lowered herself, gyrating gently as pussy muscles pulsed around his dick, and his fingers tweaked her engorged clit. Gasping for breath, they came, he first and her almost immediately after, the air filled with groans and squeals.

She sank her sweat-slickened body against him, his still spasming cock trapped inside the warm, wet glove of her pussy, as she squeezed that shrinking member dry.

"God, I love fucking you, *Chico*." Her neck arched back, tongue swiping moist lips, she grinned. "We don't do this often enough, *cara mia*." She slid off to one side and snuggled against his damp body, her fingers caressing his now flaccid cock. "This *tipo grande* has ruined any other *hombres* for me." A chuckle. "I want it all to myself."

Alex sighed. "But, that's not our deal, *chica*. I made that plain—"

"I know, I know. No commitments." She exhaled. "Just enjoy the sex—"

"Right, because, while I love doing this with you, outside of the bedroom, we have very little in common."

"But I could learn—"

Alex stilled her with a kiss. "No, I've been down that road … twice, actually. It won't do for a lasting relationship." Fingers stroked her cheek, and he pecked the tip of her nose. "If this doesn't work for you anymore, we'll—"

"Shh," rolling atop of him. "I get it," as she planted a passionate kiss on his lips. "We make glorious love, *mi amor,* and that's perfect for me. Let's not let things like relationships get in the way." Kisses peppered his neck and chest as she inched slowly lower, and the open, slick lips of her pussy tented his once again growing hardon. Back and forth, they stroked his rigid cock as he ravished her face with passionate lips and tongue, his hands busy with again erect nipples.

And then he was inside. Tight against her, they continued to kiss as she squeezed his iron-hard dick with repeated pulses. An arched hip drove him deeper inside that slippery grip as he thrust against her, upper bodies slightly separated as she planted her hands on his chest. Still, she did not meet his thrusts, but continued to pulse her vagina, squeezing and relaxing, only to squeeze again. It drove him crazy.

Head thrown back, eyes closed, she began to rock, a soft moan growing to a breathy, muted howl. Slamming together now, he gripped her arms and came in a rush, as she continued thrusting, the grip on his dick tight but quivering as she followed his orgasm with hers, announced with a shuddering snarl. One final squeeze to suck him dry, and she collapsed on his chest, face in the crook of his neck, kissing and licking up sweat.

"I love the taste of after-sex on you, *Papi.*"

Alex's arms circled her back, hands patrolling to her firm butt for a gentle massage. "I love everything about our sex together, *Chica.*" Kisses peppered her ears and eyes, and they slept, bodies intertwined.

Alex woke at six and gently disentangled himself from the woman. He'd let her sleep, but he had a charter that morning and needed to prepare. Thirty minutes later, he quietly exited his house, Chiquita still asleep. A pot of hot coffee and grilled sausages awaited her when she woke. She would eat and clean up, but would be gone when he returned. Next week, he'd celebrate his thirtieth birthday, and he decided to invite both Chiquita and Dulce. He chuckled, wondering how the two women would get on, and if that might turn into a threesome. Never done that before. The thought excited him.

~ 35 ~

Emma plucked a second dress off the size-four rack and held it up beside her first selection. Golden, knee-length, with halter straps. The other, pink with some light, unrecognizable pattern, sported tiny, puffy sleeves and a flared knee-length skirt. She shrugged. Several more needed for a two-week stay at a warm, Mexican coastal resort, so both went into her cart, and with the Fall season in full swing, all summer goods were on sale. Ten-minutes later, three more joined them in her cart. The wardrobe she'd fled South Florida with was limited, and she'd spent much of the past two years in sweat suits, two pair of shorts, and cotton T's. She'd only bought what she needed to be comfortable at the shelter, with never a reason to dress up.

Now that had changed. She continued strolling the aisles of Nancy's Fashions, in downtown Highland Park, seeking new shorts, blouses, and two bathing suits. She found the latter on another sales rack, a modest red bikini, and a sleek, black one-piece.

Thirty-minutes later she headed for checkout, then paused and stroked her chin. She'd done some research, and late November and December were prime fishing months off the southwest coast of Mexico. Char had promised Larry would take her sailfishing at least twice, so she wanted two fishing outfits: light-weight slacks, long-sleeve shirts, and a large brim hat. Fall duds, so no big sale discounts, but she didn't care. Emma had plenty of cash, and her Marsha Alcott VISA card, which she'd not yet used. Excited about the trip, she headed for those aisles and found what she needed.

The shopping list now completed, she again went to checkout and paid cash. With three large, plastic bags in hand, she exited the store and searched for the shelter's Dodge minivan. There, parked a half-block up the street, with Bobby feeding coins into the meter. *Good. Means I've got time to stay for lunch for a change.* As she strolled up the street, he turned and spied her approach, stepping to relieve her of her packages.

"Finished shopping?" said as he opened the rear hatch and deposited her goods.

"Yes, for clothing, but if you're not in a hurry, I'd like to stay for lunch, and I need to visit a pharmacy for sunscreen and stuff." She snickered. "And maybe some Dramamine."

"Planning on doing some fishing while in Mexico, huh?" A glance at his watch. "Two p.m. sound good? Gives you an hour-and-a-half to eat and shop."

"Perfect, if that works for you."

"Yeah. I got some errands in Wilmette I was going to run later, but I'll do 'em now instead." He opened the driver door. "Just be careful, Emma. There's a bunch of tourists in town for the Ravinia Fall Concert Festival, so avoid showing up on their social media."

"I will." She patted his shoulder. "Thanks for the heads-up. I'll eat at Carlo's, and find a table in back, away from any windows."

"Okay. See you at two, then." He clambered inside. "Library?"

"Yep. I'll be on the bench, waiting." She waved as he drove off, then started up the street for Walgreens, just a half-block from the cozy Italian restaurant she liked when visiting the town. She'd pick up what she needed at the drugstore for her coming adventure, and then have a leisurely lunch before meeting Bobby for their return to her home for the past two years.

"Over two years!" she muttered and shook her head. *Will I ever have a normal life again?* A two-week vacation with her sister in Mexico would be the next best thing.

~~~

Emma lounged in a rear, corner booth at Carlo's Trattoria, far from any windows. Precautions against accidently being noticed or photographed became ingrained when hiding from a stalker, but now she was preparing to go out in public. After all this time, was Brad even still searching for her? She suspected he wasn't one to quit on an obsession, and somehow, Emma had become exactly that. His obsession.

She forked up the last bite of her eggplant lasagna, savoring the flavor, leaned back on the bench seat, and washed it down with a sip of chianti. She sighed and massaged pooling green eyes, then came erect. *That bastard's not going to turn me into a mole, burrowing underground.*

She glanced at the small plastic bag, resting on the bench beside her, filled with powdered blush, lipsticks, eye shadow and liners, and a lash brush ... all things abandoned at her apartment in Hallandale. Years had passed since she had any reason to make herself attractive again, but she planned on "dolling up" in Mexico, and regain some self-esteem. There was also a tube of 30 SPF sunscreen, expecting a welcome, sunny relief from the approaching Chicago-area winter.

She laid cash atop the food bill, with a 20% tip, picked up her bag, and slid from the booth. Bobby was due in fifteen minutes, and she wanted to search for a new novel or two at the library. With an Android tablet she'd acquired at Walmart, she could download books. The library had many e-books available to borrow, and there'd be no personal Internet presence from those transactions.

Strolling toward the library, Emma mused over her coming trip. Char had reserved a two-bedroom suite at Cala De Mar, a ritzy, all-suite resort in Zihuantanejo, perched on a mountains edge, above the gorgeous La Ropa Beach. A brochure she'd downloaded from the shelter's computer resided in her shoulder tote. Despite committing it largely to memory, she loved gazing at the photos and imaging the coming trip. Swimming the infinity pool or at the white, sandy beach, boating and fishing the rippled waters of the azure sea, elegant dining and dancing in the posh dinner lounge. Maybe she'd meet a guy. Even a brief tryst seemed alluring, and the resort would be filled by tourists.

She could hardly wait, and Brad be damned.

~ 36 ~

Alex rolled over on his bed, sighed, and stretched, a wry grin creasing his lips. Thirty-years-old, and an unexpected treat while celebrating that event with his two favorite women, Chiquita and Dulce. The unexpected part was their enthusiasm for a threesome. After dancing and drinking at two cantinas, toasting his "advanced age," they eagerly returned to his little *casa*, where he'd spent several hours pleasuring both women … and of course, himself. Interesting that, after wearing him down, the women found, to their clear surprise, passion for each other, each having multiple, noisy orgasms. He fell asleep about one a.m. with the girls still at it, happy that they'd let him alone, as he had a charter that morning, and needed some rest. They'd eventually left, it seemed. Maybe Chiquita and Dulce had found new lovers in each other, and that suited him fine. He'd become conflicted over enjoying the sex … friends with benefits … with no prospect of finding one to actually love. Not that he'd pass up a hot romp when it presented itself, but it was time for a change. Chiquita, in particular, seem to want more, and that was never a question for him with her, or Dulce, for that matter.

Alex rose, dressed, and made breakfast. Time to prepare for a full day charter. The clients were especially interested in *gallo*, and it was nearing the end of their season. He'd seen several large fish, cruising the beach to the north, so it was a promising day, and these guys weren't going to complicate it with fly-fishing, which was always a challenge for roosterfish.

Alex pocketed seven Benjamins, a very nice tip, and watched two very happy men stroll down the dock, chattering and gesturing in animated replays of an exciting day. A slow morning for *gallo* was mitigated by lots of Spanish mackerel and small bonito, taken on spinning rods, trolling half-ounce feathered jigs. Just after finishing box lunches, he spotted roiling water and a shower of leaping pilchers, and he raced to get in front of the action. A group of roosterfish were hammering a pod of baitfish, their unique, cockscomb-like dorsal fins that gave them their name, slicing the water. Using spinning rods and tossing silvery lead jigs, they had a double hookup of two large roosters. Both fish took off up the coast, greyhounding several times with flashy leaps, and Alex was in hot pursuit.

Luckily, the fish stayed somewhat together, but the anglers had to work to keep lines from tangling, often one ducking under the other's rod to clear their line. Nearly a half-hour passed before Alex lifted the first *gallo* with his BogaGrip scale locked on its lower jaw. It was a challenge to photo the grinning guy and measure his thirty-three-pound trophy while still managing his boat as the other angler continued to battle his larger fish. The data would go to the taxidermist for a fiberglass reproduction, and the big fish was released to fight again another day. Trophies were seldom kept for skin-mounts any more, opting for better conservation. Although roosterfish, a member of the jack family, had been caught over a hundred pounds, fish exceeding twenty pounds were a rarity along Mexico's beaches, and they were about to land two well into the thirties.

Ten minutes later, Alex snatched the lower jaw of the second fish with his scale, this one thirty-six-pounds, and the exhausted angler could barely lift it for a photo. Considerable whoops, smiles, and back-slapping was culminated with cold beers, as all three relaxed for a while in the shade of his boat's convertible top. Their quest for roosterfish filled beyond both men's dreams, they opted for a run offshore in search of dorado or sailfish. That action was slow, with only one modest cow dolphin taken, and everyone was pooped, so the day ended an hour early.

Alex cleaned up his boat, stowed his tackle, and took his clients information home to e-mail to a Florida taxidermist who he'd recommended. The man did a great job on *gallo,* and Alex earned a ten per cent commission on the fees. In about six months the two guys from Kentucky would get the replica mounts of their trophies, and proof of their successes. He took a short nap, grilled dorado fillets for dinner, cleaned and oiled his reels, and decided to call it a night. Too tired to mingle and dance at Cala de Mar Resort, which was sold out for the next month. With nothing scheduled, he'd go tomorrow evening, to their welcome cocktail party for the week's new arrivals. Despite being well integrated into the local community, Alex enjoyed hobnobbing with some Yankees and the many Europeans who visited Mexico in the winter. And dancing with the many single women, some of whom were often interested in a tumble with a sexy, local guy. Tan, wiry, bearded, with shoulder-length blonde hair, Alex filled that bill.

Alex checked his image in the mirror as he finished brushing out his wavy, golden hair. A lazy day had been spent, sleeping late for a change, with no charter scheduled for two days, and then he'd puttered around his house, doing odd jobs. He'd rehung his front door screen, scrubbed down a neglected bathroom tile floor and shower stall, and did a load of laundry. E-mail checked, he found an acknowledgement from the Florida taxidermist for receipt of the two roosterfish mount info, with copies of invoices sent to the two anglers requesting deposits before processing their orders.

He'd dozed off in the afternoon while reading Phillip Wylie stories about Crunch and Dez, a Florida charter boat crew, just like him. Awake now, and clad in pressed khaki chinos and a short-sleeve safari shirt, he was ready to visit the Cala de Mar lounge for the welcome cocktail party for newly arriving guests. As usual, local men attended, many lured by the offer of first drink free. They were encouraged to mingle and dance with the single women, of which there were usually many. Chiquita would be at the bar, serving, and probably casting dirty looks at him if he seemed involved with a female guest. He shrugged, not really caring. He was looking for something more serious now, and besides, the girl had a new playmate in Dulce. That should take both of them off his hands.

Satisfied with his reflection, he pocketed his truck keys, wallet, and as an afterthought, a packet of condoms. Just in case. A quick splash of musk cologne, and he was out the door, ready for, hopefully, a fun evening. Maybe there'd be some Americans there. The visitors were often heavily European that time of year.

~ 37 ~

Bells tinkled as Emma shoved through the glass entry door of Highland Park Travel Agency. Another woman was perched in the waiting area, as three agents, all busy with desktop computers, had clients seated at their desks. Emma settled in a comfortable armchair, withdrew her Android from her shoulder bag, and picked up where she'd left off on the suspense novel, *Death's Angel,* she'd borrowed from the library.

"May I help you?"

Emma glanced up at a fortyish woman smiling at her. Engrossed an action scene in the book, twenty minutes had flittered by.

"Oh, yes. I'd like to buy an airline ticket."

"My pleasure to help you. My name is Marion." She gestured toward an empty desk. "Have a seat, and tell me what you need."

They walked together to her niche, and Emma settled on a chair across the desk. "I need a round-trip airline ticket to Zihuantanejo, Mexico, departing November 28, with a return two-weeks later."

"Hmm. That's less than two weeks away." She got busy at her keyboard. "Okay. It's after the Thanksgiving rush, and before the Winter season really heats up, so we may find something." She studied her screen. "The airport is called Ixtapa/Zihuantanejo. Ixtapa is an adjoining city." She peered over her half-frame specs. "Just one seat? And will you need a hotel?"

"Just me, and I'm meeting family who've reserved a suite at

Cala de Mar Resort."

"Lovely place, with a beautiful view of the ocean and La Ropa Beach." Busy again at the keyboard, her brow wrinkled.

Emma fidgeted in her seat. "Is there a problem?"

"The only seats available are on AeroMexico that departs O'Hare just after midnight on the 29th and arrives about nine that morning, with one change in Mexico City. However, that's a Premier Class seat, but because of the early time, it's not as expensive as the usual mid-day flight." She made several clicks on the keypad. "The only return available is on the thirteenth. Better times, though, again with one change in Mexico City." She rotated the monitor for Emma to view. "Nine-hundred-eighty-two dollars, after taxes and fees."

"Okay, book it." She opened her wallet. "I suppose we'll be able to work out the extra night at the resort." She paused, glancing at her billfold. "I presume you'll take cash?"

Marion's eyebrows arched, and she smiled. "Of course. You *will* need a passport and probably a credit card for the flight, however."

"Oh, I have that and a VISA card, but I just don't want to max it out before the trip." She withdrew ten, hundred-dollar-bills from her wallet, and laid them on the desk.

"No problem, then." Marion was busy again at the keyboard. "There. Confirmed and paid for by the agency. I'll print an itinerary, with your confirmation code, and I've arranged aisle seats on all flights, if that's okay."

Emma nodded. "Fine with me. Easier access to the bathrooms."

Marion nodded, rose, and retrieved two sheets from the printer. "You'll have nearly two hours for the connections, which gives you a cushion, should your flight be delayed." She handed Emma the papers.

Quickly perused, she nodded. "Looks perfect." The folded itinerary went into her shoulder bag. "Do you have a card?"

Marion plucked one from her desktop. "Feel free to call if you need anything else." She smiled. "We can arrange car rentals, tours, anything you may need."

"Thanks, but I'm leaving all that in my capable sister's hands." Emma chuckled. "Knowing her, she'll have every minute planned." She turned to leave. "Thanks again."

Back on the walk, Emma glanced at her watch, then strolled toward Walmart. Bobby wouldn't be back for her for another hour, so she'd do some last-minute browsing.

Probably won't return to town again before the trip, so I'd better be sure I have all I need. A new pair of Polaroid sunglasses were on her list, and a pair of beach flip-flops. Maybe a light-weight coverup for over swimsuits at the pool and beach. She'd rushed away from South Florida so quickly, she had nothing but basics for her stay at the shelter.

Emma's mind wandered as she moved through the massive store's aisles. Tiny tingles skipped down her spine as she pictured seeing her sister again. Over two years was too damned long. And visions of being out-and-about, swimming at the pool or on the beach, eating at fine restaurants, maybe even dancing with a guy in the lounge. She'd pulled up all there was about Zihuantanejo from the library's computer, and it looked fabulous.

She'd also digested everything she could find about the fishing. November/December was prime time for sailfish. That last time she'd gone was in her mid-teens, with Papa, who loved the offshore adventures, trolling for billfish off Miami. She'd caught her first at twelve—a forty-two-pound sail—and it took a half-hour to land after nine gorgeous leaps and three blistering runs. She'd never been more excited.

A grin lit her face. Larry had promised at least two fishing trips. They'd be nostalgic reminders of her Pop, who'd passed four years ago from a sudden heart attack, and the fun they'd shared. Char was never interested, and would probably stay ashore in Mexico too.

She sighed, and headed for checkout, hoping the trip would be all she had fantasized. Maybe she'd even meet a guy for a clandestine tryst. She shrugged.

Then what, with her still in hiding? Nothing can ever happen again unless she can shed Brad, and that was proving no easy task. Jaw clamped, lips pressed into a narrow slit, she growled softly.

Bastard!

~ 38 ~

Alex arrived at Cala de Mar's lounge just after six, and it was already teeming with guests and several local men. Chiquita, behind the bar, acknowledged him with a nod and a weak smile. Dulce was perched on a stool in front of her, sipping a martini, and they appeared to be in happy banter. So, that problem was solved with no apparent recriminations. An empty stool awaited him at the end of the bar, and Raul, another barista that night, served him his usual Corona. Alex swiveled on his seat, elbows resting on the bar-top, and surveyed the room. The band, as always during these affairs, was playing mostly dance music to encourage mingling.

The room was filled with resort guests, plus several local single men … mostly white-collar types … and a few local couples. This was a popular weekend stop for people looking for upscale entertainment. He spied a table hosting four, mid-twenties women, all moderately attractive, and the tallest was openly appraising him. He took a swig of his beer, and bottle in hand, slipped off his stool and sauntered over.

"*Hola, chicas. De dónde son?*"

"*Somos alemanes.*" The tallest nodded at him. "*¿Hablas alemán o inglés?*"

He nodded. "I'm American, actually. So, you're German?"

"Ja, from Berlin." The tall brunette gestured toward a seat. "I am Inga. And you are?"

"Alex." He offered a hand. "But rather than sit, would you like to dance?" He glanced at the string trio whose repertoire was mostly older, classic American love songs. "They play great dance music."

"Ja. I'd love to." She rose, a slim, taut body, and cobalt-blue eyes. Her hand in his, they moved to the open dance floor. Alex spun her into his arms, eliciting a chuckle, and they began to move to the music. Inga nestled close, both arms locked around his neck, and began to lead … not something he liked. Her attempt at sensuality was too mechanical, and failed. Her bony figure and aggressive actions turned him off, so after one song they returned to her table. Alex filled the resorts request of local men and danced at least once with each of the other three women, and then he returned to the bar.

He was talking to Raul, replaying the details of his last charter when he sensed … smelled, actually … a presence behind him. Black Orchid. Light pressure of fingers on his shoulder turned him, and he found himself swamped by a pair of onyx eyes under arched, black eyebrows. Blinking, the rest of the exotically stunning creature came into focus … a heart-shaped face, framed by a cascade of shoulder-length, inky hair, sensuous bow-shaped lips, and delicately arched cheeks. The most heart-stopping beauty he'd ever seen.

"*¿Qué tal un baile conmigo, ahora, chico?*" A velvet voice, soft and sensual.

Alex swallowed hard, then chuckled. "American?"

She nodded. "Wonderful." The smile was dazzling. "You speak English." Fingers brushed his bearded cheek. "So? Dance with me?"

"My pleasure, beautiful lady." Off his stool, he took her soft, warm hand, his heart dancing against his ribs. "I'm Alex." They sauntered between tables, headed for the dance floor. "And you are?"

"Mia." She slithered into his grasp, and they began to sway to the music. "Mia Saunders, from L.A. And you sound like an

175

American too." Nearly his height in her heels, her head nestled into the crook of his neck, warm breath teasing his ear.

"Yep," struggling to keep his voice in control. "An ex-pat, living and working here for several years." Her fragrance filled his head.

The swell of her luscious, slim figure was warm in his arms. Clad in black silk slacks and a sleeveless, half-buttoned blouse that did little to hide the swell of firm breasts. A full-body press tantalized him, her pelvis pressed against his.

"L.A., huh?" His head cocked back, their eyes met. "In the movies, are you?"

She chuckled. "No. Why did you think that?" Head back on his shoulder, her breath tickled his neck.

"'Cause you're the most gorgeous women I've ever met, so I figured … L.A., films."

"Really? How sweet." Another soft chuckle. "So, you live here now?" Her tongue licked his ear. "Where are you from in the States, Alex, and what kind of work do you do here?"

"From no place in particular," avoiding any mention of South Florida, "and I'm a charter boat captain." He arched back to better see her face. "You know, fishing. It's really great here, both off-shore for billfish and dorado, and inshore for roosterfish and other small gamefish."

"Oh? Kent and I thought we should try that."

"Kent?"

"My husband." Pressed tighter against him. "I'll introduce you, once we've had a few dances." She cocked her head and smiled. "I'm so happy we met, Alex, and Kent will be too, believe me." Another chuckle was followed by his ear disappearing inside her lips.

"Your husband?" An attempt to open some space between them failed. "He likes to fish?" His voice cracked, at a loss for anything else to say, as tiny mouse feet skittered down his spine.

"Oh, yes." Her pussy wiggled against his crotch, and despite his efforts to quell it, a hard-on swelled. "And he especially loves me finding someone with what I seem to have awakened there." Pressing tighter, she sighed. "And what a lovely treat I've discovered, you sexy man." The song ended but she remained glued to his body.

"Wait a minute." He was panting, becoming more aroused. "You mean he *wants* you to have sex with other men?" No sense in beating around the proverbial bush.

Mia cupped his face between her hands, her dark eyes glittering with passion. "Oh, does he ever." A soft snicker. "Kent's a good lover, but I need more than he can provide." Alex's face was drawn in for a heated, tongue-fencing kiss that lasted well beyond the beginning of the next tune. "A lot more," she panted, "and I'm horny as hell, and hot for what you've got in those pants, Alex. I've never found anything so big." His hand snatched in hers, she dragged him across the room to a table, his left hand jammed in a pocket to hide what bulged there. A handsome, tanned guy rose as they approached, smiled, and held out a hand.

"Kent, this is Alex." She nudged Alex forward and they shook hands. "He's American, working here as a charter boat captain," a lascivious grin creased her lovely lips, "and he's got a beautiful present I think he'll gladly give me, if you approve." She stood, hands on hips, and watched the two men.

Kent, a stereotypical Californian ... Alex's height, blonde, athletic, and tanned ... grinned. "Sure, and thank God, babe. If you want him, and he's willing, I'm happy." He breathed a sigh. "You've worn me out." He turned to Alex. "Don't be shy about this ... you know, a married woman." He wrapped an arm around Mia's shoulder. "She's a sexual animal, especially on vacation, so we have an understanding. When I need help, she finds someone like you to fill her needs." He chuckled. "Believe me, it's a ride you don't want to pass up." His eyebrows arched. "Are you in?"

Alex's gaze swept back and forth between them. "You're serious? You want me to make love to your wife?"

"As much as you can, all night long. You'll tire before she does."

"And where are you, while this happens?"

"I like to watch." He caught Mia's chin for a kiss. "I love this woman, and I want her to be happy. We're regular swingers, back in L.A. Made some very good friends that way."

Mia stepped toward Alex, hands outstretched.

"I don't know. I've never—" Any doubts dissolved, watching her, Aphrodite incarnate.

"C'mon, baby." She drew him into her arms, her body moving against his. "I really want that big boy of yours," a hand slipping between them found his crotch, "in my mouth ... and my pussy. Believe me, I'll make it *very* happy." Their tongues met again through seeking lips, and her skilled fingers ignited a re-stiffening cock. "Our room, now, Alex? How can you say no to this?"

He gasped for breath and shook his head. "No matter how hard I try, Mia, I can't think of a reason. You're a gorgeous, sexy siren, and frankly, at this moment, I wanna fuck your brains out."

"Then, let's go." She broke free, grabbed his hand, and headed for the elevators, Kent leading the way.

Hope the hell this isn't some kind of con. Another woman for what will probably be great sex. He sighed. *One of these days, maybe I'll find one for true love ... but hot sex is pretty great too. She's so fucking beautiful.*

He snickered silently. If this worked out, maybe they'd book him for a fishing trip too.

~ 39~

They paused in the hall, Mia swarming all over him, hands and mouth busy driving him crazy, while Kent fumbled with the key card. The door finally open, Mia dragged Alex into the suite's living room and shoved him sprawling onto his back on a large sofa. Instantly, she mounted him, perched across his groin, and stripped away his shirt. Her hips gyrated, her pussy pressing on an engorged cock through soaked, silk slacks, as she opened her blouse. No bra. He'd never seen such perfect, natural-looking tits, descending to entrap his face. He snared an erect nipple between his lips, sucking and twirling his tongue as his fingers teased and caressed firm breasts, drawing soft, panted whimpers from her.

"Damn, that's hot," she squealed and slid down, attacking his mouth with a rabid, tongue-thrusting kiss. Her blouse cast aside, she arched into the downward-dog position, and shimmied out of her slacks and a damp, bikini thong. A moment later, his chinos were puddled at his ankles, and she sprawled, full-length over his body, soaking cunt lips tenting his raging hard-on. Sloppy kissing and teasing fingers began in earnest.

Alex's hands patrolled the woman's amazing body … taut, round ass, slender hips, tiny waist, broad shoulders, and absolutely stunning breasts. Trudy's body had been amazing, but Mia's put it to shame. And the thick, open lips of that soaked pussy were driving him crazy.

"You ready to fuck, babe?" he panted, her face trapped between his hands, eyes locked.

"Oh, yeah! Am I ever. I wanted to taste that big boy first, but

I'm so fucking horny—"

"Don't worry, gorgeous. I've got plenty for you after—" He grunted a sigh as she arched her hips and drew him slowly inside her wet, tight, velvet glove.

"Oh, God, oh, God," she whimpered. "I've never … Oh, so *good!*" The walls of her vagina pulsed as she began to rock. "Oh, damn. I'm gonna cum already. You're … so … big," and she shuddered with a protracted orgasm and a panted squeal.

Alex fought to hold off and continued thrusting his hips, his cock iron-hard, amazed at her Kegel controlled muscles. She leaned in for a heated kiss, his hands busy with her tits, as they continued to dance the rumba of love.

"Oh, yeah, Alex. Yeah! Keep it coming, you fucking monster." Another lip-sucking kiss. "Keep it … oh, God, I'm cumming again." She leaned back, a wail echoing in the room, and her spasming pussy was more than he could resist, orgasming in a balls-draining gush. One more heave, and Mia collapsed against him, their sweat-slickened bodies sliding together.

"My God, you gorgeous hunk. That was wonderful." Soft kisses now, on his neck and ear. Her head turned, she spied her husband, perched on an armchair, pants down, masturbating.

"Oh, Kent, baby." She pushed onto her elbows. "Wasn't this *hot?*"

"The best ever, hon." A pink tongue darted across his lips. "Really turned me on."

An eyebrow arched, she slipped off Alex and leaned down for a kiss. "Rest up, baby. I'll be back soon for more fun." Pivoting, she stalked across the room, a glorious, sleek feline, seeking new prey. "Don't waste that on your hand, Kent," her voice husky. She dropped to her knees. "Let me." And stroked and licked his rigid cock, Kent's hands in her hair as his hip rose to meet her lips.

"God, you do that so well, Mia." Head back, eyes closed, he panted for breath.

"Yeah, but I do this better, babe." On her feet, she settled on his lap, and her eager pussy swallowed his dick. "Ahh, nice, Hubby." She began to rock, his face buried in her boobs, licking and sucking eraser-size nipples. They rocked together on the chair, the air filled with moans and gasps.

Kent grunted. "I can't hold it. You're so tight, and I love the way ... Oh, shit, I'm coming."

"Keep going, Kent. I'm ... gonna .... cum, too." They lurched together, pawing, kissing, as she squealed, "Yes-s-s. Oh, yes," and then sunk against him, wrapped in each other's arms. A soft sigh, and "You still got it, lover." She glanced over her shoulder and spied Alex, still on the sofa, watching. "Now that I've taken care of you, hon, I'd like to give our new friend, Alex, another taste." She caressed his face. "Okay with you?"

"Oh, yeah, sweetheart." He chuckled. "Take as much as he can give. I think I'm done for the day."

"Good, 'cause I want more of that big boy. Can't wait to see if I can swallow it, and I know my pussy already adores it." She rose, turned toward Alex, fists on her hips, back arched. "You ready for more of this, handsome?"

"You damned well know I am, you gorgeous, fucking succubus." Off the couch, he rose and took her hand. "Can we go to the bed, though." Her flaming body pulled close, the kiss intense, her velvet skin set ripples of tingles across his body. "I have so many things I want to do to this piece of God's perfection," he whispered in her ear.

"Oh, shit!" A pink tongue flicked his ear. "You talk like that, and I'm ready to cum again." Locked together, they shuffled into the bedroom, her fingers teasing his growing erection. "I want this beauty in me, all night long, Alex. Fucking with anybody else will never be quite the same again." She snickered softly. "But Kent'll try, all the same." On the bed, she slithered atop of him for a prolonged kiss. "Come home with me to L.A., Alex. Be my toy. California's a lovely place, and we've got a great villa in Santa Monica."

"Never gonna happen, Mia." He brushed strands of silky, midnight hair from her face. "This is just a vacation interlude for you. Let's not complicate it."

"I know. Just joking, wishful thinking." She ventured down his body, kissing and licking. "We're here for a week, so let's make the most of it." Ruby red nails teased his cock and balls, and her talented tongue licked and sucked his rigid dick. Finally, she slid up and drew him inside, emitted a soft gasp, and leaned forward to offer her glorious tits to his mouth and fingers as they surged together in growing heat, their second venture into Nirvana.

As promised, the insatiable Mia aroused him two additional times, she having many orgasms en route. Finally, unable to raise another hard-on, Alex pleasured her twice more with his mouth and hands before finally slipping away as she slept, escaping to his house at five a.m. He had a charter later that day, luckily in the afternoon, so he'd have some time to recover.

And Kent booked him for a full day trip the next day, with inuendo of another evening together afterward. Alex had mixed feelings about that. Mia was definitely the most gorgeous and perfect lover in every measure, but how much could he endure?

He'd see how it went, but at some point, there'd have to be a cutoff. No way he could survive six more days of her insatiable passion. He chuffed. How often does a guy worry about getting *too* much sex? *I guess Kent knows the answer to that.* Meanwhile, he had to catch some Z's and a charter to prepare for.

As he wound down, approaching sleep, he visualized incredible Mia, riding his cock, those gorgeous tits in his face. A fantastic interlude, but he almost felt sorry for Kent, needing to satisfy her full time. No wonder he needed help. He chuckled as he slipped toward sleep, amazed that after all they enjoyed together, the vision of her was getting him hard again.

No one ever aroused him like that, not even Trudy at her best, but it wasn't love. Somewhere, there must be a woman … and he drifted off into sleep.

~ 40 ~

Emma perched on the bed next to an open suitcase and studied her list: five summer frocks, four sets of mix-and-match shorts and blouses, and two pair of slacks and long-sleeve shirts for fishing. Of course, bathing suits, and pool and beach wear, and four cocktail dresses for the evenings, plus two sexy evening gowns for what she'd learned was a weekly upscale bash. She sighed, wishing she'd bought one or two more fancy things for parties, but everything was new. Char had collected all her outfits from the Hallandale condo but was leery of shipping them, in case that led Brad to her.

"Oh, well," muttered to herself, "this'll have to do." The case closed, Emma turned to her small backpack and rechecked her passport and boarding passes were in the side pocket. Inside, were her wallet, the new Android tablet loaded with five romance novels, her eye-mask, and other personal items she might need inflight, including a small plastic box with hardboiled eggs and a peanut-butter sandwich Madge had prepared for her.

Zipped shut, the pack slung over a shoulder, she floored her suitcase and headed down to the foyer where Bobby was waiting. Time to get rolling, and it was at least an hour trek to O'Hare, despite probable light evening traffic. She'd been advised to arrive two hours early to account for long security delays for an international flight, and she preferred a wait at the airport rather than add tension from running late. She swore not to let nervousness from venturing into the open dampen her excitement at getting away … and seeing her sister, after more than two years.

Bumping her case down the stairs, she spied Bobby talking with Madge by her desk. He turned and started toward her, reaching for her luggage handle. "Ready to go?"

Emma nodded and touched his arm as he took control of her bag. "You sure you're okay taking me?" following him toward the exit. "It's a long drive."

"No problem, kiddo." He held the door open for her. "Not gonna risk my favorite gal to some shadowy Uber guy." The rear hatch of the Caravan opened at a click from his key fob. "Too many cases of those guys trying to take advantage of a pretty young woman, especially late at night." Her suitcase loaded inside, he relieved her of her backpack to join it. "Traffic'll be light, this time of night."

"Thanks." Emma patted his cheek. "I admit I *do* feel safer this way." And she clambered onto the passenger seat.

"Eager to go, aren't you?" Settled now on the driver seat, he started the engine.

"Am I ever," she chuckled. "No offense, Bobby, but I can't wait to get away from here, even if only for two weeks."

"No offense taken, Emma." On the driveway now, headed for Clavey Road. "Despite working here for the past six years and seeing what you girls go through, I still can't imagine the stress of hiding from the world with never a time out."

"Yeah." She sighed. "Your shelter is probably a lot better than what most women like me are privy to, but it's not life. At least, not the life we had before some monster made living that impossible." Settled back, she closed her eyes. "Can't wait to see my sister," she mumbled, "and have a real vacation." Another sigh. "I just need a taste of reality." She dozed, Char's face shining in her mind.

Emma started awake as Bobby's hand tapped her shoulder.

"We're here, Emma, right on time."

"Huh?" She sat up and knuckled her eyes. "Wow, I dozed off," glancing out the window as the van slid to a stop under the AeroMexico sign. "Thanks, Bobby." She squeezed his arm. "I'm so excited." Seatbelt unbuckled, she stepped from the van into chilly evening air, as the rear hatch rose.

Bobby joined her in back and extracted her suitcase and carry-on. "Got everything, Em?"

"Yeah," shrugging on her small backpack. "Passport, ID's, ticket, all here," tapping the side pocket of her pack. "Gotta admit, I'm kinda nervous too, but I'm sure this is safe." She took control of her wheeled case. "Never did anything on line, so I can't imagine that bastard can trace me, and even if he could, he'd never chase me all the way to southern Mexico." She leaned up and kissed Bobby's cheek. "Anyway, I'm going, and I'm not going to let worry about Brad ruin my vacation." She grinned. "I'm gonna see Char, and we're gonna have a ball in the sun." She winked at him. "Jealous?"

"Trading sunshine for the big snow storm forecasted to hit tomorrow." He chuckled. "Now why would I be jealous about that?" He closed the rear hatch. "Anyhow, have a great time kid, stay safe, and we'll see you back here in a bit over two weeks. Text me your arrival, and I'll pick you up." He waved and watched as she strode for the glass doors to Departure. Satisfied she was safely inside, he climbed into the Dodge and drove off.

Ninety minutes later, Emma was settled in her aisle seat aboard AeroMexico's Boeing jet, buckled in and awaiting departure. Nestled against a neck pillow retrieved from her backpack, her eyes closed in an effort to relax. Too hyped by her first venture into the open in more than two years, it wasn't easy, but she needed to sleep. She didn't want to be logy when she finally saw Char, and waste her first day of freedom. Two weeks would pass quickly, and the specter of re-confinement in the relative luxury of the shelter didn't sit well. *Can I ever be rid of that monster and find a guy I can love?*

Relaxation seeped in as the plane pushed back from the gate. Somehow, the drone of the automated safety announcements eased tension, and she drifted off, images of her sister and the sparkling Pacific dancing in her head.

Two weeks of freedom, and she wasn't going to waste it, Brad be damned.

~ 41 ~

Alex slid into the driver seat of his Dodge pickup, slumped back, and groaned. Five a.m. and finally able to extricate himself from Mia's passionate grasp, he'd watched the insatiable witch awaken Kent as Alex slipped away. The poor bastard. Alex chuckled as he fired up the engine. No guy with normal hormones would think to feel sorry for a man wed to such a gorgeous, sensual creature, fiery sex again and again without end … until he actually experienced it. He was drained.

As he headed out of the resort's lot, he sighed, thankful for a charter-free day. A chance to sleep late and recoup. He chuckled again, replaying Mia's and Kents's pleas for him to move to L.A. Especially Kent, who was desperate for a regular relief pitcher. The poor guy was stuck in a classic Catch-22, because Mia was really a sweet, loving, and interesting babe, and no starlet was more gorgeous. Her nymphomania, however, muddied the pool, and because Kent loved her and wanted to stay married, he was constantly on the prowl for help in bed. Alex feared for them, because somewhere along that road they were likely to encounter the *wrong* sort of guy … and that may prove dangerous.

Not my problem, and they did go for two full-day charters, which was a nice boost for the preseason. Business usually began picking up in early December, still a week or two away.

Arriving home, he parked under his open car canopy, went inside, stripped to his boxers, and collapsed on the bed. Soft snores echoed through the room almost instantly, and images filled his dreams of a gorgeous, raven-hair succubus riding his cock, her luscious breasts in his face. He blinked, opened his eyes, shook his head, and cast away those visions before falling back to a less turbulent sleep. Thoughts of Mia would bring no rest.

Alex rose through the sea of dreams, creasing its riffled surface, coming awake. He lay quietly for a moment and gathered his thoughts, then glanced at the bed beside him. Vacant, thank God. He chuckled as he pushed up against the oak headboard and knuckled his eyes. A first for him, happy no sexy woman lay beside him, ready to make love. Mia's incessant need had purged his desire, at least for the moment. Pivoting, he perched on the edge of his bed and looked at his clock: ten-forty. The latest he can ever remember sleeping. Time to rise, dress, and have breakfast, before returning to Cala de Mar. He'd promised to drive the Saunders to the airport at Noon, but he didn't want to arrive early in case Mia wanted to draw him in for one final party. He was totally spent.

Clad in workout clothing, he'd decided to visit the dojo after dropping them off. A strenuous kung fu workout with its master was what he needed to reinvigorate himself. After nearly two years at that esoteric martial arts training, he'd become the equivalent of a black belt, but still no match for the Shifu Master, a Shaolin monk who'd fled China to avoid it's oppressive rule. Alex relished the physical strength, endurance, and peace the discipline created, but didn't intend to become Buddhist. While he never expected to use it in self-defense, he'd be ready if needed. Even karate black belts were no match for a kung fu master.

Alex glanced in his rearview mirror as he drove away from AeroMexico's Departure terminal, the L.A. couple waving goodbye. His ear still tingled from Mia's whispered, final words.

"Please, Alex, think about joining us in L.A. We'll make it

worth your while." She'd planted a soft kiss there. *"I'll* definitely make it worthwhile." Their bodies pressed close, her finger made a surreptitious caress of his crotch. "I desperately want this big boy close by, all the time." Then a heated, tongue-dueling kiss. As they eased apart, she said, "Believe me, Kent does too."

"Sorry, gorgeous." His fingers caressed her arched cheek. "I loved our time together, both in bed and on the boat, but my life is here." He'd stepped back, her hands in his. "You'll find the stud you need back home, and I'll soon become a fading dream." He turned to enter his truck.

"Never! You're one of a kind, lover." Her eyes welled. "Check your pocket, in case you change your mind." A pout crossed her face. "I *need* that big buddy of yours in my life."

Now, as he exited the airport, he drew a slip of paper from his pant's pocket and scanned it: two phone numbers, one marked "exclusive," an address in Bel Aire, and e-mail and WhatsApp info. Everything necessary if he wanted to get back together in California. He chuckled as he crushed it into a ball and discarded in a small trash bag hanging on his dash. Mia was definitely too much of a very good thing.

As he arrived at the dojo, a resolve formed in his head. *I'm gonna lay off sex for sex's sake for a while.* A smile tickled his lips as he glanced at the glass door, lettered in Chinese, Spanish, and English: "Find here a place of strength and peace." Shaolin monks were mostly celibate, so cutting back fit right in with his training. He sighed. *Somewhere out there is a woman who will love me for me. I cherish my life here, but is this where that can really happen?* He shrugged and exited his truck.

No students were present, and Shifu Master Deshi materialized from the back room, gliding across the floor in total silence. Alex was amazed by the almost mystical movement of the monk, often seemingly appearing out of nowhere, moving like a shadow. He bowed.

"Shifu Deshi, I greet you with reverence."

The monk nodded, returned the bow, and settled to sit on the mat, legs crossed in front. Alex did likewise, facing him, three feet apart, arms crossed at the wrists in his lap. A moment passed in silence, before the monk spoke.

"I sense disquiet in your aura, Tudi. You have experienced a troubling encounter?" The monk spoke excellent English, as Alex preferred.

"Yes, Shifu." Alex sighed and closed his eyes. "A sexual adventure with a couple, swingers from Los Angeles. She was a veritable succubus, constantly demanding, never satisfied. Totally draining." Eyes open again, he held the monk's mahogany orbs.

"And this bothers your soul, my son?" His lips edged into a wry smile.

Alex shrugged. "Not the sex, exactly, Master. It was incredible, and the woman was a passionate and loving companion. But, she exhausted me." He paused, searching for the right words. "I think it's more about me—who I've become—than her." A small head shake. "That I'm so involved in physical gratification that I've lost sight of love." He sighed again. "As you know, what I've thought was love in the past was only an illusion." Alex had bared his soul to this Buddhist monk about his history with Trudy and Anne, skirting how his wealth had factored into their relationships. "And now it seems it is solely sex, not true love, that drives me."

"And it is this true love that you desire?" He rose and offered a hand to his student, called a Tudi."

"Yes." Alex was on his feet. "More than anything. Must I forsake sex to succeed?"

"Abstinence is the Shaolin way, but you are not Buddhist, and do not practice the Chan. Still, caution is a virtue, and I believe you are ready." Hands clasped, palms together in front of his chin, he bowed. "The discipline of kung fu, to which you've become quite adept, will help release those bonds that restrict your real soul." He nodded at the mat. "Shall we begin?"

Alex mimicked the bow and stepped onto the mat. If nothing else, an hour of strenuous exercise would settle him down and get him back to normal ... whatever that was. They began the ritual warmup of slow-motion moves, soon escalating into lighting flashes of hands and feet. Fully restrained, no deadly or even incapacitating blows were exchanged. Nevertheless, Alex acquired a few new bruises, but only delivered one to the monk. Sixty minutes later, Alex toweled off hard earned sweat, tired but also refreshed.

Mutually respectful bows were exchanged, and Alex left his fee, which the Shifu emphasized was optional, before departing, now clearheaded and ready for a new world before him. No more sex for the sake of sex, at least for the near future.

If I can't find true love here within the next year or so, I may have to think of some other future. For now, I'm just gonna love the fishing. And there *was* that cocktail party that evening at Cala de Mar Resort. He enjoyed that, and often booked charters there.

He headed for his moored boat to ready it for tomorrow's charter, a father and son from Indiana, visiting Ixtapa for a week. The fifteen-year-old was eager to get his first sailfish, and with the moon waxing toward full, conditions were excellent for that to happen.

Little made Alex happier than fulfilling a boy's dreams.

~ 42 ~

Brad Barnes fished his vibrating phone from his jackets pocket and peered at the screen. *Good News?* He stepped away from his companions and entered his office.

"Detective Rosa. You got something for me?"

"Yeah, Barnes. We just got a hit on an Emma Logan, flying outta O'Hare yesterday on AeroMexico."

"Mexico, huh? Ya got a destination?" Brad closed his door to avoid eavesdropping.

"Ixtapa/Zihuantanejo. Fancy resorts on the southern Pacific coast." A short pause. "Got a return in two weeks."

"Son-of-a-gun." His eyes sparkled. "You got a her hotel?"

"Nope. Just the flights. No record of her making any kinda res there."

"Okay, thanks, but probably won't help. That's a long way off. Not pressing, so I can hit her up when she returns. O'Hare, huh." He grunted. "Musta moved to Chicago."

"Yeah, a big place. Good luck in finding her there. I'll let ya know if anything else hits."

"Thanks, Dom. Like I said, it can wait until she returns." He disconnected after spilling that lie. Th*e bitch thinks I won't chase her that far, but she's wrong. Two weeks, huh?* So, a week to finish prosecuting a double homicide left a week to go get her. Needed some planning, but he was getting good at that.

First book a flight. He settled at his desk, opened his personal laptop, and found the AeroMexico page where he selected flights, with two seats on a return on the same day Emma scheduled, but to Miami, not ORD. They'd be coming home together. Then he Googled Ixtapa/Zihuantanejo. Shit! Tons of fancy resorts there. Probably staying somewhere on the beach, but if she wasn't registered, calling each wouldn't help.

Hmm. She's not going alone. Meeting the bitch sister, I bet. He began trolling Facebook, looking for posts by Charlene Hamlin, but the woman had little presence there. How about Twitter—X, now? But what's her handle? He'd find a reason for Tech to dig that up. Instagram next, but not there at all. *The blond bitch is a doctor, isn't she?* Maybe a website? Yeah, maybe the *hubby's* website. He's a big-time auto sales exec.

A Google search of Larry Hamlin turned up a website and a Facebook page. Trolling through his posts, Brad discovered he was away for two-week. No mention of where, but Brad figured it was Mexico. A happy, family reunion. He keyed up a Metro-Dade law-enforcement search app and fired off queries to the area's resorts, seeking a registration. Could be either Zihuantanejo or Ixtapa. Normally confidential info, but they'd usually open their records to cops seeking persons of interest. Twenty minutes later, his computer pinged and lit up with results … Cala de Mar Resort. Mr. and Mrs. Lawrence Hamlin, a two-bedroom suite for two weeks.

"Gotcha," he muttered, scrawling the info on a notepad, then scrubbed the search from the computer's memory. Next, he found a modest inn in the town of Ixtapa with separate casitas, not connected rooms. Not a fancy resort, but it provided the privacy needed when he brought Emma in. No nosey neighbors in an adjoining room to cause trouble. He reserved the second week of Emma's stay, and salivated over mental images of how he'd spend it, once he had her again. Making up for a lost two years.

~ 43 ~

Emma shifted from foot to foot, antsy at the length of the visitors' cue at Mexican immigration in the international airport. A glance around provided no familiar faces, so no one who might recognize her. This was the very beginning of the winter peak season in southern Mexico, so still pretty early to find any Floridians there. Passport in hand, she was eager to get out of there and find her sister. A quick check of her phone's notepad reconfirmed for the fourth time they were staying at a resort called Cala de Mar. Char and Larry arrived the evening before, and Emma insisted they sleep in. Because of her redeye flight, it was early morning, and the hotel offered free shuttle service from the airport.

Forty minutes later, Emma wheeled her bag outside into what was already a warm day. Once through Immigration, Customs had been a snap, with no check of her luggage. Bright sun in an azure, cloudless sky lit the Limo Pickup curb as she searched for the resort's van. A few minutes later, a brightly colored mini-bus pulled to the curb, "Cala de Mar" emblazoned on its side. The driver came to load her bag, along with those of four others, into the rear hatch as the five climbed aboard. It was a fifteen-minute ride to the resort, breathtaking as it clung to the side of the mountain in staggered rows of suites. Emma texted Char on her arrival and was told to send her luggage to their suite, 312, and to look for them having breakfast.

Inside the lobby, Emma's eyes, wide with awe, swept the ornate room—plush seating around small, carved mahogany tables topped by exotic pottery lamps with Aztec motifs. Huge, crystal chandeliers hung in vaulted domes. Striding to Reception, Emma arranged baggage care and got directions to the breakfast area. She arrived at an open patio overlooking a huge infinity pool, and a view of the Pacific in the distance, bathed by a pleasant, salty breeze from the ocean. Char and Larry were perched at a table for four, under a broad umbrella.

"Char!" Emma squealed and scurried between tables and into the arms of her sister, who rose to meet her. "Oh, my God, it's so good to finally see you again." The hug was protracted, with Char's hands patting Emma's back, a soft kiss planted on a teary cheek.

Larry was also on his feet, arms around them both. "So glad you made it, Em," he said. "Any problems?"

"You mean Brad sightings?" The sisters eased apart, and Emma knuckled away tears. "No sign of the bastard, and I really don't expect any." She glanced around and sighed. "Hopefully, he's given up, but anyway, I doubt he'd chase me all the way down here." They settled back at the table. "I'll have to be extra vigilant when I return, though, just in case he's still hunting me." She reached out and caressed Char's cheek. "Whatever, it's worth the risk. I was going crazy, not able to see you guys for over two years." She shook her head. "Barb's been there almost five years. Don't know how she does it."

"To survive, that's how," Larry said, and picked up a menu. "We've been waiting for you, and I'm starved. Let's order."

Emma studied the plastic-coated sheet. "Pricey."

"Our treat, and prices aren't a consideration. We're going to spend whatever it takes to make this trip memorable, Sis." She chuckled. "Wait 'til you see the suite."

"Fancy, huh?"

"Oh, yeah. Two bedrooms, two baths, our own little open patio with a private pool, and a glorious view of the ocean. You're never gonna want to leave," glancing up as the waiter, adorned in classic Mexican duds, arrived. "Let's order."

Ninety minutes later, in the suite, which was everything Char described, Emma donned her black, one-piece swimsuit, a tasseled cotton robe, beach sandals, and brimmed straw hat provided by the hotel, ready for a visit to La Rope Beach, just below the hotel.

On the sand, chaise lounges, umbrellas, one-man sail boats, and jet-skis were available for hotel guests. Water ski charters and para-gliders filled the rest of the bill. Heavily doused with 30 SPF sunscreen, necessary for a natural redhead, she was eager for a day of fun. Half-pound burgers with all the trimmings, crispy fries, Boston Baked beans, and Mexican beers were consumed at a beachfront grill at lunchtime. A bronze-skinned beach boy showed her how to run the Sea-doo, and she buzzed around the shoreline on placid waters for an hour, then finished the afternoon lolling in the shade of a huge, striped umbrella. Freedom never tasted so good.

Back in the room at five, all three showered and then napped for an hour before dinner. The hotel offered a welcome cocktail party in their lounge. Drinks, music, dancing, and the flier mentioned local men were invited to mingle and dance with single women. Emma looked forward to that, not expecting anything more than just a good time. She loved to dance, and some of the guys she'd seen around were pretty hot.

Diner was divine: oysters on half-shells, tomato bisque soup, a huge southern lobster tail with melted butter, and a steaming chocolate lava cake for dessert. Larry popped for a magnum of champagne to celebrate Emma's venture back into the real world. Then they repaired to the lounge where a trio of musicians, decked out in ethnic Mexican sarapes, played mariachi and pop dance music.

They settled at a small table near the dance floor, and Emma's eyes swept the room while Char and Larry took to the floor to the beat of a rumba. Mostly guests from dinner peopled the room, but the expansive mahogany bar hosted a bevy of single men, many in local garb. There were four other women who appeared as singles, already dancing with guys apparently supplied by the resort for that purpose.

Emma spotted a tall, caramel-haired *hombre,* talking with a cute barista. Finished, he swiveled around, elbows on the bar, and surveyed the room. *Kinda sexy.* Nicely trimmed beard and nut-brown skin, he had the bluest eyes—not typically Mexican. His stare found hers, and he smiled, slipped off his stool, and wended his way past couples on the floor and tables to her side. He gave a small bow and eyebrows arched, said, "American?"

"Yes." She smiled. "Just arrived today." She held out a hand, which he gathered lightly in his. "And you?"

A nod. "Yep. An expat, living down here for over two years." He glanced around. "You alone? I don't want to intrude—"

"You're not. I'm here with my sister and brother-in-law for a couple of weeks of fun and relaxation."

"No better place for it. Care to dance?"

"Love to."

He tugged her to her feet, and the strolled to the now crowded dance floor. In his arms, she appreciated him not overdoing the contact. "I'm Emma." She looked into his eyes and smiled. He was a good foot taller than her.

"Alex." They swayed to a romantic Latin ballad.

"So, are you retired, or do you work here?" Emman arched her neck to better see his face. Not really handsome, but masculine and peaceful. She liked it.

He chuckled. "Retired is for the rich. I run a small, fishing charter boat out of Ixtapa harbor. It provides a living, and I'm comfortable here." He shrugged as the music segued to another ballad. "Not looking for anything more exciting than chasing roosterfish along the beach, or tussling with a marlin, and making new friends along the way."

"Sounds nice," moving closer into his arms, feeling somehow safe. *Wish my life was so uncomplicated.* "Larry, my brother-in-law, and I plan on doing some fishing. I really want to catch a sailfish, but those roosterfish sound interesting too." She glanced up at his face. "Maybe we'll book a trip with you."

"It would be my pleasure, Emma. Mine isn't a fancy, flybridge charter boat, just so you know." The tune ended, and they headed for her table. "But, without patting myself on the back, I'm one of the best fishermen down here." Char and Larry were still on the floor, so Emma gestured him toward a chair and they sat. He looked at her near-empty Martini. "The same?" She nodded, and he signaled the barista for a refill for her and a Corona for him, which quickly arrived.

"The fishing's quite good right now with the approach of the full moon, and though we're nearing the end of their season, *pes gallo,* roosterfish, are still abundant. "I've seen—and caught—some big ones lately, so you should give that a shot. They're a lot less common than sails, but we can also get you one or more of those, as well."

"Sound exciting." Their drinks arrived simultaneously with Char and Larry, and Emma made the introductions. After a brief discussion, Larry booked Alex's next free full day, two days hence. They spent two more hours together, and Alex filled them in on what to do besides fishing. He and Emma danced several more times, and then Char asked him onto the floor. He suspected that was more vetting, protective of her sister.

Alex sensed an underlying concern for Emma … a sense of danger to her, and big sis wasn't leaving anything to chance. Mattlock couldn't have conducted a better cross-examination, done quietly as they swirled across the floor. Luckily, he appeared to pass muster, and he was looking forward to time with them ... especially Emma, who was a warm and very lovely woman.

Nothing like Mia, should it ever come to that.

He should be so lucky.

~ 44 ~

Alex lingered in his pickup, parked under his carport, and thought about Emma and her family. Really nice people, but the redhead seemed ... what? Tense, maybe? And her sister came across as her guardian. Larry too, both cautiously protective of Emma. *It's like they came here as an escape from something.* Well, probably none of his business. His job would be to create some exciting memories for them, and hopefully they'd all relax and just have fun.

His growing client list came from a wide swath of the world: Americans, Canadians, Europeans, and even Latin America. Probably no surprise he enjoyed working with Americans and Canadians best—the home town crowd, although he was happy to see the Saunders return to California. Mia texted him they'd return in about three months and was looking forward to another week together. He chuckled and shook his head as he stepped down from his truck. If he knew when they were coming, he'd manage to be away, or at least very busy most of that time. One or two nights with that gorgeous siren was all that he could take. *Am I getting older, or just wiser?* He shrugged.

Inside his *casa,* he prepared for bed. It was after midnight. He had the morning charter with the Indiana father and son, and he wanted to be fresh. Catch that kid his sailfish, something over a hundred pounds seemed likely. Maybe even more than one, with this near-full moon. Something about that really brought out the sails.

Then Emma and Larry booked for the next day, a full eight-hour charter. For some reason, he especially loved working with female anglers. Prospecting for that elusive true love he sought with a like-minded woman? Anyhow, they'd indicated they would probably go for more than one trip, since they we in Ixtapa for two weeks. He was going to go all out to make this trip special, sensing Emma's need for escape from something.

Alex checked his alarm clock, slipped into bed under a flannel sheet, closed his eyes, and drifted toward sleep. Emma, that lovely redhead. Someone without airs. Real and down to earth, and a very nice dancer who'd felt natural and warm in his arms. The kind of woman he could develop an interest in, if she were local.

But, she wasn't, and won't be there beyond her two-week vacation. No reason she'd ever stay, and he certainly wasn't going back to South Florida until he resolved this issue with true love … or the lack thereof.

Oh, well. She was into the fishing, and that would be fun. If it led somewhere … not likely, and twice-burned, he wasn't going to push for something else.

He slept and dreamed of whirling across the dance floor, Emma in his arms. Then raven-haired Mia, clad in a skinny bra and a bikini thong, cut in.

Oh, shit.

~ 45 ~

Emma glanced at her watch as she followed her sister and Larry into their suite. Just past midnight. No wonder she was bushed. Paused just inside the entry, eyes sweeping the room, a wry smile tickled her lips. Tired, but she realized, not tense. Maybe the first time since fleeing Florida she felt safe, and looking forward to tomorrow. Two weeks' worth of tomorrows before returning to northern Illinois ... and probably tension again. Stepping over to her sister, she curled Char into her arms for a warm hug.

"Thank you for this, Sis." Tears trickled from her eyes. "I ... I can't tell you—"

"I know, baby." Returning the hug. "Out and about, without looking over your shoulder for a change has gotta be—"

"Great," Emma injected. "So exciting to have so much to do here."

"Like fishing with that handsome boat captain?" Char grinned, an eyebrow arched.

"Handsome?" Emma giggled. "Gee, I didn't notice."

"Yeah, I bet." Char's turn for a chuckle. "Seriously, though, he did seem like a fine young man."

"Nothing but nice things said about him by one of the servers," Larry added.

"You *checked*," Emma stared at her brother-in-law, fists on hips.

"Sure." Larry patted her shoulder. "Wanted to be sure we were hiring a good fisherman. That's all."

"Oh, that's all, huh?" Emma snaked an arm around his waist for a friendly squeeze.

"Sure." Larry laughed. "Said he was one of the best boat captains around." He gave her cheek a gentle pinch.

"Good." Emma turned toward her room. "Something else to look forward to. Meanwhile, I gotta finish unpacking and hit the sack. I'm pooped. A red-eye flight, two martinis, and all that dancing was a lor more than I've been used to, the past two years." Paused at the bedroom's door, she peeked over her shoulder. "What time in the morning, Sis?"

"Set a wakeup call for nine, Em. The breakfast buffet ends at ten." She took Larry's hand and headed for the master bedroom. "Then we'll plan an easy day to get caught up. Maybe stroll the *Mercado*, and do some more beach time. You want to be fresh for the fishing."

"Sounds like a plan," Emma said and disappeared into her separate bedroom, happy to have her own en suite bathroom. Cala de Mar Resort was the definition of luxury, and she planned to enjoy every minute.

Propped up in bed, Emma scanned the pages she'd printed before departing Highland Park, a review of the fishing opportunities off Ixtapa. A soft chuckle bubbled out as she absorbed the information. She suspected her eagerness about fishing was more a tie to her memory of times together with Dad, when they'd ventured out of Government Cut in Miami in search of sailfish. Those were exciting moments and fond memories. Anyway, she was looking forward to doing it again in two days. That their captain, Alex, was a pleasant and attractive man was also a plus.

According to what she'd read, this was peak season for

sailfish, and the Pacific species grew to three times the size of their Atlantic brethren. Marlin, both blacks and blues, were also around, but less often caught. And the colorful dolphin-fish, called dorado in Mexico, were always plentiful. Plus the exotic roosterfish, a rarer prize, though this was the end of their season. She hoped to talk Larry into at least three trips, and maybe they could even lure Char to join them, at least once.

Her sister selected this Mexican resort less commonly visited by Floridians to minimize the chance of meeting someone they knew from home, but in the process also found one of the best fishing sties. And this resort, Cala de Mar, couldn't be more luxurious. Finally wound down from travel and the welcome party, she laid the pages aside, clicked off the lamp, and scooted down to sleep.

A vision of whirling around the dance floor in Alex's arms was her last thought as she drifted off, a soft smile lingering on her lips.

~ 46 ~

"Woo-eee!" Emma leaned back and shook her arms. "Finally." A small grunt, and she unsnapped the reel clips from the leather fighting harness stretched across her shoulders. The device took much of the strain off her arms during the fight. Right leg scissored over the heavy, 80-pound class rod, still notched into the chair's gimble-socket, she lurched unsteadily to her feet.

Larry delivered a high-five and said, "You gotta see this, Em." He crouched at the port side, phone camera poised.

Emma shuffled to the gunwale where Alex leaned over the side, laid a hand on his shoulder for balance, and peered down. The huge fish, blue-silver with dark stripes, lay on its side, gills fluttering, its long, black beak secured in Alex's gloved hand.

"Black marlin, Alex?" Despite the three-hour struggle, she was still stunned at its size.

"Yep." A grinning glance at her. "A real beauty, and a good 300 pounds. Biggest ever taken on this boat, lady." He peeked over his shoulder, "Larry, you getting photos?"

"Yeah. Em, lean in and grab her dorsal fin." Several photos recorded her triumph. "You're gonna release her, Alex, right?"

"Sure. Hook's too deep to get out, so I'm gonna cut the leader as close as I can." A side-cut plyers was snatched from a sheath on his belt and the wire cable snipped. "Larry, go to the helm and get us underway at a slow troll speed. We need to get water flowing over her gills." As Larry complied, Alex up-righted the fish, held it by the bill and it's larger dorsal fin, and slowly working its head back and forth as water flowed through her mouth.

Emma sat on the gunwale and watched. "Won't that hook be a problem for her, stuck in her throat like that?"

"Nah. Their stomach acid is so strong, it'll be dissolved inside of a week." Five minutes later, after a few head shakes, the marlin swam off, once again ready to fill an avid angler's dream. Famously said, "A trophy fish is too valuable an asset to be caught only once." He turned to Emma. "Really great job, Emma. A lot of women couldn't have stuck it out—"

Words cut off as Emma swept him into a fierce hug, followed by an almost shy kiss on the cheek. "What a day!" Giggles bubbled up. "I couldn't have planned anything more exciting."

Alex blushed as he patted her back, and as they stepped apart he glanced at his watch. "You've got an hour left to fish if you want, or we can head in. Up to you." His eyes swept between his two clients.

"You had enough today, kid?" Larry asked.

She chuckled as she slumped onto the chair. "Two sailfish, that big dorado, and then that marlin? Anything else would be anti-climactic." She massaged her upper arms. "I'm done, if it's okay with you, Lar." She shrugged. "I can watch if you wanna try for a second sail."

"Nope. Let's head in." He turned to their captain. "Would you join us for dinner tonight, Alex? Help us celebrate a great start to this vacation."

"Be my pleasure. I've enjoyed your company." Throttled up to cruise speed, he looked over his shoulder. "Seven okay? Gives me time to clean up the boat and get her ready for tomorrow."

"Perfect." Emma moved next to him, grabbing a stainless-steel handle for balance. "When's your next open date?" She glanced at

Larry who nodded. "We want to do this at least two more times, if you can fit us in."

"Of course. I'm open in two days, and not booked for much of the rest of the week, so whatever is your pleasure." He studied the approaching shoreline and adjusted his course, headed for Ixtapa Marina. "We can confirm dates at dinner tonight, if you'd like."

"Sounds like a plan," she said. "Hope they'll all be as good as today, but we can skip the marlin next time, unless Larry wants to try." She laughed and patted his back. "Once was exhilarating, but I think twice might be exhausting."

"No marlin for me," Larry grunted. "I got pooped just watching you fight it. You're definitely a survivor, Em." They exchanged looks and small nods, not missed by Alex.

Everyone settled down for the thirty-minute run back to the docks, three small and one large blue flags fluttering from the now upright starboard outrigger, bragging of their successful day.

Char and Larry followed Emma from their room and paused in the hallway as the redhead hurried toward the elevator.

"This trip was a great idea, babe." Larry took her hand.

"Yeah. She really seems happy and at ease." A kiss brushed across Larry's cheek, they started after her sister. "This fishing reminds her of going with pop when she was a teen."

"Yep. She was really into it out there." Larry glanced at his wife. "I kinda think she was really into our captain, too." He squeezed Char's hand. "Seems like a really great guy, but a fishing guide? In Mexico?" Their eyes met. "Maybe grasping at any path to safety?"

Char chuckled. "Let's not get ahead of ourselves, buster. She's no dummy. Besides, you've boosted her nest egg to well over a million buck with those REIT trust investment. She's wealthy enough to do what she wants, *where* she want, once she figures that out." Her arm hooked through Larry's, they reached Emma, holding the elevator for them.

"C'mon, guys." The OPEN button released as they stepped inside. "Not nice to keep Alex waiting.

Char caught Larry's eyes, her eyebrow arched, as they descended in silence. Reaching the lobby, they headed for the dining room where Alex awaited for them at the entry.

"Ah, the fishermen have arrived." He shook Larry's and Char's hands and kissed the back of Emma's. "Get some rest?"

"Yeah, a much-needed nap." Her smile was radiant. "Between the sun, the roll of the boat, and all those fish, I was bushed." She hooked his arm at the elbow as the entered the restaurant. "But, this is the best I've felt in years. C'mon, I'm starved."

Larry and Char exchanged looks, and he shrugged as they followed the maître D to a table. The air was rife with odors of roasted meat, garlic, and cinnamon. All things to whet already growing appetites. A string quartet, in a far corner of the expansive room, strummed soft, ambient music. They barely settled in their seats when a waiter arrived, distributed menus, and poised with a pad and pen.

"Drinks?" he asked.

A quick survey, and Larry ordered a bottle of chilled pinot grigio. After lingering over the food list, the women ordered southern lobster tails with the usual trimmings, and the men went for porterhouse steaks, with clam chowder all around to start.

Emma rose and took Alex's hand. "I love this music. Come, dance with me."

"My pleasure." He stood and led her to the small open floor.

Close in his arms, Emma laid her head on his chest as they moved around the floor. "I hope I'm not being too forward, Alex." She sighed. "I ... I've sort of been ... off the scene, more or less, for a while. I'm just loving feeling kinda normal again."

He nodded. "I kinda got that impression, Emma. Some kind of

bad relationship got you spooked?"

"Yeah, you could say that." She eased closer against him, savoring the contact. "I don't want to talk about it, though. I'm just gonna have a good time and relax." Her neck arched back, a smile twitched her lips. "And do some more fishing. I really loved it out there."

"Well, that's what I'm here for." He twirled her away in a spin, then gathered her back into his arms. "We should work in some time for *pez gallo* … roosterfish. This is the end of their season, but there's been some unusually big ones on a beach up the coast a bit. They're really special, and very beautiful …" glancing down at her raised face, "just like you." A small smile. "I'm a sucker for auburn hair."

Emma blushed and looked away. "Thanks," she murmured. "You're not too bad, either … for a fisherman." They giggled together and returned to the table. The wine was poured and hot chowder served.

Dinner was unrushed, and conversation spanned fishing, the US economy, and immigration … both from and to Mexico. Avoided were any further mention of Emma's plight, or why a clearly capable American chose to live a simple life in Mexico.

Char watched Emma and Alex interact and build a growing connection. Emma was too smart to fall into what could be a perverted version of the rebound effect, but she obviously liked this guy, as he also did her. Was it truly a growing affection by him, or might he be an opportunist, sensing a well-to-do woman's need, looking for a golden ring. She had nearly two weeks to figure it out, and in the meantime, they'd arranged three more full-day charters over the next 10 days. She may have to go along at least once to get a better handle on their growing connection.

As the three of them headed for their suite after an evening of wine and dance, she wondered if her PI had come up with anything more on Brad Barnes and his questionable relationship with at least two other missing women. Emma would never be safe, maybe not even in Mexico, until that monster was put away … or dead. Jaw clenched, she realized she was fine with either.

She checked her watch. Too late to call Miami tonight, but tomorrow she'd check with the guy and get a progress report. Meanwhile, she intended to see her sister had a great time during these two weeks. If that included an affair with an attractive boat captain, Char would have no problem with that. *More* than a passing affair might be something else, but she'd worry about that if it happened.

Inside the suite, Emma gave her a fierce hug and again thanked her and Larry for doing this. She was having a ball, and hadn't felt so free in over two years. Emma confessed to Char that she had a growing crush on Alex, but promised not to rush into things. Tired from a long and physically trying day, she was ready for bed. Tomorrow would be a day of rest, preparing for a second exciting day of fishing.

She could hardly wait, not sure if it was for the fishing, or being with Alex again. Either way, she was happy, and it was about time!

~ 47 ~

Poised in front of her room's full-length mirror, chin cupped in her fingers, Emma pivoted back and forth as she regarded her image. Knee-length, black skirt and ivory, short-sleeve blouse, standing on two-inch platform shoes—attractive but still understated. She didn't want Alex to think she was a cheap floozie. Of course, he knew she wasn't, but she didn't want this to look like something else, either. Was this even a date? He'd just offered to show her an evening of local culture, with no innuendo.

This was her sixth night in Ixtapa, and they'd completed a second exciting day of fishing. Larry had an hour-long tussle with a fifty-pound yellowfin tuna, and they'd caught five sailfish, hers the biggest, which Alex said was one of the largest he'd ever taken on the boat. All released alive to fight another day. They found a bunch of dorado shaded under a large, floating log, and the action was hectic, taking eight fish on the lighter tackle, all over twenty pounds, with one bull Alex said was probably forty.

Exhausted from a non-stop day, both she and Larry caught an hour nap before dinner. Although Alex had dined as their guest several times, he begged off tonight, having errands to run, but offered this evening of entertainment later. So, here she was, primping like she was going to a prom or something. No reason to expect this to be more than a guided tour by a very nice guy. Or was there? Their three evenings at the resorts restaurant had included much dancing after dinner, and he hadn't shied from holding her close and even nuzzling her hair. Just a fishing guide encouraging more bookings, or was there something more?

"Oh, well, time'll tell," muttered quietly, as she retrieved her handbag and headed out. Char and Larry were settled in the suite's living room, reading.

"I'm off," she waved. "See you guys later."

"Have fun, Sis," Char said. "No need to rush back. We've got a lazy day planned for tomorrow."

"Yeah, so don't wait up for me." Emma smiled at her sister's open gaze. "He's a nice guy, but I don't expect to do anything crazy, so don't worry."

"Me? Worry? About you?" Char chuckled. "Why would I *ever* do that?"

Emma grinned, nodded, and headed for the door. "Yeah, no Brad to muddy up these waters." She waved. "I've got a key card." And she left, striding to the elevator. Alex was probably already awaiting her in the lobby.

Stepping from the lift, she scanned the room and spotted him, lingering near the reception desk, gabbing with a guy there. Seeing Emma crossing the lobby, he made a parting comment and turned to meet her.

Alex grinned. "You clean up well after a busy day of fishing, Emma." He took her arm and led her toward the exit. "All rested up and ready for a fun evening?"

She nodded. "An hour nap before dinner, and as you suggested, I only had a salad."

"Good, 'cause I'm gonna treat you to real Mexican cuisine and entertainment."

"I'm ready." She smiled and squeezed his arm. "Cala de Mar is ultimate luxury, but I'm eager to see some of the rest of this area."

"You'll love it." He paused outside his Dodge Ram. "You okay with riding in my pickup?"

"Sure." A chuckle. "Just part of the local culture." Climbing aboard, she fastened her seatbelt. "You *are* part of the local culture, aren't you, Alex?"

"For a bit more than two years." He started the engine and headed from the resort's lot. "I really love it here."

"Two years, huh?" She twisted in her seat to better see him. "Something else we have in common."

"That I came down here for a change, and I'm guessing you went somewhere else for the same reason." A sidewise glance at her. "Right?"

"More or less." She shrugged. "A necessary change." Emma peered out the side window, passing along the palm-lined avenue. Minutes slid by in silence as he negotiated the winding avenue, working inland and away from the mostly resort-filled coast.

"Wanna talk about it?" He studied her from the corner of his eye.

"What? Why I moved?" She hesitated. "Let's just say, there was a situation there I wanted to get away from." Her eyes caught his. "And you? I suspect Ixtapa is a long way from home."

"Yeah, pretty much the same as you." Momentary concentration was needed to work through congested traffic. "Something that seemed to require leaving town to avoid." Followed by a chuckle. "Just personal. Nothing illegal or anything, but I was ready for a change." Enough soul-bearing. "Anyhow, here we are. Mexican street bar-b-que."

He parked on a grassy strip in front of a neon-lit storefront. Out of the truck, he hurried around and helped Emma down from the high step. Hand in hand, he led her past a scattering of outdoor tables, and inside to a smoky, warm room, filled with aromas of sauces and spices. A long counter, replete with metal trays of meats, fish, sausages, and roasted veggies stretched across the rear of the area. Alex drew her along the row and explained what each tray contained, and they placed their orders.

Platters in hand, they moved to the open patio and settled at a small table, bathed in a gentle, salt-laden breeze, each with a *cerveza*, and ate in silence, except for a muttered "wow" and "yum" from Emma.

~ 48 ~

Three-hours later, Alex pulled his Dodge into Cala de Mar Resort's lot and parked in a guest spot. Turned toward Emma, he grinned. "Tired?"

She nodded, and sighed, touching his arm. "But in a good way." She grinned. "Where'd you learn to tango so well? That was a lota work, but kinda sexy too."

"Lots of practice since I moved here. Tango's really an Argentine thing, but they love it here, too." He stepped from the cab and went to her door to help her down. "So, you had a good time?" Their bodies were close, the scent of lilacs wafting over him, his hands sitting lightly on her hips, and he could almost feel heat emanating from her.

Head tilted back, her emerald eyes held his ocean blues. "The best." Her voice turned husky. "I … I can't remember enjoying an evening so much." She glanced down, then back to his face. "I really like—" The words stifled by his lips as he gently drew her against him. A soft, lingering kiss, fueled more by tenderness than lust. Somehow, her arms were around his neck while his lightly circled her waist.

"I really like you too, Emma," said as they eased apart, his lips curled. "I'd apologize for being so bold, but your arms around my neck seems to make that unnecessary." He smiled as they hung together, eyes plumbing each other's. Alex's fingers ran through her auburn hair and caressed a cheek.

'This is kinda awkward." A small kiss on her forehead.

"You're here for another week, and then you'll return to Chicago, and I'm not going anywhere. So, what are we doing?"

"Me?" She sighed. "I'm enjoying the first sense of romance I've had in ages. We may live in different worlds, but for now, I'm here with you, and there's no place I'd rather be."

A gentle smile split his face. "You plucked the words right out of my mouth, Red." Another protracted kiss before they stood apart, holding hands. "My past life was so all-consuming with work, I never had a chance for a real relationship … one based on who we were, and not …" He trailed off. "Anyhow, this, with you, is how I want to feel about a woman. So if it's okay with you, let's just enjoy our time together. Real romance instead of carnal lust, which I kinda think many short-term affairs often turn into." He shrugged. "I've had my fill of lust."

"You can't know how good that sounds, Alex. Except maybe the 'short-term' part." She stepped in for a hug, her head against his chest. "Lust's okay I guess, when it's combined with love, but when it's the only thing …" She stepped back, her eyes wide.

"So, too much lust is why you moved to Chicago?" He cupped her face in his hands. "Were you in danger?"

She nodded with a groan. "A stalker. Very persistent, and I suspect, *very* dangerous."

"You couldn't go to the cops? Get a restraining order?"

Emma shook her head. "He *is* a cop." A sigh. "A prominent D.A., actually, with lots of connections. If Char hadn't stepped in, I could be dead by now."

"Wow!" He drew her in for a gentle hug, her auburn hair puddled against his chest. "He was really that scary?"

Emma eased back and nodded. "Char says two women from his earlier affairs have disappeared." Taking a hand, she started toward the resort's entrance. "I've been hiding in a very nice, but very remote, women's shelter. Unless Sis can find something on him to put him away, I'll never be safe."

Pulled to a stop just outside the door, he laid his hands on her shoulders. "You could always move to Mexico, Em." His face serious. "I hear Ixtapa is very nice."

She chuckled and leaned in for another, more heated kiss. Head arched back, she smiled. "Don't think I haven't thought of it since I met you, Captain." A sigh and they entered the lobby. "But I'm not sure, even way down here, I'd be safe from him." They strolled across the marble floor to the bank of elevators, and paused, hand in hand.

"Okay," Alex said. "Let's enjoy the time we have together, and maybe we can figure something out." He caressed a cheek. "See how serious this becomes, because it could just be a release from the pressures of hiding out."

"Sure, we can do that." On tiptoes, her lips brushed his. "But I think we both know this is going to be more than a passing fancy. You are, by far, the best guy I've ever met, and I'm not sure I wanna let you get away."

"Glad to hear that, 'cause I'm feeling that way about you." The swoosh of elevator doors opening drew their glances. "Anyway, we've got another charter scheduled in two days, and I think we should try for roosterfish before they disappear for the season. Convince your sister to join us. Plenty of room for three anglers on my boat, and I'm betting she'll have a ball."

Emma entered the elevator, her fingers trailed free of his. "Good idea. I think she'll come." She paused, holding the OPEN button. "Will I see you tomorrow?"

"I'll try, but I've got my second full-day charter with two brothers from Omaha, and they asked me to show them the town afterwards. I'll call if I can get away early enough."

"Okay, but I'll miss you, darling." A kiss was thrown as the door slid closed.

Alex remained in place, staring at the shiny metal door. *Darling? Is this finally what real love looks like? What a woman.* He could make some inquiries back in Florida. Use some of that stagnant wealth, lingering in off-shore accounts, to do something about this Brad who was harassing the woman he was coming to love. He shook his head. Doing that might leave a trail as to where he was the last twenty-six months, and was he ready for that? He realized Emma was worth any risk, if it came to that.

Something to think about as he walked back to his car. It'd been a full day, and with a charter tomorrow, fishing would give him a chance to unwind … and think more about this glorious little redhead angler he was falling in love with.

Darling?

Who woulda thought?

~ 49 ~

Bent over the gunwale, Alex snagged the big fish's lower jaw with his BogaGrip scale and hoisted it from the water to a chorus of squeals and shouts.

"What a beauty," he grunted as he brought the slivery, black-striped roosterfish inboard, and turned it broadside. "C'mon, Char. Get in here and hold the dorsal fin for some photos." He studied the scale. "Thirty-eight pounds. Biggest *gallo* I've ever had in my boat."

Charlene Hamlin sidled in next to Alex, still holding her rod, smiling broadly, and exposed the fish's unique cockscomb-like fin. "That was unbelievable." She looked at her sister. "I'm coming to get why you love fishing so much, Em. The whole thing—the explosive strike, the speedy runs, the three jumps—it's heart-pounding."

"Nothing like it, especially in shallow water where you can see everything," Alex said. "Larry, grab that tape measure from the shelf and let's get a length and girth. Then I gotta get the lady unhooked and back in the water."

"You're gonna release her, Alex?"

"Yeah. Like we said, too valuable a trophy to catch only once." Measurements taken, the immobile fish, gills flaring, went over the side, and Alex worked the forged hook from her jaw. "Give me a little speed, Larry. Get some water flowing over her gills." The boat eased forward, and a few minutes later, Alex released its jaw, and the beautiful fish finned slowly away, good to fight another day. Alex waved. "God speed, baby. Maybe we'll dance again next season," turning back to his three clients. "Another week and they'll be gone until August."

"Any idea where they go?" Emma asked.

"South, some say, or maybe up to Baja." He began straightening up the boat, securing Char's rod in its holder. "Maybe as far south as South America," returning to the helm to get underway. "That's the fifth *gallo* over thirty pounds in my boat this season."

Emma joined him at the helm, an arm lightly around his waist. "Big ones like that are quite rare along this coast." Their eyes locked, spawning sweet smiles, then he glanced back at the other two. "You guys had a pretty full day. Never caught so many roosterfish in one charter. We got an hour left. Wanna keep fishing or head in."

Larry shrugged and looked at the two women. "Seems like a perfect time to quit, huh?"

Both ladies agreed, so they all found seats and Alex revved up the engine for the forty-minute ride back to port. Larry joined him as he piloted the skiff, buffeted by a salty breeze from their twenty-knot speed. They rode in quiet, enjoying the ambience, punctured only by the soft rumble of the powerful outboard and the swish of their wake through the sea.

Larry touched Alex's arm. "You mentioned that a taxidermist could create a replica of that fish," snatching a quick glance at his wife. "That beauty would look great on her office wall at the hospital."

"Yeah, and conveniently, the guys in Fort Lauderdale." The mountainous shoreline, lined with hotels, was now clearly visible as they sliced through a light chop on the indigo seas. "Give me you contacts in Florida when we dock and I'll send him a pic and the info. He'll reach out to you for a deposit after you return. You can send a few more shots to get a good likeness when he's done."

"You make a commission on the mount, when it comes from you?" Larry steadied his footing against the surge of the boat.

"Uh hu, but it doesn't cost you any more. Just comes out of

the usual fee." Alex eased back on the throttle as they entered the harbor. "This is a fairly lean existence, so any perks help."

"Not a problem, buddy." Larry patted his shoulder. "Actually, glad you can benefit from it, because you've made this vacation one we'll all remember for a very long time." He peeked at his sister-in-law, settled aft in the fighting chair. "Especially Emma. She really needed this break."

Alex nodded. "I gathered she's avoiding something unpleasant back home, huh?"

Larry shrugged. "She'll tell you about it, if she wants. It's up to her."

"Of course." *She already has.* Engine cut to idle, the skiff slid alongside the wharf and Alex skipped forward to lash a bowline around a rusted cleat. Emma, now an "old hand," was tying off the stern. Alex hopped onto the planked surface and offered a hand to each passenger, one at a time, drawing them onto the dock.

Emma was the last off and somehow, certainly not by accident, ended against Alex, arms around his neck. "Will you join us for dinner again, Captain." Her smile, soft and alluring, set his hear tripping against his ribs.

"It would be my pleasure, ma'am." A glance at his watch. "Seven-thirty not too late? I've got some things needing to be done first.

Emma pivoted to look at Char, who nodded. Turning back to Alex, she said, "Seven-thirty is fine. Gives us a chance to rest up a bit." She chuckled. "It was a very busy day." Up on tiptoes, her lips brushed his cheek. "See you then, darling," whispered for his ears only, and she turned away to joined her family as they strolled off the dock.

Alex watched them saunter away, pausing to observe another guide fillet a dorado. *Darling.* He shook his head, a grin tilting his lips. That single word set his heart tumbling.

Darling. Something he'd savor for the rest of the day.

Darling had never sounded so good to him. What did that

mean? He had less than another week to find out.

Alex and Emma lingered, arms around the other, alongside the infinity pool, rippled in the evening's darkness from a gentle, salt-laden and flower—scented, onshore breeze. Sumptuous dining, followed by two hours of drinks and dancing in the resorts lounge, had eventually led them there. Char and Larry had retired for the evening, and they were alone … finally.

"Beautiful, isn't it?" She glanced up at him. "Peaceful." A soft chuff. "Haven't felt so at ease in over two years, Darling."

He grinned and drew her against him. "I love when you call me that." Leaning down, their lips tangled in a gentle yet passionate kiss, her arms circling his neck. Heat from her slim, athletic form and firm breasts against him caused a stirring at his crotch. Unsure how far this was going at the moment, his hips drew back to minimize that contact. The movement cause a separation, and Emma's hazel eyes found his, her eyebrows arched.

"Something wrong, Alex?"

"No. No, I … ahh, you excite me, Em. My heart's racing, and that's not the only thing getting stirred up." He caressed her cheek and then kissed the tip of her nose. "I'm … I'm coming to care too much to rush things."

"Yeah, I get that." She sighed, and her hands cupped both his cheeks. "But I love being her in your arms, Alex," drawing his face down for a more heated kiss, one arm around his waist, pressing him close.

Heart jackhammering his ribs, Alex's hands found her firm butt and lifted her, both legs circling his hips as the kiss lingered, tongues in a delicate fencing match. Minutes passed in continued passion before the separated and Emma slipped back onto her feet, each panting for breath. Hands on her waist, Alex inched back.

"Christ, Emma, what are we doing here?"

"Falling in love, it seems." Eyes flared, she took his hands. "Don't you think?"

"Yeah." He chucked her chin. "And that's the problem." Drawn in for a soft hug, her cheek rested on his chest. "What happens in a week, when you return to Chicago?" He kissed her forehead. "What happens to love, then?"

Stepping back, her eyes pooled. "I don't *know*, Alex. Something I gotta figure out. I *do* know I don't want this to end, so—"

"Look." A glance at his watch. "It's late, and I got an early charter tomorrow, so as hard as it is, I gotta go." Her face cupped between his hands, he planted a gentle kiss. "How about I take the three of you out tomorrow evening, like I promised—authentic Mexican food and entertainment. We'll have some alone time afterwards." He took her arm and led her toward the lobby. "Gives us a chance to think about this and maybe come up with a plan. You can discuss it with your sis, too, if you want." Arriving at the elevators, they paused. "I really want to find a way to stay in your life."

"Me, too, darling." Up on her toes, a soft kiss brushed his lips. "Me, too. Desperately."

He lingered after she disappeared behind the closed, silvery doors. *Damn, I want that woman, but somehow this feels different. I sense if we made love, it would be something totally new for me.* A shrug and a sigh, and he headed home. Charter tomorrow, and then an evening with the most incredible women he'd ever met.

Somehow, he wasn't going to let her slip away.

~ 50 ~

Alex flopped a pair of nice mackerel on the cleaning table and watched the two Italian guys march down the dock, hands flying in concert with excited yammering. Chuckling, he returned to the simple task of filleting the fish for his little freezer, as he had dinner plans that night. Em, Char, and Larry. *Sounds like a comedy team.* Dinner and a night on the town. Eyes on the departing men, he grinned, shrugged, and returned to the two slender macks, savoring the scent of fresh fish and salty air, cleansed by a short downpour in the early morning.

Strange charter. They's booked him for the entire day, and when they'd spotted the school of mackerel chasing baitfish close to shore, they insisted on stopping and casting jigs with light spinning rods. Whatever the clients wants, so the next two hours were spent catching about thirty macks and small bonito, all accompanied by whoops and hollers. All but these two fish had been released. Finally, they made it offshore and finished the day with four sailfish and a half-dozen dorado. A smile crept across his lips. He loved fishing with such exuberant guys. Stereotypical Italians.

Working his fillet knife through the firm flesh, thoughts drifted to that spectacular little redhead and the coming evening. He paused and stared blankly at the azure bay, it's rippled surface lit by the western sun, flittering like bright gems. He sighed. Images of women skittered through his mind: rapacious Trudy, athletic Anne, unquenchable Mia, hot little Chiquita, and sweet

Dolce … all remembered in their naked glory, fucking his brains out. He grunted and shook his head, trying to cast them away. Five women, all about sex, two with secret motives, and the others admittedly in it for physical pleasure, but still only sex. He chuckled. Pretty great sex, too.

But, now there was Emma, and everything seemed different. She was lovely, sweet, and clearly passionate, but there was so much more. Was she the first really authentic woman he'd known? Certainly, her attraction to him had nothing to do with his wealth, which he was sure she was totally unaware of. But was it, for both of them, some sort of rebound from unhappier affairs? Her's a stalker, and his … well, Trudy and Anne were in fact stalkers, too, but of a different ilk than Emma's Brad. Still, was he falling in love because this was his first real relationship, based on personality, not just physical beauty and passionate sex?

The fish cleaned, Alex slipped the fillets into a plastic bag, and wiped his hands on a damp cloth. His eyes swept the area, and he shrugged. *You're overthinking this, Alex.* He was falling for Emma exactly because of who she was, and not something she might represent. He hoped that was true for her too. And if so, how would that work? Or could it *ever* work, with him here in Ixtapa, in a life he enjoyed, and she, with friends and family back in the states? If this was what he suspected, the dawning of true love, he could live anywhere to be with her. But what *about* her, with an apparently very dangerous guy stalking her? Would she move here to be with him? No guarantee that would make her safe from a committed antagonist. With his wealth, they could live anywhere: Europe, Asia, New Zealand. All lovely possibilities, but far away from her family and friends.

He sighed, and started down the quay, headed for home. All questions with no answers, at least at the moment. Was he getting ahead of his skis, here? First, they each needed to verify this was love, and not just passionate lust. And with less than a week left to her vacation, not much time to do that. Then they'd face the conundrum, if this *was* real, of what to do next?

Anyway, they were up for dinner and a night on the town, and maybe some time alone together later, after Char and Larry took their leave. His heart started a small rumba, picturing her in his arms. He wouldn't rush things, but he eagerly wanted to make love to that darling little redhead.

Not just sex. Slow and tender love, something he realized he'd probably never really done before. They had six days, and he wouldn't rush things.

This had to be perfect because of who she was.

Perfect.

Brad Barnes slouched low in the driver seat of his rental Jeep Cherokee, parked near the edge of Cala de Mar's front lot, nestled in the shade of a huge banyan tree. Glancing at his watch, he stifled a yawn. He'd arrived in Mexico two mornings ago and checked into a modest, intown lodging, in an individual casita ideal for his purposes. The first day was for scouting Ixtapa and Zihuatanejo, getting the lay of the land, as it were, and planning his abduction and escape with that wicked little redhead. Cala de Mar was the last stop on his list, but he was tired from travel, so he just located it and got a feel of the environment. Clearly, a luxury operation, snuggled at the base of the mountain and right on the beach. Then he returned to his digs, dined at a nearby cantina, and turned in early. He intended to be fresh and alert for his coming caper.

Yesterday, he returned to the resort and chanced a visit to the lobby. He located the huge infinity pool and found a secluded spot to scan it for Emma. Not there. Disappointed, he exited the building and slipped around the outside to a spot where he could search the beach, using small binoculars.

And there she was, under a huge, striped umbrella, sprawled on a lounge next to her blond bitch sister and her hubby. Couldn't miss that auburn hair and sexy little body, looking hot in a skimpy bikini. Brad found a shaded spot to hunker down to maintain surveillance, but three hours later, all he'd seen was her swimming with a paddleboard and taking a towed parachute ride down the beach. No opportunity to make a move in such open and busy environs. Returning to his Jeep, he retrieved a telescopic mic he'd carried down there in his luggage, hoping to pick up some conversation to learn later plans. Something he could work into a snatch later.

An hour later, slumped in a folding chair he'd brought, earbuds in place, he finally learned what he sought … dinner plans, out on the town with some local guide. Six p.m. departure from the resort, so he packed up his gear and bugged out. Get a couple hours rest and be back on site by five-thirty. He'd follow them, hoping to find the chance he needed to spirit her away. Best op may be to get inside and take her when she went for a potty break. A chloroform-soaked rag would make it silent and quick.

A grin creased his face, his tongue darting across dry lips. He could hardly wait. More than two years, but the vision of her in his arms, squirming under him as he finally took her again, brought a rising bulge in his pants. None of the women he'd fucked, and there'd been plenty, ever did it for him like Emma.

~~~

Brad hunkered low in his Jeep and watched the three of them stroll from the resort's entrance with their local guide, headed toward an aged but well-kept Dodge Ram crew cab pickup.

"Humph." *Not what I'd expect for some tour guide.* Then the guy took Emma's hand, and her smile at him said volumes. *Not just a tour guide after all.* Brad gritted his teeth, his knuckles white from their strangle of the steering wheel. Two deep breaths sucked in steadied his heart. If his little redhead queen was into this guy, did that change the scope of this mission? Did that bearded. blond bastard need to pay for meddling in his corral? He exhaled a slow sigh as he cranked the Jeep's engine, preparing to follow. *The dumb bastard probably doesn't know he's transgressed into my world. Best not to complicate this. Getting Emma's the mission here.*

Brad rolled after the exiting Jeep and kept some distance between them. Once on the main street, a comfortable two cars separated them as his prey drove into, then through the bustling resort town and on to the older, native area. *Going local, are we?* As darkness crept over them, they wove through narrow streets, lit by small fires in open pits and occasional flickering gas street lights. and into a commercial district. Soon the air filled with aromas of cooking meat, charring over half-drum bar-b-ques: steaks sizzling on grills, and birds, ribs, and roasts turning on spits. The pickup slipped to the curb in front of an open-air cantina, and Brad paused, looking for a non-existent parking spot. Emma, her sister, and the brother-in-law stepped down and waited in the entrance while the guy drove his truck onto a scrubby lot, a hundred feet up the street.

Brad waited until the driver joined the other three and entered the restaurant before finding a place to park, fifty feet away, on the same barren patch, confident he wouldn't be recognized if he laid low when they returned. He found what passed for a scruffy pub a half-block up the street and settled at a shadowed, outdoor table with a beer and a plate of tacos, to await Emma's next move. This wasn't a place to make a play for her with three others to deal with. Maybe later, when they returned to the resort.

Three of the most frustrating hours of Brad's life dawdled by as he followed Emma and her posse from the cantina to a bar, and then to an open-air plaza where two Mariachi bands played traditional music and love songs. Emma and the blonde danced body-to-body and exchanged lingering kisses and lightly roaming hands. *Definitely* not just a guide, and watching that guy and *his* girl act like lovers was a hot poker in Brad's gut. Total will power was required to quench the need to punish him. Emma was his prize. That blond mutt would soon be forgotten, once they were again together.

Now it appeared they were en route back to the resort, so Brad sped ahead and found a secluded parking spot. He hunkered back behind some tall, red-blooming bougainvillea bordering the entrance, his canister of chloroform and rag ready for action, if he could just get her alone. The Dodge arrived in front of the entrance, and all stepped out.

"That was a really beautiful evening, Alex," the blond bitch patted his arm. "Larry and I are bushed." She took her husband's hand. "So, we're gonna head in and give you guys some time alone." Brand grimaced. *What the Hell* ...

As they started for the door, Emma called after them. "Don't wait up for me, Sis."

Char chuckled as they strode off. "Didn't plan on it, honey. See you in the morning."

Fuck! Brad's brow crinkled, and his hand shook as he watched Emma and the guy dissolve into a passionate embrace, hands a lot less shy than earlier. "*Shit! Didn't bring the fucking tranq gun.* Afraid it would get picked up on a scan of his checked baggage, he'd left it home, but he had a substitute. Chloroform had always been enough in the past, but not if he had to deal with this jerk *and* Emma at the same time, especially since she was pretty good at martial arts. Jaw clenched, eyes squeezed into slitted squints, he struggled to keep his labored breathing silent as he watched their protracted kiss.

Emma's head drew back, still tight in his grasp, and he heard her whisper, "Your place?"

"You're sure, Em. This is so--?"

"I've never been more sure of anything in my life, my darling." She caressed his cheek. "I've only needed nine days to know you're the love I've searched for my whole life."

"Oh, God, that's music to my ears, because I feel exactly the same." He kissed her brow. "It doesn't bother you that I'm happy

GEORGE A BERNSTEIN

at this simple existence—a charter boat captain."

"Hell no!" She laid her head on his chest, still tightly clasped together. "I'd love it, because I'd be sharing it with you."

Her head now between his hands, they kissed again, long and lingering, and then the guy stood back, took her hand, and hurried back to his Dodge.

Brad pocketed his abduction tools and hurried to his Jeep, able to follow them for the short drive up the coast to a neat, well-kept little bungalow. He parked on a grassy patch and watched them rush inside, arm-in arm. No doubt what was going to happen next. He drove by as they entered the house and found a parking spot a hundred feet up the road. He planned to wait it out and follow them back to the resort, but it soon became evident she intended to spend the night. After two hours, and a slow drive-by by local *guardia*, he left.

Eventually, she'd return to Cala de Mar, so he'd spend the night in his Jeep if necessary, looking for a chance to take her then, hoping the guy would just drop her off and drive away. Parked in a secluded spot in the lot, he reclined his seat, plopped is cap over his eyes, and drifted into a troubled sleep. His jaw cramped at dreams of *his* Emma making passionate love to that blond nobody.

Now was the time to set that straight.

~ 52 ~

Alex coasted his pickup to a crunchy stop on the gravel drive beside is home, shifted into PARK, and swiveled to face Emma, hitched around toward him. Luminous emerald eyes found his, and her lips tilted into a bare grin. His pink tongue dampened dry lips as he gazed at her face, partially lit by a full moon lingering overhead in a cloudless, star-scattered sky. Gentle breezes wafted through their open side windows, shimmering her auburn locks. Heart trip-hammering his ribs, her hand in both of his, he sighed.

"We're here?" She glanced at the modest stucco home. "Your house?"

He nodded. "Not the lap of luxury, like Cala de Mar, but it works for me." Alex shrugged. "It's all I need here." They paused, eyes still locked, and moments crawled by on tiny, silent feet. He sighed again and kissed the back of her hand. "Are you sure about this, Em? I know how it feels ... how *I* feel, but we hardly—"

Emma caressed his cheek and leaned over for a soft, protracted kiss, stifling his words, one hand lightly on his neck. Lingering inches away, she murmured, "Yes, Alex. It's only been nine days, but ... but I feel I've loved you for a lifetime." Her lips pursed. "But, I'll ask you the same question. I don't want to push you—"

"No, no." He cradled her head between his palms, and his lips brushed hers. "There's nothing more I want than this. Just that I rushed into things before. Things that seemed magical at the time, but were really only lust and ... other things."

"So, you're gun shy, is that it?" She eased back, her brow wrinkled.

"You'd think I'd be, but I'm not, at least not with you." An arm circled her shoulders, and he pulled her to him, across the cab's center console. "There are so many ways I know this is different, my love." A short, fierce kiss. "So many ways." His door shouldered open, an arm slid under her knees, and he shimmied out and onto the drive, Emma cradled in his grasp. "If this feels right to you, it's *definitely* right for me."

"Oh, yes, darling. Yes! Nothing could be more perfect."

Alex marched for the house, Emma's arms circling his neck, his face peppered with ardent kisses. As he reached his door, the squeal of tires from the road drew his gaze. A Jeep accelerated up the highway. He shook his head, pushed inside, and strode directly to his bedroom as Emma tugged at his shirt. Laying her on the mattress, he slid alongside, and lips, tongues, and fingers became busy voyagers. Her blouse opened and the bra released, feathery fingers and a teasing tongue found firm breasts with amazing, upright nipples … luscious targets for eager lips.

Emma moaned and panted, her hands venturing inside his shirt, pink nails skimming over his back. Alex squatted back on his knees and shrugged out of the shirt as Emma leaned up and shimmied loose from her blouse, both cast aside. Snuggled again together, he partially on top, lips savored the sweet honey of the others as they continued to kiss, some fueled by intense passion while others lingered with tenderness. Their eyes plumbed each other's, filled with awe at the intense *togetherness* surging through them.

"I've … I've never felt so … so complete," he breathed.

Emma nodded wordlessly, fingers stroking through his golden locks, and her arms, locked around his neck, drew him in for a kiss filled with both intensity and tenderness. Twenty minutes trundled by, charged with lavish kisses, fierce hugs, and mumbled sounds of awe.

Finally, Emma squirmed free, rolled Alex onto his back, and shed her skirt and thong. She straddled his thighs, unbuckled his belt and opened his zipper as his fingers tripped erotically over her skin. A moment later, his pants and jockeys were gone, and her eyes flared. She trailed her fingers lightly over his erection as Alex lay still, panting softly, and watched her.

"My *God*!" she stammered. "I never …" glancing at him. "I'm far from a virgin, but I've never seen anything like *this*, Alex." Sliding back on her haunches, she leaned down, fingers still busy. Then her tongue trailed its length, licking at the glans, and she snickered. "Girls always dream of a guy with a big cock, but never wonder if they can handle it."

"And you, Emma?" His voice breathy. "Are you worried?" Propped on one elbow, his fingers trailed across her cheek. "I promise to be gentle and take it slow."

"That's so sweet, my darling." Panting, she leaned forward, her body sliding up across his, coming in for kisses. "But, I'm not concerned. We ladies push bigger things than that lovely cock outta our vaginas, and I really wanna christen our love by swallowing that lovely, big thing inside my now very wet pussy." An intense kiss slavered his lips, and she slid back and eased the head of his dick inside her soaked, flared lips.

Snatching her braced biceps, Alex arched his neck. "Condom?"

She shook her head and lowered herself into him.

"Oooh, so big." Hips wiggling, moaning and panting, she worked back, taking his rigid cock deeper, as Alex's hands were busy with her breasts. "Ahhh, that feels so good, darling." Hands planted on his chest, she began a slow, long stroke, the muscles of her hot cunt pulsing from the pressure, loosening a surge of fluids.

"Oh, geez, darling," she gasped. "It's so … I've never … holy crap, I'm gonna cum already." Moving more quickly now, head back, she squealed, "Oh, ooh, oohh *yes* … *YES!*" Her whole body trembled and she writhed, seated on his lap, fluids gushing from her before collapsing across his chest, their lips locked in feral passion, his still fully erect dick still locked inside the velvet vault of her quivering pussy.

Alex cupped her face in his hands, lips tilted in a sly grin. "There's more to come, if ya pardon the pun, *cara mia*." His hips began a rhythmic thrust.

"You didn't cum, Alex?"

"Not yet, darling." Voice hoarse, he continued slow, deep thrusts. "But, even after I do," panting now, hands busy with her body, "it's only the beginning. I'm hoping this'll be the most special night of both our lives." Grunting, he increased his pace. "I'm making love to the woman I've waited my whole ... life ... for." A final heave and a groan, and he erupted in a torrent.

Emma's eyes flared at the burst of fluids inside her as she continued to surge. His orgasm drew a soft wail from her at her second orgasm, even more intense than the first. "Ohmygod," muttered softly and sank back against him. "What a stud." She sniggered. "*My* stud." Her head in the crook of his neck, she licked at his perspiration. "Right, Alex?" murmured against his skin. "You're *my* stud?"

"For sure, Red, if that's what you want." He sighed. "I've never been surer that this is what *I* want." He lightly kissed her eyes. "You're the woman I've waited for, my whole life."

Emma wiggled free of his shrinking cock and slipped to his side, snuggled again in each other's arms. Gentle kisses and patrolling hands filled the next minutes as they murmured soft sounds of love.

"Who woulda thought I'd find the man of my dreams, and he'd be an American living in southern Mexico?" Passion laced their next kisses, and soon they were entangled in another erotic venture, carnal, yet filled with something deeper ... a sacred pledge of love.

The night meandered by, imbued with unexpected pleasures and serious talk of any possible future for two people from what appeared was disparate environs. Was there a way to overcome all their hurdles?

Finally, well past midnight, Emma sat up, draped in his sheets, and caressed his face. "It's hard to tear myself away, darling, but I think I should return to the resort. My sister may be concerned, and we never said I'd be out all night."

Propped on an elbow, his finger trailed lightly across her skin. "Okay, I get that, but what about—?"

A finger pressed against his lips, she said, "Not to worry, darling. We're gonna spend every possible minute together, and figure out what's next." She sighed. "I just wanna keep some boundaries with Char until we do that. Okay?"

"Of course. Makes sense. I kinda get the sense Char's not one to get on the wrong side of."

Emma giggled. "You don't know the half of it, but all she wants is what's best for me, and I know she likes … and trusts you, so don't worry."

They dressed, slowed by touches and kisses, and were finally out the door and headed for Cala de Mar. Alex drove, filled with peace. Never had he felt so complete.

Emma shared the feeling, but it was shadowed by fear of Brad, lingering in the back of her mind. She shook her head. Her life had changed. What could he do, especially if she decided to remain in Mexico with her one true love?

They rode toward the resort in silence, each filled with their own thoughts.

~ 53 ~

Brad twitched and his eyes popped open at the flash of headlights sweeping across his windshield. He'd positioned the Jeep in the resort's lot exactly for that reason, to spot a late-arriving car. Or in this case, the Dodge pickup he was awaiting. With the interior lights darkened, he stepped from the SUV, a small tote in hand, and checked his watch: 2:20 a.m. Brad scurried quietly to the ambush spot he'd earlier cased out, a tall hedge of purple bougainvillea, close to the walkway as it approached the resort's entrance. In a crouch, he withdrew a thin, three-foot bamboo tube and a small aluminum case, then set aside a bottle of chloroform and a soft cloth. He watched the guy park alongside the entrance canopy and walk around to the passenger's door, which opened as he arrived.

And there was Emma, stepping down and into his arms. Brad's jaw clenched as he watched. He withdrew something from the metal case, inserted it into the tube, and rose.

Arms around Alex's neck, the kiss was more avowed love than carnal passion. Lust was slaked several times during the evening, and now they were pledging commitment. After a prolonged meeting of lips, their faces separated, eyes locked. Alex's fingers traced across her forehead, down a cheek, and gently grazed her ruby lips.

"God, you are amazing." His hand in her auburn hair, his lips made soft contact with each eye and the tip of her nose, then snugged her head against his chest. "I've never felt so ... so full. So complete, Emma."

She gave him a fierce hug, then drew back her head. "Me too, my darling." A saucy grin split her face. "Like I said earlier, although it's been barely more than a week, it feels like I've loved you forever." Stepping back, she took his hands in hers. "It takes all I've got to tear myself away."

"So, why must you leave me now? We could spend the night—"

Two fingers pressed against his lips cut him off. "I'd love that, and we will, another time, but Char is expecting me, and it's already very late." A sigh. "She worries about my safety, even way down here."

"I get it." He wrapped her in a gentle hug. "Want me to walk you in?"

"No need, darling." On her toes, she planted a small kiss. "You've got a charter tomorrow … this morning, actually." They chuckled. "You need to get some rest."

"Yeah, okay. So, I'll see you around six-thirty for cocktails and dinner. Should we go out on the town again, or eat at the resort?"

"I think here'll be best. You'll probably be tired from a full day of fishing, and I'll be eager to have you in my arms again." A brief but more intense kiss, and she stepped back. They lingered, each enwrapped with their view of the other, then Alex sighed, turned, and was in his truck. Emma paused, arms crossed and watched him drive off. A smile lit her face and she shrugged, amazed at how sure she was that this was real love.

A sigh as she started toward the entrance. How could this really work? He was here, and like her, clearly avoiding something back in the states. Might she actually be willing to stay here with him? And would that keep her safe from—?

Emma lurched to a stop as a figure stepped from behind some bushes—a man, cloaked in shadows.

"Who's there?" No reply, just hunkering there, clearly watching her. Jaw clenched and muscles tense, she took a tentative step. "I'm going inside, so please step aside."

"Is that how you greet your beau, Emma, after so much time?" He eased into the dim light, a tiny grin twitching his lips.

"Brad!" Eyes flared, she stumbled backward. "You ... you're here? Why—?"

"Because nowhere was too far from me to find you, Em." Something ... a tube, it seemed ... was in his hand, held just below his chin. "You're mine, Emma." His grin widened. "You'll always be mine, and I'm taking you home with me." He raised the tube to his lips.

A blowgun, flashed across her mind as she dropped what she held, twisted into a semi-crouch, and took a TaeKwanDo fighting pose. *How the Hell did he find me?* His cheeks puffed, then he blew the dart at her. Less than ten feet away, he couldn't miss. Emma darted aside but felt a sting in her upper arm. A quick glance saw a dart dangling there, piercing her blouse's sleeve, barely penetrating her skin. She shivered as she yanked it free. *Tranquilizer!*

Brad leaped forward, and she threw the dart at him, batted aside. Emma's knees buckled, but she managed a straight-arm thrust to his chest that elicited a small "whoof," but there was no power in it. She began to sink, and then a cloth was over her face, and she gasped, inhaling the chloroform. A moment later, she hung in his arms, senseless.

Brad drew her to him, face buried in her auburn locks, and sighed. "You're too special to let you get away, Emma. None of the others ever hooked me like you, Baby." He gathered her up and started for his rental Jeep. "We're gonna have years together now, once you learn to accept me as your destiny." He paused at his SUV's door, rocking back and forth, savoring the feel and smell of her, showering her face with kisses.

"I hope that bastard didn't fuck you out, darling, because when we get to my casita, we're gonna have a long overdue party." He panted at the image. "I can't wait to feel my dick in that tight little cunt of yours." He fumbled to open the passenger's door and heaved her onto the seat, buckling her in. Brad flinched at the flare of headlights from an arriving vehicle, spurring him on. The door slammed shut, he hurried around and mounted up, eager to be away.

No need to rush now. He had his long-sought prize, and savored anticipation, already causing a stirring in his groin. Emma slumped against the door, unconscious, as his fingers trailed lightly down her arm and across a thigh. Tongue swiping his lips, he sighed, then started the Jeep and drove off.

~ 54 ~

A groan echoed in the cab of the Dodge as Alex drove slowly from the resort, reluctant to leave the woman he'd come to adore. Finally, true love, not tainted by avarice for his wealth. The question filling his head was, what next? He supposed he could move back to the States if this indeed was serious … and he was pretty damned sure it was *that* … because he'd no longer worry about another gold-digger. But, would that be safe for Emma, with this Brad guy hounding her. That would have to be dealt …"

Those thoughts were fractured when he noticed Emma's black evening clutch, sitting on the center console. She probably didn't need it --- *Oh, shit.* Is surely held her room key card, and without that she'd have to awaken her sister to get in. She could always get another at reception, but that might be a hassle at that late hour.

A quick glance showed no traffic, so Alex pulled a sharp U-turn and headed back toward the resort, sure he'd catch her in time to avoid any problems. As his headlights swept across the parking lot drive, he noticed a guy at the far end, helping someone into a Jeep. Probably someone who over-imbibed. He continued toward the resort's entrance, then slowed and glanced back. That other car seemed … out of place at this hour. As he swung into a slow turn toward the resort, he shrugged. "Not my business," muttered to himself as he parked across the front of the walk and jumped out, Emma's purse in hand.

Striding up the path he paused, spying something colorful laying on the walkway, just outside the entrance. He spun, searching for the SUV, now out of sight, and it flashed to him that that may have been his business after all, because puddled on the stone walkway was the sarape he'd bought that very night from a street vendor, a gift for his new love.

He raced back to his Dodge, leaped in, and sped away, searching for telltale glow of tail-lights. The lounge closed at one a.m., so anyone there that late would likely be dropping off, not picking up. Had that been Emma, shoved into the SUV?

"Shit!" Had he seen a splash of auburn hair as his light swept by?

"Emma!" he growled as he reached the road. Eyes squinted, he searched the night in both directions, right toward the city, and left down resort row. No taillights visible in either direction. He hesitated. If that *were* her stalker ... damn, all the way down here? ... what would be his next move? His place, wherever he was staying. Probably not a fancy hotel on the beach. Too public. A smaller venue in town was more likely. He veered right and hit the accelerator. *Are you heading for the city?* Spinning tires squealed against the macadam surface, as he floored the gas.

"Did that bastard really follow her clear to southern Mexico?" his voice a hiss, jaw clenched, lips a knife-slit. Hopefully, the guy was in no hurry, unaware he'd been spotted. There were two miles of relatively deserted road before they reached the edge of the city. Plenty of time to catch them if he'd guessed right, and it *was* Emma in that car.

Unsure what to expect if this *was* Brad, but Emma felt he was dangerous ... maybe even deadly. If he caught them, and it ended in a tussle, Alex was confident in his Kung Fu skills. So, he'd better catch them. No way he was gonna lose the woman he'd sought for so long to some psychopath.

Just in case, he retrieved an extra edge from his glove box.

~~~

Brad reviewed his plan: a day or two there to revel in her hot little body—catching up for lost time. Probably needs to keep her semi-sedated and calm, because she *was* a firecracker, but that's what he loved about her. All the other bitches became complacent and were no longer fun, but he was sure Emma would always keep it spicy. Just had to balance the sedative to allow her to be active, but still in his control, an art he'd mastered.

He'd have to put her out to bring her home, posing her as a sister who'd suffered a stroke while on vacation, and he was returning her to Florida for medical care. A wheelchair for airport transport, and an IV in the plane to trickle the drugs into her arm, keeping her asleep. He chuckled at the sympathy he'd probably garner from crew and passengers. Images of her finally in his arms, naked and lovely, squirming under him, his dick plunging into that well-remembered, tight, wet little cunt, got him panting.

~~~

The pickup shimmied, racing across the pavement at 80 mph, as Alex, white-knuckled on the steering wheel, scanned the road ahead. The guy thought he was away clean, so he may not be in a hurry. If Alex missed him now, he knew of two small inns in the city with individual casitas, the likely choice for someone seeking privacy. He had an idea of the vehicle he was after, a Jeep SUV, so he'd …

Wait! There! A faint glow of red ahead. Taillights! Alex pushed the Dodge up to ninety. Gotta be them.

God, please let it be them!

~~~

Brad's eyes swept over Emma, his tongue trolling his lips. He

242

chuckled. Just seeing her there, picturing how he'd slowly strip her, licking and kissing everywhere before he …

Carnal visions evaporated at the flare of lights in his mirror. A car, coming up fast.

"What the fuck?" Who else was out at this hour? Less than a hundred feet back, the vehicle passed under a street light, and Brad realized it was the pickup of the guy who'd dropped her off. The bastard who'd been fucking *his woman. How the hell did he find me?* Jaw clenched, Brad fought off an urge to stop and kill that spoiler of the woman he'd finally recovered. Too public out here on the open road, and he needed to stay free of the local cops. An intersection loomed, and he swerved left onto a highway that led into the Mexican interior. Get away from any possible witnesses, in case it came to a fight. He floored the Jeep, but the truck was still gaining. He wove back and forth across the two-lane highway, trying to impede his pursuer.

"Damn!" If they got into a vehicle shoving match, the Jeep would sustain damages and would complicate his getting away unnoticed. Alongside now, the guy in the truck was yelling at him and signaling him to pull over. Brad accelerated, but the faster pickup pulled in front and began slowing. Two failed attempts to get around it failed.

Brad gritted his teeth and snarled, realizing he had to deal with this nut. It wouldn't be enough to get away. He would take him out so there'd be no blowback that might impede his escape with Emma. Braking, he skidded onto the gravel shoulder and slew to a stop. He peeked at Emma. Still out. No time to give her another dose of chloroform because the truck halted, fifty-feet up the road, its door flung open. Brad released his seatbelt and snatched a six-inch-blade hunting knife from his glove box. He also retrieved his Colt .38 revolver that had come with him in checked luggage, and tucked it into his back belt.

The knife should be enough, combined with his brown-belt

karate training. Three scattered houses bordered the road, so the gun would make noise that could attract unwanted attention. He *would* use it, if absolutely necessary, but martial arts and the knife should be enough. This mutt had to be dealt with—fast and permanently—so he could get on with business. A long overdue romp with Emma urged him to be quick, deadly, and then gone.

Brad stepped from the Jeep and spied the other guy already out and advancing, with no visible weapon in hand. This ought to be easy.

The man paused twenty feet away, arms hanging loosely at his side. "So, you're Brad, I'm guessing."

"Uh huh. Emma told ya about me? How good we had it? What's it to you?"

"I got a different story. A mean bully and a damned poor lover." Alex edged sidewise and shuffled forward. "No real man has to force a woman. That's why she loves me and hates you." He continued to advance, eyes on the glint of the blade in Brad's hand.

"Okay, lover boy," said with a snicker, "come get her. She's used merchandise now, so I ain't sure I even want her anymore." He glanced into the Jeep, drawn by a soft moan. She was awakening, so he needed to finish this fast and get her back under control.

"Emma," Alex called. "I'm coming," taking two quick strides.

Brad chuckled, hopped forward, and threw a deadly kick at his throat, but somehow the guy slipped past, Brad's foot barely grazing his shoulder. Landing in a low crouch, he spun to face Alex, now poised at one side, just standing there, unphased, arms again at his side. Brad growled. Though never taking the black belt test, he'd become very adept, and had actually beaten his sensi quite badly. Eyes slit, he studied this guy, who apparently had skills, but he'd still be no match for a karate expert.

Brad leaped forward, feet and hands flying in a complicated feint and lunge attack, the knife finishing with a deadly thrust. He stumbled, falling to a knee, when instead of solid contact, he'd hurled into vacant space. His opponent barely seemed to move, but somehow had snatched his knife hand at the wrist and swept Brad's legs out and spun him to the ground, but not before Brad landed an elbow above his right eye. Back on his feet, Brad's brow wrinkled, a growl deep in his throat. The bastard stood there, relaxed despite blood seeping into his eye, arms dangling, a smile edging across his lips.

"You done yet, asshole?" Alex's lips pressed into a slit. "I was gonna just take Emma back, but I see you need to be put down, like a junk yard dog," taking a step forward.

Brad clenched his teeth, wanting to end this without gunfire. People in the houses might hear the shot. He advanced more cautiously, then went on the attack, hands and feet flashing, using all he'd learned, but Alex managed to swat away every move but one, a sharp chop to his left clavicle. That arm now hung limply, apparently stunned by the blow.

Brad labored for breath. He was doing all the work, and his opponent was just defending, so he needed to finish this with the small edge he'd gained. Time to end it, and a new attack came to mind. As his target faced to meet him, Brad charged, leaped into the air to draw his defenses, and threw the knife. Just ten feet, and a chest was a big target. Brad blinked, stunned by a kick to his chest that put him flat on his ass. The other guy was in a crouch, holding his knife by its haft, apparently plucked out of the air.

'What the fuck?" Brad scrambled into a squat. This fucker was a magician. Noise or no noise, this had to end, and he reached for his .38. Eyes flared, he watched this ghost-man produce a much bigger weapon. A noisy boom covered the crack of his revolver, and something slammed his right shoulder, smashing him backward onto the pavement … and everything went black.

~ 55 ~

Alex shook his head, and bloody fingers came away from his left temple. *Creased. Damn, that was close.* He strode in and kicked away Brad's pistol. The slug from his Glock 40 had immobilized Emma's abductor, but that wouldn't last. Some duct tape retrieved from the truck' bed bound whimpering Brad's wrists behind his back, and as an afterthought, Alex also wrapped his ankles. Rolling the man onto his belly, Alex sucked in a breath and glanced over his shoulder as a light went on at a nearby casa.

"Que paso," a woman called from the doorway.

"Llame al guardia y a una ambulancia, por favor." He waved. *"He capturado a un criminal. Pronto para la ambulancia."* A bandana pressed against his head stemmed the trickle of blood from the shallow furrow above his ear.

"Bien," and she disappeared inside.

Alex knelt at Brad's side and found a pulse at his throat, noting no exit wound. The slug was probably buried in his scapula, but not a lot of blood yet, so he grabbed under his arms and dragged Brad against the Jeep's tire, sitting him up. If his lungs filled with blood, he could drown before help came. Alex shrugged. No real loss, but the guy deserved justice, not death. *At least, not by my hand, despite trying to kill me.* He heaved upright.

"Emma!" Alex spun on a heel and hurried to the passenger side of the Jeep. Opening the door he found her awake but drowsy. The bandana secured around his head, he used Brad's knife and slit the zip tie that bound her wrists, unbuckled her seatbelt, and gathered her in his arms.

Soft sobs and trickling tears bathed his neck. "Oh God, Alex, you ... you saved me." A small kiss found his lips. "That bastard. He woulda ... he woulda ..."

"Yeah, so he thought." They shared a lingering kiss. "But luckily, you left your purse in my truck, and I was bringing it back when I figured out what happened."

"My white knight!" A smile managed to crease her lips. "How can I not love a guy like that?" Eyes flared as her fingers traced his cloth bandage. "You're hurt?"

"Nothing serious, my love. You're what matters—"

They craned their necks at the warble of fast approaching sirens. Emma's eyes still wide with wonder, searched his.

"I saw the fight, my darling. It was amazing, 'cause Brad is an expert at karate, and you made him look ... foolish." She caressed his cheek. "I knew you were special, but—"

A small kiss stilled her, and he smiled. "Luckily, I met a ShoLin monk when I arrived in Ixtapa, who'd fled China. I continued the kung fu training I'd started as a pre-teen. Mostly as exercise, and for, I guess, self-defense. I was a nerd, after all, but it didn't take bullies long to learn I wasn't an easy mark." Out of the SUV now, they edged in front to meet the arriving police and ambulance. He lowered Emma to her feet. "Kung fu makes karate seem like a kid's game."

"Your teacher will be proud of how well you did." Still unsteady, his arm circled her waist for support.

"Knowing him and the discipline, he'll wonder how I got hurt." He took her hand and elbow, and with wobbly feet, led her to meet the *guardia*. The Mexican version of EMT's were already tending to Brad, and as suspected, they'd inserted a drain into his right lung. Another addressed Alex's two wounds and treated them before applying proper bandages. They were superficial, but he suspected the arrival of a black eye. And, certainly a headache. He gazed at an approaching cop, who looked unhappy.

"¡Qué pasó aquí?" The officer fronted them, arms folded, eyes sweeping between Brad and the two lovers. Ten minutes later, Alex, with Emma's input, had explained the train of events, and they were free to go, with an appointment the next day at HQ to make a full statement.

Brad, now cuffed and legs shackled, was loaded onto a gurney and hustled away, headed for the hospital.

Emma joined Alex in his Dodge, and one of the police took control of Brad's rental Jeep. A deep sigh emanated from Emma, followed by a small groan as she knuckled watery eyes.

"Where to, Em?" asked as he buckled his still groggy lover into her seat. "The resort, or my place?"

"I'd love to be with you tonight, Alex, but Char's probably outta her mind by this time, wondering where I am." A hand caught the back of his neck and she leaned across for a gentle kiss. "You're a bit battered, and I'm wiped out and need a good night's sleep, what's left of it. So take me to the hotel, please. You can come by around noon … oh no, you've got a charter in a few hours." She caressed his cheek. "You up to it?"

"I'm gonna set 'em up with one of the other captains. Hate to stiff a client, but I'm in no shape to fish today. You're all that'll be on my mind, and we still have to go to the police station to make our statement." He started his truck and pulled a U-turn. "Gonna be interesting to see what the cops may learn about Brad, now that we've actually got charges against him." He glanced at her, leaning back, eyes closed. "I'm guessing you're gonna be safe now, Babe. Safe to go back home to Florida, if that's what you want."

Lips ticking into a small smile, she nodded. "If that's what I want," she murmured, and then sighed again.

They rode the rest of the way to Cala de Mar in silence.

Alex knew whatever she decided, he would be a part of it.

~ 56 ~

Late in the afternoon, Alex joined Emma, Char, and Larry at a table in Cala de Mar's lounge for happy hour cocktails. Emma and he had visited the local cops after a late brunch and filed their report. Brad was stabilized and in custody at the hospital under guard, and after Alex's and Emma's visit with the *guardia,* the prosecutor was preparing charges for kidnapping and attempted murder. They would also contact Miami P.D. with their information. See if they'd investigate Brad at that end, now that they knew who he *really* was.

"I bet they find more than they expect," Char said. "A guy like that, well, no way Emma was his first victim." She took one of her sister's hands. "Thank God you're done with him now, hon." She glanced at Alex's bandaged face, whose eyes, one now ringed by black bruise, never left Emma's face. "You can return to Florida now ... or not." A pat on Emma's hand and a smile. "Things I suspect you two are gonna have to work out." Rising, she took Larry's arm. "C'mon, Hubby, we need to leave these two alone. I'm going for a swim at the beach."

Larry grunted and rose. "Me too, Babe. All this drama is wearing me down." Chuckling, the pair left Emma and Alex alone.

Emma turned, a shake of her head swirling her auburn locks. "So, my battered but heroic white knight, here we are," cupping his face, a thumb grazed across his blackened right eye. "For the first time in nearly three years, I can finally relax, thanks to you." She took his hands, her brow wrinkled. "I *can* relax now, Alex, can't

I?"

"Oh, yeah." Giving her fingers a gentle squeeze. "The cops got him dead to rights, as they say. Nothing's gonna keep him out of a Mexican prison. The prosecutor said twenty to forty years, hard time, and no *gringo* is likely to survive that long in that joint." He slid his chair next to hers and wrapped an arm around her shoulder. "Maybe, if the Miami cops find something worse … like those missing girls murdered … they might win extradition. In Florida, he'd get life without parole, or even the needle." They kissed. "Either way, he'll never bother you again.'

"So, what about us, Alex?" She curled a hand behind his neck and planted a soft kiss. "This vacation ends in five days, but I can't imagine a life without you."

"I love you more than I can say, Em." He rose and pulled her into a warm hug, she nuzzling at his neck. "So, we're gonna work this out." A kiss, and he chucked under her chin. "But, at the risk of sounding inappropriate, I got a full-day charter tomorrow. The guys I canceled for today, and I can't do that to them again." They strolled, arm-in-arm, toward the doorway. "I'm bushed. An adrenalin drop, I guess. Anyhow, I gotta get the boat ready and then get some serious rest." They paused at the glass double-door entry. "I can come by for dinner tomorrow evening. Gives us time to clear our heads. Consider the future." He took her hands. "Deal?"

Emma nodded, then stepped in for a more passionate kiss. "Just so you know," panting softly, "nothing's gonna keep me from my white knight." Her lips tilted into a tired grin. "My one true love."

Another kiss, and Alex shuffled out the door, steeled against looking back, or he might not leave.

True Love? Yes, I think I've finally found it … no strings attached.

Three days later, Alex joined Emma, clad in white slacks and an ivory, sleeveless blouse, for drinks at seven at the resort's lounge. Discussion of their futures hung in the air, so far unresolved.

They'd just completed their last day of fishing that day, only the two of them. Much of their time on the boat, at Emma's request, was spent showing her how to rig baits and set up tackle. She'd caught two sailfish on split-tail mullet she'd prepared from scratch, and squealed, so excited she swarmed over him with kisses. To both their surprises, considering they were drifting at sea in a mostly open boat, things became much more passionate, and somehow, they found themselves making love atop life vests strewn across the boat's floorboards.

"My heart's bursting with love for you, you amazing man," she murmured, her sweat-slickened body pressed against his, as they snuggled together afterwards. "No way I'm spending my days … my *life* … without you." A strong hug as she kissed his bearded cheek. "Especially now that we know I'm safe."

Pushed up on elbows, he kissed the tip of her nose. "I can't imagine myself without you, either, Em." Sighing, Alex rolled off and wiggled on his pants. "Two days before you're scheduled to return home. We're gonna have to figure it out."

"Yes we do." She sat up and also dressed. "And I've got some ideas about that." A glance at her watch. "Three hours left to fish, and I don't wanna waste them. I *love* it out here." Emma planted a brief kiss and caressed his cheek. "Especially, because I'm here with you." Another sailfish and a nice bull dolphin completed their day.

Now, back at the resort, showered and rested, they lingered peacefully, savoring their cocktails and awaited Char and Larry to join them. Emma had news she wanted to share with all. Alex rose as the other two arrived, greeting both with hugs.

Char settled down as Larry held her chair, and then he sat. "So, lovers and fishermen both, huh?" she chuckled. Char laid a hand atop her sister's. "The suite seems empty without you sleeping there, Em, but I get it." She studied Alex's face. "Seems to me you finally found the right guy." Her attention turned to Emma. "So, how do you plan to work this out? Is Alex coming back to the States with us?"

Emma shrugged. "I haven't asked him to do that, Sis. He loves his life here." Her eyes swept all three faces, and her lips ticked up. "I've decided to stay."

"Here?" Char's eyebrows arched. "In Mexico?" She looked at her husband.

"Yep." Her sister's hand gathered in hers, Emma continued. "I've found my soulmate, and I love his life here as much as he does. I'm hooked on the guy *and* the fishing." She glanced at Alex. "That is, if he'll have me. Maybe I can even be his fishing mate on the boat when he has clients." She giggled. "A two-man crew, like the big yachts."

"Wow!" three voices, uttered in unison. "This isn't exactly the life of luxury, darling," Alex said. "It's not Chicago, or South Florida—"

"The only thing I'll miss about those places is my sister and her great hubby, and we can visit, both ways. I can live with that." Swiveled in her chair, she cupped Alex's face in her hands. "What I can't live without is you, darling. You in my arms, you on the boat. You in my bed. You, you, you."

Face split by a huge grin, Alex hooked the back of her head and drew her in for a soft, lingering kiss. "Ditto, babe. I coulda moved back, if that was the only option, but I love this one better." His eyes swept them all. "Everyone on board, if ya pardon the pun?"

"Whatever makes my sister happy." Char's eyes welled with moisture. "And that certainly seems to be you and this life. I *will* miss her, but now we'll have an excuse to visit this gorgeous resort more often." She looked at Larry. "And we have a lovely guest suite in Miami, always ready for your visit. I hope that'll go both ways."

"For sure," Alex said. "I've still got friends and my old partner I'd like to see, back in the States." Adoring eyes focused on his lover. "Seems the reason I wanted to get away has evaporated with the arrival of my own true love."

Drinks finished, they repaired to the dining room for dinner, all filled with an aura of content. Alex planned to visit the *guardia* the next day for an update on Brad.

That needed to be put to bed, once and for all.

He'd also considered coming forward with who he really was, but decided against it for now. Plenty of time, once everything was cemented in place. He'd been managing fine on what he earned and wanted to keep it simple and let things develop on their own. Emma loved him for who he seemed and wanted to be sure this was going to last.

Alex had no doubt about his feelings for Emma, but realized that's how it was with both Trudy and Anne … until it wasn't.

~ 57 ~

Alex entered the resort's lounge and spied the three of them sitting at a side booth. He'd dropped Emma off in the morning after a night of passionate release at his place, before continuing on to the police station to get a new briefing from the Federal detective.

"Hi guys." He slipped into the booth and set a note pad on the table.

Char pointed to the papers. "So, looks like you got some information. Tell us." She sat back, arms crossed, while Emma snugged up, kissed his cheek, and hooked her arm though his elbow as he plucked up the pad.

"Quite a bit, actually." He flipped a page. "Miami-Dade got a warrant, raided his home, and found a secret, walled off area in his attic. Behind a hidden, locked door, which they broke down." A pause as he studied their faces.

"And?" Larry asked. "C'mon. What did they find?"

"Two women. One," glancing at his notes, "a Lourdes Valdez, drugged, nearly naked, and chained to a bed, and the other, Tamme Dean, apparently her custodian."

"What the Hell!" Char growled. "Sex slaves?"

Alex nodded. "At least in the case of Valdez. She'd been a court reporter he'd dated over a year ago, who disappeared. Texted her family she'd met the guy of her dreams, had ditched Barnes, and was moving to South America." He shrugged. "Obviously, Barnes took her and sent the message."

"And the other woman ... Dean, you said?" Char leaned

forward.

"Disappeared four years ago, with the same basic message to her folks. Dated Barnes, then left him for someone else and moved away."

"But it sounds like she was helping him, Alex," Emma said.

"Yeah, apparently a victim of the Stockholm Syndrome." He shrugged. "He had her so long she became an ally. Took care of 'his girls' and even joined in on threesomes with his most recent captive."

"His girls? Most recent?" Char's brow wrinkled. "There were others?"

"According to what they pried outta Dean, at least two others while she was there."

"What happened to them?" Larry wrapped an arm around his wife's shoulder.

"Barnes tired of them … and they disappeared. He went fishing in the Everglades … each time with one of the women … and came back alone." Alex peered at his notes. "Probably gator bait. Dean said she feared he was about to do the same with her, once he got Emma back." He gave his lover a one-arm hug. "You were all he ever talked about, she said." He flipped the booklet closed. "Anyhow, they're preparing a litany of charges against him, including four counts of kidnapping and two of Murder One, and are negotiating with Mexican authorities to extradite him."

"That gonna happen?" Char asked.

"Doubtful. The Mexican prosecutor wants to make an example of why you don't pull this crap down here. The cartels don't have any real presence locally, and he wants to keep it that way." Alex grunted. "Believe me, if you want Brad punished, Mexican prisons are the place to do that. If he lives to finish his sentence, Florida will get him then."

"Thank God it's over." Emma shuddered and laid her head on Alex's shoulder. "What an evil, conniving bastard. So, we can go on with our lives now."

Char leaned over the table, elbows resting atop it's polished surface. "And you've decided this is what you want, Em?"

Emma patted her hand. "Yeah, with no reservations." A glance at Alex. "I know it's been fast—"

"Less than two weeks," Char said.

"Uh huh. But I've never been surer of anything in my life." She caught Alex from the corner of her eye. "Alex feels the same. Kismet, the classic thunderbolt, whatever. Maybe we were lovers in past lives." She giggled. "All I know is, this feels right ... for both of us." Emma eased back in her seat. "I read somewhere that whirlwind affairs are twice as likely to survive than long romances.

"We're gonna live together. See that it *does* last." She grinned. "Despite your appreciated concerns, Sis, I think I'll have plenty to do." She sipped her martini. "Alex makes enough to live by, and I've got Nana's trust if there's an emergency, so relax and enjoy your last two days here." She glanced at Alex, who nodded. "I'll stay here with you guys for those. Spend 'em together, having fun and making memories. And I'll keep in touch when you're back home. Okay?"

"Better than okay, Em." Char drained her merlot and they all rose from the booth. Char hugged her sister and kissed her cheek. "If you're happy, kid, so am I. Just be sure you write every week and send pics."

"I promise," turning to Alex. "So, if it's okay with you, I'll just stay now. Most of my things are still in the suite, so I have all I need."

"Sounds right, darling," taking her in for a warm kiss and hug. "Call if you need anything." He hugged Char and shook Larry's hand, then turned back to Emma. "I've got a half-day charter tomorrow, so I'll come by after. Lunch?"

"Perfect. I'll wait, so call when you're on the way."

He nodded and waved as they left, then chuckled. *Her Nana's trust. How funny is that? A woman able to pay my way, instead of the other way around.* A smile filled his face, and he was surfeit with warmth.

Finally, and without question.

True love.

~ Epilogue ~

One year later

Alex pulled his Dodge pickup alongside the AeroMexico arrival curb just as Char and Larry exited baggage claim, each wheeling carry-ons, all that was required for a short, weekend visit. He and Emma stepped from the Dodge and hugs were shared all around.

"Good flight?" Alex took control of their luggage and stowed it in the truck bed.

"Yep." Char smiled. "AeroMexico does a very nice First Class." A hand caressed Emma's cheek. "A year here has done you good, Em. You look radiant."

"Yeah, well, four months preggo does that to you." A happy snicker as she patted a slightly bulging belly. Char gave another hug and a kiss on her cheek.

"Okay, all loaded up. Get in guys, and I'll take you to the resort." Alex touched Char's arm. "Cala de Mar again?"

"Of course," as she slipped onto the rear seat, next to Larry. "That's where this all started, and I've reserved a private event room there for the ceremony." The doors closed, everybody buckled up, and they drove off.

"It's really nice of you to do this for us, Char, but we coulda handled it." Alex glanced back at her. *And I've got that covered.*

"Yeah, yeah, I know. But it's not often a girl gets to treat her favorite … and only, sister," chuckling, "to her wedding." She touched Emma's shoulder. "I've arranged the private room and food, dear. You get a band? And a minister?"

Emma nodded. "Our favorite Mariachi trio, and the prosecutor who tried Brad is a justice of the peace. Not doing anything religious."

"I hear Barnes got thirty-years at their max security prison," Larry said.

"Yep. And it seems he's being tried in abstention in Florida: two counts of Murder One, four counts of kidnapping, sex-trafficking, and other things."

"Yeah, he'll never see the light of day, and six families will finally get closure."

"Six?" Alex peeked over his shoulder. "I thought it was four."

"They've just tied him to two others missing women from five and six years ago. The murder charges might be upped to four." Char leaned back, arms crossed. "Still investigating."

Arrived at the hotel, all exited the truck and started for the entrance. "So," Char asked, "how many guests, Em? Mom and cousins Micky and Sally'll arrive later today. No hubbies, though. Miriam is coming alone too, but won't arrive until Saturday morning." She touched Alex's shoulder. "How about you?"

"Just my old business partner, Justin, arriving tonight, and a few friends and local boat captains. Plus my kung fu master." He chuckled. "And two of my old girlfriends, before Emma." He glanced back. "No drama there, though, 'cause they've discovered they love each other, and they never really loved me ... or I, them. They're just good friends now, and seem happy for us."

In the hotel lobby, Larry registered as Char huddled with the events manager. Heads turned at angry words erupting from that office. Alex sent Emma to get a booth in the lounge while he checked out the hubbub. A moment later, Char stormed into the lobby, her lovely face screwed into a bitter snarl.

"What's going on, Char?" Alex caught her hands to still her.

"The bastard said the room I'd reserved was already taken.

Tons of apologies, but not an alternative offer." Angry tears were knuckled away. "I had everything organized—"

"Don't worry." Alex drew her in for a soft hug. "I know of a place we can use. Just as nice, too." He leaned back and patted her cheek. "I'm sure you'll be happy. Nothing's gonna screw up this weekend, Sis." Grinning. "Okay if I call you Sis?"

Nodding, she asked, "You're sure you got it covered?" Watery eyes held his.

"Positive. Everything's gonna work out fine." He patted her cheek. "Why don't you go up to your room, freshen up, and catch a few Z's. We'll meet down here in an hour." A chuckle bubbled up. "I've got some things around town I wanna show you guys."

"Okay." She sniffled. "Meet you in the lounge?"

"Yeah, for drinks and a toast before we head out." He took Emma's hand, who'd joined them to hear what the fuss was about. Eyebrows arched, she searched her lovers face.

"What's going on, Hun?"

"A little mix-up on the venue, but I got it covered." Her elbow in his grasp, he headed for the lounge. "Let's get a table and wind down. Char and Larry will be down in an hour."

Drawn into a warm hug, then a gentle kiss, he added, "A toast to my magnificent fiancée, our soon to arrive son, and a very special future." He grinned. "I got surprises for all."

"What?" Emma tugged at his arm.

"In due time, sweetheart. In due time." In the lounge now, he headed for a side table.

Sixty minutes later, Char, a bit red-eyed, arrived with Larry, and everyone settled in.

Alex offered a toast, "Like old times with good friends," and glasses clinked.

"So, you've settled in to this life, Sis?" Char studied Emma's face.

"Yeah, I love it." She hooked her arm with Alex's. "We've had a lot of charters, and I'm officially the boat's mate, now. Rigging the baits and working the rods." She smiled at her fiancé. "Alex boats all the big fish, though, especially now," fingers tracing her belly. "Our son gets special care."

"That's so neat, Em. The tan looks good on you." Char's eyes swept their faces. "You gonna have enough room when the baby comes? That's a pretty small house."

"I've been thinking about that, too, Sis." Alex's eyebrows arched.

Char grinned. "What? About the house?"

"Yep. So, let's take a road trip." All rose and headed out, boarding Alex's pickup.

"I've been looking around and think I've found something a bit up the coast." The road south bordered La Ropa Beach on the right and the resort-ladened mountainside on their left. All rode in silence as they skirted the sea, absorbed by a view of the rippled water, sparkling under a marshmallow-scattered, robin egg sky. Ten minutes later, he turned into a small, cobblestone road that headed into a secluded dale. Four modest houses dotted the road, and a fenced lane between them led back toward a sprawling hacienda.

"I found the perfect place to raise our kid, Babe. Dulce, one of the two girls I mentioned, is a realtor, and she'll prepare our offer."

"Which house, Alex?" Emma's head was on a swivel. "They all look very nice, but can we afford this?"

"Yeah. I've saved up." He stifled a grin as they continued up the lane. "Wanna see the hacienda? It's vacant."

"They don't care if we look around?" Char asked.

"Nah. Dulce's got access, as their realtor." Stopped at the entrance, all piled out, and thirty-minutes was spent exploring the grounds. The five-thousand-square-foot, U-shaped ranch house surrounded a terraced courtyard, complete with an outdoor kitchen and a child's playground. The adobe house included four bedrooms with en suite baths, a gourmet kitchen, spacious media room, formal dining room, and a two-room guesthouse with its own small kitchen, all floored with red Mexican tile and scattered Persian carpets. In back was an eight-stall barn and a white-fenced corral, with a three-bedroom staff bunkhouse alongside.

"Lovely place, but way outta our league," Emma mused. "Couldn't afford something like this, even with Nana's trust."

"Yeah." Alex wrapped her shoulder with an arm. "Probably need a staff of three or four." He kissed her cheek. "But I thought you'd like to see how the really rich live."

"Beautiful, but I'm happy the way were are. We could even manage with the baby in your place, if we can't afford something bigger." She caressed his face and planted a soft kiss. "I don't wanna be tied to a big mortgage."

"No, me either, but it's nice to dream, huh?."

Emma didn't notice his bare grin.

"Anyway, let's go. I wanna zip past the marina. I hear some new boats have arrived."

Soon they'd parked at the Zihuatanejo Harbor and were strolling along the wharf. Alex paused, and with Emma wrapped in one arm, pointed at a boat, bobbing at its mooring.

"Look at that beauty. Rybovich, about 38 feet, fully decked out for fishing. Twenty-foot riggers and everything. How'd you like to fish from something like that?"

"Wow! She's something," glancing at his face. "Full sleep-aboard cabin and everything."

"Yeah. Probably got circulating live-wells, and see, even a transom door for landing big fish. A real fishing machine."

"Gonna be some rich guy's play thing, Alex. No way charters could every support a boat like that."

"Something else to dream about, huh?" Cradled in both his arms, head on his chest, they waited for Char and Larry to return from a stroll farther up the dock.

"Okay, guys," turning toward shore, Alex led off. "Now that we're done dreaming, let's head back to the resort and see what I've found for a wedding venue."

Settled back in the lounge, drinks served, both couples took to the dance floor. Emma molded close to him, her head in the crook of his neck, totally at peace. Alex kissed her auburn locks and sighed. *Time to spill the beans. Hope it goes well.*

"Let's get back to the table." A wave at his in-laws-to-be brought all to their seats.

Emma snuggled close, head on his shoulder, as his eyes swept the other couple, and he breathed a soft sigh.

"So," eyes down, fingers interlaced, "There are some things that need to be said. Cleared up, actually, and I hope you all understand the why of it."

Char's brow wrinkled, and she glanced at Larry, *what* silently mouthed.

Alex sighed again and took Emma's hand, his eyes finding Char's, a small smile tickling his lips. "No bad, last-minute confessions, Sis, but I guess it's time I finally come clean. I ... I haven't been entirely honest with all of you."

Emma's eyes flared. "*Now* you're gonna tell me some dark secret? Pregnant and right before our wedding?" She squeezed his hand, grinned, and shook her head. "I don't give a damn what you've done or why you're hiding down here. I'm still gonna love you."

Alex chuckled. "Well, I sure hope so, but it's nothing bad. In fact, it's kind of a nice surprise."

"So, spill it, buster. I thought I knew—"

"First off, it's my name. Last name, really. It's not Weaver."

"Not Weaver?" Emma's lips puckered. "Our son's name's not gonna be Andrew Weaver?"

"No, it's Jordan." He paused. "Alex Jordan. From just north of your original neck of the woods, West Palm Beach. Wellington, actually."

"Really?" Emma's brow wrinkled. "So why did you change—?"

"Alex Jordan?" Larry interrupted and rubbed his chin. "I seem to remember … what, yeah, maybe three years ago … young tech billionaire, Alex Jordan just … disappeared." His eyes flared. "That's you, Alex? *You're* that Alex Jordon?"

"One and the same." Alex slouched back on the bench and grinned.

"But why … why this charade?" Emma gasped, her eyebrows arched.

"Gold diggers." Larry's grin creased his face. "I remember the rumors. There was one … or was it two … women you were involved with." He nodded. "Yeah, one had moved in with you and was already planning a wedding, as I remember the gossip." His fingers drummed the table top. "Rumor was, you dropped her like a hot rock when you caught on to what she really wanted. And wasn't the other one a fishing captain?" His hand waved through the air. "So all this makes sense. Beautiful women who wanted you for the lifestyle you could provide. Right?"

Alex nodded and grinned. "You're hooked into the rumor highway, huh Larry?"

"Need to keep up to date in my business, Bro. So tell us."

Alex sighed again. "You've got it mostly right, Lar. They were fine ladies, but eventually I realized that their so-called love was primarily fueled by my wealth. They hooked me with great sex and lust." He shrugged. "I'd spent ten years building my business and was totally inexperienced with real life. They wanted the golden ring, and I wanted something else. When I was twice-bitten, as they say, I had to hide away, be just a plain Joe Blow, until I found it, true love—" turning to Emma, "with you, you darling woman." He kissed her. "Someone who loved me for me, not knowing of my wealth."

"You're a billionaire?" Emma, mouth agape, wrapped his neck in her arms, cheek to cheek, tears trickling across his neck, "and you came here to live a simple life in hopes of finding someone like me?"

He nodded and turned to Char. "So you should know, I'm the guy who tied up that room. No way I'm gonna let my sister-in-law pay for my wedding, considering my real circumstances." He studied her face. "I hope you understand?"

She grimaced, then nodded. "That's a relief. I thought I was gonna have to kill someone."

Alex chuckled, then his eyes found Emma's. "And while we're at it, I bought us that lovely hacienda."

"The hacienda, Alex?" Emma eyes widened. "The one we just—?"

"Yep, with that guesthouse for my in-laws next visit." A pause as he kissed her hand. "And two horses for you and a pony for our son, when he's ready."

"Wow, I'm stunned." Eyes brimming, she glanced at her sister who shrugged. "This is really incredible." She planted a fierce kiss on his lips and sniffled. "Anything more I gotta know, Houdini? Not sure I can handle much else."

"Well, one more small thing. With my new mate crowding things up on my little boat, we're gonna upgrade that, too."

"We *are?*" Emma hitched around to see him better.

"Uh hu." He grinned and kissed the tip of her nose. "Our thirty-eight-foot fly-bridge Rybovich, all fitted out and ready to go, the one we saw in the Zihuatanejo harbor. My wedding present to you, darling. Even got a crewman lined up and eager to go. You'll still be my mate, though. No one makes a split-tail mullet better than you." He winked.

Emma squealed and threw her arms around his neck for another passionate kiss. "God, I knew I loved you, but this is mind-blowing."

They kissed again, long and tenderly. He thumbed away the moisture from her eyes.

"Yes, my darling. And I *adore* you. Finally, my …

true love."

AFTERWARDS

I hope you enjoyed *True Love?*, my 4th venture into steamy romantic fiction. As always, the characters are fictitious, and any resemblance to real people is coincidental.

And for the critical purist, while real places are used in this novel, physical attributes may have been changed to meet the demands of the story, so it's not so much that I "got it wrong," as that I modified it to meet my needs. This *is* fiction after all.

I'd also appreciate if you took a few minutes to leave an honest review at Amazon, and Goodreads, if you're a member there.

Feel free to view my other three steamy romances, *Trapped* (winner of "The Next Great American Novel," and top 100 on Amazon), *A 3rd Time to Die,* a paranormal romance, centered on Past Lives and Grand Prix horse competitions, and *Hidden Treasures,* #1 Best Seller at Amazon steamy romances. See all my work at:

GeorgeABernstein.com
and at: amazon.com/author/georgeabernstein

Here's a brief sample of *Trapped* for your pleasure.
Enjoy.

TRAPPED
~ Excerpt ~

~ Prologue ~

Turn signal flashing, she eases into the right lane in front of a large, battered pick-up, with less than a half-mile to the Old Orchard exit ramp. Jackee Maren rarely drove so aggressively, but first delayed by her two sons' late departure from school, and then navigating around a minor fender bender on Dundee Road, she is already ten minutes behind, and she's *never* late. The Northern Illinois Chapter of the United Way won't start its planning session without its chairwoman, and Jackee hates the idea of keeping so many busy people waiting.

Peeling onto the ramp, her two boys bickering and shoving in the back seat draw her attention. Glancing back at the road, a ridge of goose bumps cascades down her spine. They're hurtling toward a string of glaring tail lights, cars unexpectedly stopped by a red light at the first intersection off the expressway.

She jams on the brakes and is stunned when her big Mercedes slews sharply right, smack into the path of the pickup truck. It slams into the rear fender of her sedan, sending it careening off the road, the seatbelts gouging her shoulder, crushing the breath from her lungs.

"Hang on boys," she gasps.

Oh god! My sons! They can't die here.

They spin down the embankment like an eccentric top, ricocheting off a bridge column. The wheel torn from her grip, the air filled with the screech of rending metal and the stench of burning rubber, the car rears like a great, angry beast, its hind legs hamstrung. Slamming down, it hurtles backward into the culvert, bucking and skipping along the steep embankment.

Despite seatbelts, Jackee is flung around like a rag doll in the jaws of some huge Rottweiler. The air bag erupts in the midst of their tumultuous downward plunge, rushing out at 200 MPH, just as frontal impact slings her forward.

Her face catches the brunt of the blow, skewering lips on her teeth, smashing her nose. A searing bolt of pain fires across her brain, igniting a burst of red heat behind her tearing eyes. A sharp pitch right crushes her left cheek against the window, knocking her momentarily senseless. The sedan teeters, enveloped in a cloud of dust, hunkering precariously on its haunches before crashing down on its wheels, coming to a thunderous, grinding stop.

Jackee awakens to wailing and blubbering from the two small boys in the rear seat.

"Mommy!" The call gasped through ragged breathing.

"Mommy!" Now a frantic screech.

"I'm . . . I'm here."

We're alive! Thank god, we're all still alive.

She sags against the seatbelt, every joint singed with agony, unable to will herself into action.

Help should be coming. She moans. *Gotta hang on . . .* She slips out of consciousness.

The continual bawling and moaning of her sons stir her, drawing her out of the fog of semi-consciousness. Her left eye is swollen shut, but the other flickers open, glazed with shock.

Where the hell's Fire/Rescue.

She winces, her whole body racked by pain.

Seems like we've been trapped down here for . . .

The warble of a fast-arriving rescue vehicle answers that question. She closes her eye, struggling to control the thunder in her head and the molten bands of fire across her chest.

"Lady? You with me?" A hatchet-faced EMT materializes at

the shattered passenger-side window. She strives to focus on the man, who is futilely struggling with the door.

"Malcolm, Bryan," the words slurred through bloodstained lips. "Sons . . . back seat . . ."

"Yeah, they're still strapped in. We're gonna take care of everybody, but it's you I'm focused on."

Jackee's head lolls forward, her one open emerald eye fluttering closed as she struggles to remain conscious. The swell and ebb of her breast confirms that, while battered, she still lives. Her sons in the back continue their chorus of terror, though it's winding down to a pattern of whimpers as their surge of adrenaline burns out.

"Can't budge this damned door," the EMT, grunts. His thick-shouldered partner, hefting a crowbar, joins him.

"Move over and give me room to work." Forcing one end of the steel into the jamb, struggling to lever it open, he glances at his partner. "Those kids look okay?"

"Probably. All that loud wailing is a good sign, but we'll check 'em out once we get everyone free. The woman's obviously suffered some airbag trauma and . . . oh, oh, she's coming around."

Jackee's unswollen eye blinks, her head inches up, and she tastes the blood oozing from her nose and lips.

"Oohhh. What . . . what . . .?" She struggles to turn her head. *Oh! My sons. The brakes . . . bad crash . . . are they . . .?"*

"Mommy!" Malcolm's voice a hoarse squeak. "Are you hurt? We're okay, I think." His voice and Bryan's whimpering through ragged breathing is reassuring.

Jesus. So close. Don't know how I could . . ." She sags, her thoughts fading again.

"We're gettin' nowhere with this bar." He looks back.

"We need the hydraulics down here, and in a fuckin' hurry," he screams up at the road.

"On the way. How 'bout a power saw now?"

"No way. Too dangerous."

Ten minutes later, a hydraulic pry bar dispenses with the door. Frantic minutes drag by as they disentangle Jackee from the air bags, and her two sobbing, shaken sons, from their seatbelts.

Jackee smells the fuel that continues to seep from the ruptured tank, pooling beneath the wreckage.

Fire—or worse—is an eminent threat.

She floats to full awareness. Her body is festooned with welts, and her face feels like she's gone ten rounds with Joe Frazier. Strapped to a gurney, her head and neck immobilized, one medic checks her vitals, which, despite her tattered façade, are surprisingly robust.

"Looks like you're gonna be okay, Lady. Got someone you want me to call?" he asks.

"Husband. Phil Maren." Mumbled with a thick lisp over a swollen tongue and lacerated lips.

"North Chicago Printing. In city. My sons?"

"They're shaken and bruised, but don't seem to have any major problems. We're checking 'em out now. They'll come to the hospital as a precaution, and your husband can pick 'em up there."

Moments later the ambulance races toward Skokie Valley Hospital.

A freak thing. Was it the brakes? Phil just serviced the car.

She sighs.

How did it . . . ?"

She slips off into a sedative induced slumber.

Chapter One
Five Months Later

Where am I?

Intense, deep-cave blackness envelops her . . . smothering,

almost thick enough to touch. She seems adrift, suspended a pool of dark, still water.

A bath? That doesn't make sense.

Despite a shroud of absolute darkness, she senses herself rising, finally breaching the inky surface, floating weightlessly.

And she is awake.

What was that? A dream? It seemed so real.

Jackee Maren lay very still, confused by the eerie perception of bobbing gently on tepid, calm waters. Despite a sense of warmth lapping at her, she shudders.

What's happened to . . .? Oh, how stupid of me.

My surgery. It's finally over. Five months since the accident, and breathing hadn't gotten any easier. But why is it so—so dark in—where? A recovery room?

Why have they left me alone?

A pungency unique to hospitals floods her with unpleasant memories: Momma, Daddy, and her own last visit. Not a happy moment in the bunch.

Icy tentacles caress her spine, kindling a mountain range of goose bumps.

What's going on? Why . . .? Oh . . . .

Voices murmuring, barely whispering, apparently close by. What are they saying?

Spooky, laying here in this—this black place. Why haven't they taken me to my room? Phil'll be worried.

Won't he? He promised to take time from work to care for their sons . . . to be supportive for a change, while she recovers from this reconstructive facial surgery he seemed so eager for her to have. She shivers, momentarily reliving that scary car accident.

Spinning, lurching, crashing down that embankment. The shriek of rending steel.

God, it was terrifying!

The boys tussling in back, and I was distracted, worried at being late . . . and wondering about Phil's frequent late nights. He was seldom home evenings before the accident. But that changed after I spun the Mercedes into that ditch.

Whatever. That was then. Gotta figure out the now. Why I'm still in Recovery. Get someone's attention. If she moves, will stitches tear? An undercurrent of voices pulls at her.

Why are they whispering?

She shivers again, her skin peppered by an icy sleet of uncertainty.

Has something happened—something bad? No one's here. No one to check on me. Did something go wrong?

Oh damn, it must be terrible.

Her heart tumbles, skipping into high gear. This crushing darkness robs her of any sense of place.

Maybe I'm dead, locked away in the morgue, lying on a slab, waiting to be cut up. It's so black, and they . . . Oh, shut up.

Jeez, it was only reconstructive surgery after the accident. Dead people don't lie around, thinking. Always ready to worry if there's a little hitch somewhere. Nothing bad happened. Still, I've gotta get someone's attention.

Hey. Why didn't I see that before?

How had she missed what was right in front of her . . . two shaded windows, a bare sliver of light glimmering at their lower edges. Dare she move, seeking aid? Still stymied by the strange aura of weightless floating on a glassy film of water, she tentatively stretches out a hand.

Am I moving? Eerie. I can't really tell in this utter darkness. Her unseen fingers trip lightly across the base of the shades.

Success. Both spool noiselessly upward.

Finally. She winces, blinking at the glaring light, before her vision clears.

There, three men, standing in a small, white room, two wearing blue surgeon's scrubs, the other, the tallest, a dark suit. No second bed, no moveable tables, no guest chairs anywhere. No outside windows, either. Stark illumination from flickering fluorescent fixtures cast demonic shadows across their faces. She shivers, unassured by the sight of the trio of apparent doctors.

What is this place? A recovery room? Suddenly their voices become clear.

"I spoke to her husband," says the one in the dark suit, fingering the stethoscope looped around his neck. "He said she occasionally took both amphetamines and tranquilizers."

He said that? It was just this one time, and he said . . .

"Damn," from the taller of the two, "that wasn't on the admitting form. We could've rescheduled. Drugs and anesthetics always cause problems."

Problems? God, I knew it. Damned hospitals. Damn, damn, damn.

"We're checking," the third man says. "I'm not convinced tests will tell us anything that will do us much good in court, if it comes to that."

What the hell are they talking about?

She is suddenly struggling to breathe, her heart pummeling her breast.

Oh Jesus, something did happen. Something bad.

Head spinning, her world lurches surreally askew. She shudders.

I'm so cold. Her little lagoon churns from comfortable warmth into a bed of ice.

Something's terribly wrong. Hospitals are supposed to fix things, but I had the same scary feeling while waiting for Daddy's test results, and I was right.

Gotta find out what's happened. Sucking in a ragged breath, worried about damaging her facial surgery, she grits her teeth before calling out.

"Hey."

Don't panic. They'll see me in a minute.

But they *don't.* Are they deaf?

"Over here." Louder now, willing them to look at her.

"You, out there. Please help me."

The taller surgeon cocks his head and turns.

Thank god. He'll see me now.

He pauses, still as stone. Then his eyes flare wide, his jaw dropping. Snatching at the other doctor's sleeve, he thrusts an almost accusing finger at her.

"Look," he shouts. "Look."

"Her eyes! Her eyes.

"They're open."

Chapter Two

The three men rush to the two little windows, the sports jacket of the tallest flapping in his haste.

My eyes? What about my eyes? Why is he so damned excited?

The taller of the two surgeons pushes in front, very close to the glass, his head seeming to fill both openings. She winces, blinking, from a bright light shined into her eyes.

"Mrs. Maren, can you hear me? Are you all right?"

"Of course I hear you. You're standing right there, aren't you?" He squints, bushy dark brow creased, lips pursing, but doesn't respond.

Is he deaf?

"Mrs. Maren, if you hear me, please signal somehow." A furtive glance at the other men, then back to her, his brown eyes boring into her. "Can you move anything?"

Ohmygod. She shivers, the truth crashing over her, sending her heart on a rumba rampage inside her breast.

I wasn't talking. Were they—oh, god—they were only thoughts inside my head!

I didn't . . . Oh, Jesus. I can talk, can't I? Stomach roiling, she gags back rising gorge, acid burning her gullet. Another reality stabs her, freezing her mind. She gasps . . . or did she?

Did I actually swallow? Despite the bitter taste, she senses no connection to her throat, her tongue, her lips. She feels nothing. The sour taste of bile fills her head, not her mouth, as if everything is disjointed. She can sense, but can she *feel*?

No. There's only this ethereal aura of weightless floating.

What's happened to me? Why can't I talk? Why can't I feel anything?

"Mrs. Maren?" His voice breaks through the jumbled panic surging through her head. "I'm sure you hear me. I see your eyes moving. Can you do anything else? Please, try."

Struggling to clear her mind, she focuses on his face, so close to the two little windows.

Move? Yes, I must be able to wiggle something.

Oh, god. Oh, god. Why can't I . . . Something. I gotta do something. Twitch, finger. Nothing. *Move arm, move.* It refuses.

Wag a foot. Make a fist. Nothing cooperates. She grunts silently, straining at the effort.

Scrunch, toes. No luck there, either. No need to see them to know the results.

Nothing. She tries to shake her head. *Stupid. Can't do that either.*

Shit. Can't move. Can't talk. Can't do anything. Nothing at all. Her mind spins dizzily, whirling down . . . down . . . down, into a black, chaotic whirlpool of terror.

"No physical activity," the other man in blue scrubs says, glancing at an electronic monitor, "but her heart rate's way up. She's agitated."

"I'm not surprised." The taller man studies his patient. Shrugging, he reaches for her hand. It's beyond her vision, and she feels nothing.

"Can't you signal us somehow? Maybe blink your eyes?"

Jesus. What have they done to me? What have they done?

Only she hears the screams of terror echoing through her head.

Nothing works. Gotta do something. Gotta get control. Fix this, somehow.

Tenuously in charge of her fractured psyche, she concentrates on the simple task of shutting her eyes.

They close.

Thank god. At least that's something, and . . . What the hell.

Those emerald orbs fly wide, the "window shades" closing and opening at the same time.

Unbelievable! They're not windows. They're my eyes.

"She did it. She did it. Mrs. Maren, please blink twice if you understand me."

Ohmygod. It was simple surgery. What's gone wrong? This can't be happening.

Can't panic. These are good doctors. Gotta calm down and cooperate.

Her heart still jackhammering at her ribs, she musters fractured courage, willing her eyes to blink twice. The "shades" closed both times.

"Great," said the taller one. "She understands. Get an EEG on her. Let's find out what's going on." The other doctor hurries away.

Oh, Jesus. She pants, her throat closing, choking her breath, crushing her lungs.

I'm gonna be sick. Gasping for breath, she struggles against rising gorge swamping her.

What's gone wrong? Why can't I even wiggle a finger, or make any sound? Not even a grunt. It's like a bad dream.

That's it. I'm having a nightmare. Wake up, Jackee. Wake up.

"Heart rate and BP are really spiking. She's panicking."

"Can't blame her," the dark suit says. Leaning close, he speaks with a quiet firmness.

"Mrs. Maren, I know you're scared, but you've got to control your panic. I don't want to be forced to give you a sedative."

No, this isn't a bad dream, is it? The scary truth is I'm living the nightmare.

"Now we know you're alert, we can take care of you. Try to calm down. We need to ask you some questions and do further tests on your condition."

My condition? You call this *a condition?*

"Blink once for 'yes,' and twice for 'no.' Okay?"

Oh, god. What did you bastards do to me? A banshee's wail echoes inside the soundproof vault of her beautiful, blonde head. Purged, she struggles to stifle her panic.

Gotta calm down. Daddy taught me to be tough. You can do this. Finally, precariously in charge, she blinks once.

"Good," says the doctor she labeled Number One.

"Now concentrate hard and try again to move something. Even a small twitch of a finger or a toe. Anything. Can you do that?"

*Okay. Gotta stop acting like a crazy dog, chasing its tail. Take a slow, deep breath, just like Daddy taught me when I was little and afraid from a bad drea*m. But this is no dream, and she seems unable to govern her breathing.

Another damned thing that doesn't work. Mentally gritting her teeth, she bears down on the minor task of jiggling a tiny digit. Her thumping heart slows as concentration supplants fear.

But controlling her emotions seems all she can do. No twitch anywhere, not even a millimeter. Closing her eyes, focusing her mind, she wills just one finger to curl. No success. She gives a mental sigh, as reality sweeps over her.

Gotta accept the facts, no matter how terrible.

Strangely calm now in the face of unassailable truth, Jackee's green eyes find the doctor's, blinking twice.

"No? You can't move anything except your eyes or eyelids? Okay, don't worry. I'm sure there's something …" The clippity-clop of fast approaching wheeled carts cuts him off. Several white-coated people, led by Number Two, burst into the room.

"I've got the EEG team and the head of neurology," he says. An efficient group of newcomers, a conglomerate of men and women in blue scrubs and white uniforms, bustle about, setting up their equipment. Number One nods, taking her hand.

"We're going to run some tests to see what's going on. Figure out how to get you well. You're our top priority."

Jackee supposes he's giving a reassuring squeeze or patting her hand. It's out of sight. No way to tilt her head to look.

God, how scary. I can't even feel that.

She "shivers," chilled, as if lying in a snow. How is *that*? Physically, nothing changed.

"I'm Dr. Hersch," he continues, "and this (gesturing toward Number Two) is Dr. Lambini, Chief of Surgery. Our boss, the man in the suit, is Dr. Markowitz. We're doing our best to figure this out. Get you better so you can go home."

What a jerk. If that were to be reassuring . . . well, it's not very convincing.

His hollow charade is ridiculous enough to fracture her dam of tension, spilling the frigid bath of panic and terror into the ether, leaving her slack and listless. She's again bobbing gently, sending ripples across the newfound watery cove of her mind, no longer cold.

His words sow no confidence. She senses nothing they can do will actually work.

She blinks once through welling tears.

At least I can still cry.

TRUE LOVE

www.ingramcontent.com/pod-product-compliance
Lightning Source LLC
Chambersburg PA
CBHW050356260626
47156CB00003B/752